# Deadly Reigns V

# The Saga Continues

### A Novel

### By

# Caleb Alexander

Copyright 2013

4-11-17
KMA

Caleb Alexander

This book is a work of fiction. Any references to historical events, real people, establishments, organizations, or real locales, is intended to give the fiction a sense of reality and authenticity. All other names, characters, places, and incidents are either the products of the author's imagination, or are used fictitiously.

Published by Golden Ink Media

All Rights Reserved

ISBN: 978-0-9826499-9-2

# Chapter One

The four diamond-black colored Rolls Royce Ghosts pulled up in front of the old, white, ramshackle, dog run house and parked. The street was empty, in fact, the entire area appeared as though a massive tornado had swept through many years ago, and took away all of the houses. It was a street in a small town that seemed as though it were in the middle of a sparsely populated rural area. There was a house here, a house there, and all were spaced so far apart that the term neighbor seemed a far stretch. Wabash Street in Odessa, Texas was the poorest street, in the poorest area, on the poorest side, of an impoverished town.

Odessa, Texas was one of those towns whose reason for existence left once the oil boom subsided. It was an impoverished old oil town that the world had long forgotten, and that time and progress had left behind. Its residents were mostly preoccupied with scratching out an existence, and playing high school football. The football team was the only thing left to remind them of the glory days, back when the Permian Basin was in its heyday.

The employers in the area were all of those that made a small city operate. There was a Walmart, some car dealerships, a few local banks, and all of the necessities that made a small city habitable. Very little outside money flowed in. What was left of the oil industry was still present, and there was great hope for the new extraction technologies coming down the pipeline, the prison industry was a major employer, as was The Department of Homeland Security. Odessa was located in what was considered the red zone for illegal border crossings. Once the immigrants made it across the border near El Paso, their next stop was usually somewhere in the Permian Basin, which served as a way station for the journey north. It was for this reason, that Odessa, Texas was at the crossroads of the illegal human smuggling trade, *and* the drug trafficking trade. And it was also for this reason that the city's residents felt as though they were living under siege.

Anjounette sat in the rear of one of the Rolls Royces, staring out of the window periodically, but primarily focusing on the crossword puzzle that she held in her hand. The trip from San Antonio to Odessa had been a boring one. Nothing to look at, nothing to see, an occasional oil pump alongside of the road, and an occasional tumbleweed blowing in the distance. She would be glad to get her task over with, so that she could return to a place with some semblance of civilization. Even the cattle on the way out to West Texas seemed to understand just how desolate and miserable a place in which they found themselves. They peered at her passing motorcade with great interest, forgetting the tiny patchwork of grass that they were forced to graze upon, if for only a few moments. Their eyes seemed to be begging for someone to take them away from this windswept patch of mystery.

The dark suited men that accompanied Anjounette poured from the Rolls Royces, and raced up to the front door of the horrid residence with their weapons drawn. Upon arriving at the front porch it was decided that kicking the door in was unnecessary, and perhaps even dangerous. The entire structure appeared as though the slightest force would cause its collapse. The Reigns' men simply pushed open the front door and walked inside. They found their target curled up in a fetal position on the couch.

Anjounette watched the door. No gunfire, no muzzle flashes, no nothing. Apparently her men had found Juan Rodriguez just as they had anticipated he would be found; either passed out from a night of shooting up heroine and smoking crack, or passed out in a drunken stupor. They had expected one or the other because it was the weekend, and he was off of work. They found him in both, a drunken stupor, and a heroine induced deep sleep.

One of the Reigns men walked to the front door and waved his hand, giving Anjounette the all clear sign. She no longer participated in the fire fights or gun battles anymore, and it was not like she participated in those things much in the past, but she was a Reigns now, and her marriage to Dajon meant that she was now too valuable to risk. In addition to her being a full fledged Reigns, she was also a member of The Commission, and the head of the great State of Louisiana. She no longer put herself at risk of catching a bullet. Besides, as a Reigns wife, she was an enormous target, and a giant trophy for all of the family's enemies, so she always made sure to exercise extreme caution.

Anjounette opened the suicide doors on the Rolls Royce and climbed out. She ran her hand down the length of her dark gray Chanel skirt, smoothing out the wrinkles. A quick tug at the hem of her matching Chanel jacket straightened it out as well. Her trip across the unkept lawn to the front door of the dilapidated shack took only moments, and her men opened the door for her as she neared the entrance to the residence. Anjounette stepped inside to find Juan still passed out on the couch. She nodded toward one of her men, who in turn, pulled Juan off of the couch onto the hard wooden floor of his trash filled living room.

"What?" Juan said, stirring and waking out of his stupor. The smell of alcohol reeked throughout the home, and from his clothing. His breath smelled just as horrid. "Who are you? What do you want?"

He was still drunk or high, or a combination of both. Spoons with crack residue, as well as metal crack pipes with burnt tips could be seen on the trashy wooden coffee table. Next to the crack pipes, sat a glass crack pipe, several empty crack vials, some empty liquor bottles, and two empty syringes. Anjounette carefully lifted one of the empty Jim Bean liquor bottles from the table and poured the rest of its contents onto Juan's face, jarring him to semi-consciousness.

"What?" Juan shouted. "What the fuck? Who the fuck are you?"

Again, Anjounette nods to some of her men. Two of the men lift Juan off of the ground by his arms, while another rakes a bunch of trash off of one of the wooden chairs arrayed around Juan's equally filthy kitchen table. The chair is brought into the living room, and Juan is plopped down into it.

"What the fuck are you doing?" Juan shouted. "Do you know who the fuck I am?"

"Do you know who I am?" Anjounette asked, peering around the trashy residence.

"I'll bust your ass!" Juan shouted, slurring his words. "I'll have you thrown into prison."

Anjounette spied Juan's uniform shirt sitting disheveled across the back of a well worn lounge chair. She lifted it and smiled. It was the uniform of an Immigration and Customs Enforcement Agent. The uniform had lieutenant's bars on it. Juan was an ICE lieutenant.

"I'm here, Juan, because I believe you have some information for me," Anjounette told him. "I'm here, because you have *a lot* of information to give me."

"Fuck you," Juan told her.

"I was hoping that you would make this easy for me, Juan," Anjounette told him. "I don't want to be in this shit hole town of yours, any longer than absolutely necessary. I'll tell you what, you tell me what I need to know, and I'll be out of your hair in the next ten minutes. I even brought you a present."

Anjounette nodded to one of her men. The man pulled out a small pack of Black Tar Heroine and held it up so that Juan could see it.

"You tell me what I need to know, and you can get us out of your hair, and start your little party," Anjounette continued.

Juan tried to get up, but was forced back down into the chair by the two hulking men standing on each side of him. He started to reach for the package of drugs, but caught himself, and lowered his hands.

"What do you want?" Juan asked. He was growing more and more sober with each passing moment, and his sobriety was starting to make him cranky.

"Odessa is the crossroads of this shit hole," Anjounette explained. "And because it is, then you would know if any strangers passed through. And as we all know, nothing and no one, passes through here without checking in with you, and paying you and your crooked little band of deputy dogs to look the other way. I want to know who they were, who they worked for, when they passed through, where they are now, and whether or not they passed back through here? You tell me that, and you can have your little Scoobey Snack."

"I don't know what you're talking about," Juan said, rolling his eyes.

Anjounette closed her eyes and exhaled. "Oh, Juan, please don't do this to me. Please don't let it come to this. Is it really worth it? Is it?"

"Fuck you, *Puta!*" Juan told her.

Anjounette turned to one of her men and smiled. The man produced a small hand held blow torch and lit it. The small blow torch came alive, spitting out an intensive blue flame.

"I don't give a fuck about that," Juan said defiantly.

Anjounette turned toward another man, and nodded. The man walked toward Juan's fireplace, and pulled a black wrought iron poker from a stand next to it. He carried the poker back to the man holding the torch and held it up. The torch bearer heated the tip of the poker until it became a fiery red. The man holding the red hot poker turned toward Anjounette.

"Last chance, Juan," Anjounette told her captive. "We can do this the pain free way, or you can go through a tremendous amount of pain and suffering for no reason. At the end, I'm going to get what I want out of you anyway. At the end, no one holds, Juan. Everyone breaks."

Juan spat at Anjounette's feet.

Anjounette nodded at her man holding the poker. The man laid the poker again Juan's shirt, burning a hole through the shirt and setting a portion of it on fire, and then searing Juan's dirty skin. Juan cried out in pain.

"When did they come through here?" Anjounette asked.

"Fuck you," Juan repeated.

Anjounette nodded. Her man again placed the red hot poker against Juan's chest, searing his skin. The smell of burning chest hair and dirty flesh wafted through the air, as Juan cried out in agony.

"Don't make this hard for yourself," Anjounette told him. "You could be smoking right now. Enjoying yourself. Drinking, shooting up, getting high, doing whatever it is you want to do. Instead, you suffering. What for, Juan? Why are you suffering for them? They're gone. They can't harm you. Take your drugs and live."

"The feds are going to have your ass," Juan told her. "I'm a federal agent."

"You're a junkie," Anjounette told him. "Don't fool yourself. You may work a 9 to 5 during the week, but don't fool yourself. You're a crooked ICE Agent, and a junkie. Nobody is going to weep for you, Juan. Nobody is going to miss you. Nobody is going to come and save you. When you're gone, don't expect anything, but death, and decay, and worms eating away at your rotting corpse."

"They are going to bury your ass!" Juan told her.

"They are going to bury you, Juan," Anjounette told him. "You and you alone, are going to the grave. Did you think that you were in the clear, Juan? You, and your crooked little team?" Anjounette shook her head. "No, the feds know all about you. They know all about your little operation. They know about you being on the take. They've been investigation you for a long time, Juan. A long time. You're not one of them. No, they see *you* as one of *us*. And anything that happens to you, they are just going to feel like you got what you deserved. You had it coming for being a crooked cop. That's how they're going to look at this, Juan. That's it."

"You're lying," Juan began to break down. He could feel tears welling up in his eyes. "You're lying!"

Anjounette shook her head. "I wouldn't lie to you, Juan. Why would I? What reason would I have to lie to you?"

"Because," Juan said, and then paused. "Because you want to know!"

Anjounette seated herself on the arm of Juan's ragged sofa. She nodded. "I do, Juan. I do want to know. And you want to tell me. You want the pain to be over. You want a hit, don't you? Just tell me. Tell me, and you can have it."

Finally, Juan broke down into tears. He was defeated. He *was* a junkie. He was an alcoholic, a crack head, a heroine junkie, a failed husband, a lousy father, a crooked ICE agent, a total and complete failure. He had no reason to protect anyone, he thought. He had nothing to live for, and no honor left to defend.

Anjounette leaned forward and lifted Juan's syringe from the table and held it up. "It's so easy. All of the pain can be over. It feels so good, Juan, you know it does. When this sweet, delicious shit is coursing through your veins, it feels like Heaven. Don't prolong it anymore, don't deny yourself the pleasure of some of the best smack you'll ever have. All you have to do its tell me." Anjounette leaned in and whispered. "Tell me."

"Let me just..."

"No," Anjounette said, stopping him in his tracks. "*First* you tell me, and then you get to party. How many of them?"

"Six," Juan said, lowering his head in disgrace.

"Who did they work for?"

Juan shook his head. "I don't know,"

"Yes, you do," Anjounette said calmly. "You can tell me."

With tears pouring down his face, Juan shook his head.

"Tell me," Anjounette said calmly. She lifted the syringe up toward him.

"I don't know," Juan blurted out. He began crying heavily and sweating profusely. The monkey was definitely on his back. "Who do you think!"

"Did they come back through here?" Anjounette asked.

Juan shook his head.

"Are you sure?" Anjounette asked.

"No!" Juan shouted.

"This is very important," Anjounette told him. "A little girl's life is on the line. I need to catch up to them. I need to *find* them. Did they say where they were going? Do you have any idea where they were going?"

Sweat poured down Juan's face, as he shook his head.

"Do you have any idea where they could be?" Anjounette asked.

Juan shook his head.

"They didn't go south, and they didn't go east, so they have to have came west," Anjounette told him. "Where are they, Juan? Tell me. I have to find that little girl. I have to take her back home to her family."

Juan's lowered his head into his hands and began balling.

Anjounette peered around his house, until she found what she was looking for. She rose from the arm of the couch, walked to a nearby set of shelves, and lifted an old family picture off of it. She walked to where Juan was sitting, and showed him the picture.

"You have two daughters?" Anjounette continued.

Juan was silent.

"What if someone took one of them?" Anjounette asked. "What if someone took your daughters, and they needed you? What if they needed their father to come a save them? Think about this little girl. She needs her father. He's all she has left. I'm sure she's missing him, crying for him, wanting to go home. Where is she, Juan?"

"I don't know!" Juan shouted.

"What did they pay you?" Anjounette asked.

"Nothing," Juan said, shaking his head.

"They paid you," Anjounette said, peering at all of the drug paraphernalia on the table. "They paid you a lot. In fact, they paid you so much, that you haven't been into work the entire week. You been on a drug binge, partying and blowing money this entire week. Prostitutes, heroine, coke, crack, crank, mollys, Xanax, you name it."

Juan broke down into tears and lowered his head into his hands once again.

"Who do you think we are, Juan?" Anjounette asked. "You think we're amateurs? You think we wouldn't check? We know exactly what you have in your bank account, how much your average account balances are, what you spend it on. I know you paid your cable bill last week. And that's unusual, because the usually have to disconnect it, before you have it cut back on. Same with your water, your electricity, you phone. You came into some extra money, Juan. How much was it? How much did they pay you?"

Anjounette nodded toward her man, and he grabbed Juan's arm and straightened it out. He had tracks running up and down it.

"That would be normal for you," Anjounette told him. "But you partied even more than that. I talked with you supplier. Nice kid. Smart mouth though. Didn't want to kill him, but he wouldn't shut the fuck up."

Again, Anjounette nodded. One of her men lifted Juan's leg, pulled off his black dress sock, and held up his foot. He spread open Juan's toes, and revealed a bloody callous with permanent puncture marks from where he had been shooting up continuously the last week.

Anjounette turned away from the disgusting sight, and waved her hand, telling her man that he could let Juan's foot go.

"We're not amateurs, Juan," Anjounette said, facing him once again. "We know the answers to the questions, before we even ask. All of our bases are covered. It was the Odessa police department who escorted us here. It is the Odessa police department that is keeping the area clear. Four Rolls Royces in this shit hole town, was sure to attract attention. I'm telling you this, so that you understand the situation. It's over."

Anjounette lifted the photo of Juan's daughter and showed it to him. "I'm through playing games with you. That little girl is missing, and if you don't tell me what I want to know, these two precious little girls is this picture, are going to be on the other side of that fucking milk carton. You got that? Now, where the fuck are they?"

"I don't know!" Juan shouted.

"Who does know?" Anjounette asked.

Juan eyeballed the picture of his daughters. "The chief."

"The chief works for us," Anjounette told him. "You're full of shit."

"No!" Juan said, lifting his hands and pleading. "Not *that* chief!"

"What chief?" Anjounette asked.

Again, Juan starred at the photo of his daughters before answering. "El Paso. He sent them! They said he sent them. He gave them safe passage."

Ajounette nodded. She turned toward her man and nodded. He tossed the package of heroine to Juan, who caught it. Anjounette eyeballed the syringe, and one of her men lifted it, cleaned her fingerprints off of it, and then handed it to Juan.

Juan leaped from the chair, grabbed a spoon, and a lighter from off of the cluttered coffee table, pinched off a piece of the heroine, and placed it on the spoon. He placed the lighter beneath the spoon, melting his heroine. He lifted the syringe, and drew the melted heroine into it.

"Juan, that's pure, uncut heroine," Anjounette told him, heading for the front door. "It's extra strong. It's designed to make you overdose. We wanted your death to look like an accidental overdose. If you take that, it's going to kill you."

Anjounette and her men headed for their waiting cars, knowing full well the Juan was going to inject the uncut heroine into his system. Even her warning wouldn't matter. Juan was a stone cold junkie, and he was dying for a fix. He was also dying for the pain to end. Not the pain from the red hot poker, but the pain of a failed life, and failed expectations. He stuck the needle in his arm and injected the heroine into his veins. He fell back down onto his sofa as the uncut drug worked its way through his system. He would be dead before the caravan of Rolls Royces made their way off of his street.

# Chapter Two

Dante's thirty-thousand-square-foot Spanish Colonial type mansion sat on a bluff overlooking the Jack Nicklaus Signature Golf Course within the prestigious community of Cordillera Ranch. The estate sat on just over fifteen private, gated, highly secured acres, and contained all of the usual amenities and accoutrements of a residence its size. There was an indoor swimming pool, an outdoor swimming pool, an indoor bowling alley, an indoor basketball court, an outdoor tennis court, a putting green, a movie theater, a fully equipped home gym, some fifteen bedrooms, some twenty bathrooms, and all of the usual living areas, kitchens, and dining areas. But most importantly, it also held a helicopter pad. One of the Reigns family's massive Augusta Westland 101 helicopters sat idling on that landing pad, waiting for Dante to board.

Desire walked into Dante's bedroom and spied the array of weaponry that he had laid out on his bed. He walked out of his closet carrying another assault rifle, which he laid on the bed next to the four others that he already had laid out. There were also four semi-automatic handguns, some claymore anti-personnel mines, and a few hand grenades. Numerous clips and magazines, as well as many boxes of ammunition also sat on his bed. Dante stopped and stared at her. At this point, he didn't care what she knew, he didn't care that she was a reporter, or that she had just come into his life. All that mattered right now, was his little girl.

Desire covered the lower half of her face, while staring at the weapons on the bed. She had grown up around weapons her whole life. Her Dad had been in the Army, and he had taught her how to shoot at the age of twelve. The weapons themselves weren't disturbing to her, it was what they were about to be used for that was. These weapons were about to be used to take away a human life. She was wholly unprepared for that thought.

In her job as a national reporter, Desire had covered numerous tragic events that had resulted in the loss of many lives. But in her eyes, that was different. That was reporting, it was her job, and it was all done *after* the fact. In this case, she was watching weapons being packed in order to bring about death and destruction in the future. It was a surreal experience. It was news yet to be made. She felt like she was in the movie *Minority Report*, witnessing a pre-crime. She cared about Dante, and she had come to feel strongly about Lucky, and so her emotions were all over the place because of the situation she know found herself thrust into. She didn't know what to say, or what to do. Should she try to stop him, should she try to talk him out of going, should she call someone and report what she was witnessing? She was confused to the fullest to say the least. The man she had come to care about, was about to go out and perform a heinous act, in order to rescue a child that she adored. It all had her on an emotional roller coaster, and so once again, tears began to roll down her eyes. She was emotionally racked.

Dante stared at her. He too was at a loss for words. Not because he felt that he needed to justify what he was doing, or what he was about to do, but because he simply didn't know what to say to her. It was, what it was, he was going to find the men who has taken his little girl, and he was going to do whatever it took to get her back. If Desire didn't understand that, then fuck her. He would have to deal with her when he got back. Did that mean putting a bullet in the head of the woman he had come to have deep feelings for? He didn't know. Should he attempt to explain, he wondered? Did he owe her an explanation? The silence between the two of them was deafening. Dante turned, walked back into his closet to retrieve more weaponry.

Desire knew that she loved him. She knew that she couldn't stand there in tears saying nothing. She knew what type of person Dante was when she first started dating him. She knew his reputation. And now, to actually see that what people had said about him was true, was shocking to her. She had convinced herself that ninety percent of what she had heard had been rumor, that had grown over time into myth. How could such a gentle and caring man be the monster that everyone made him out to be?  It was impossible, she had convinced herself.  To watch him with Lucky, was to see a man so full of love that it was impossible for him to be filled with the evil and hatred and demonic nature that so many had accused him of having.  And now?

Perhaps that was it, Desire thought.  They had taken away that love, that happiness, that joy, that gentle kindness that he had inside of him when they took away his daughter.  Was the good that he displayed merely a reflection of *her* light?  In taking Lucky, had they taken away all of the goodness and kindness within his soul?  And if that was so, shouldn't she want him to get Lucky back?  Shouldn't she want the light to come back into his heart?  And not just as a selfish matter, but if she truly cared about him, and about his daughter, shouldn't she be helping him load weapons?  What would she do if it was her child?  What would *her* father have done?  What would any real father do?  And with that question, she had her answer.

Desire wiped the tears running down her cheeks as she thought of her own father.  Her dad would move Heaven and Earth to keep her safe even now, let alone when she was a little girl.  So how could *she* or anyone else fault Dante, for doing what any man, any father, any parent would do?  She couldn't.  Whatever it took, she thought.  If he had to kill to bring his daughter back home safely, then so be it.  And she would give him her support.

Dante walked back into the bedroom and placed more explosives on his bed.  He started to turn and walk back into his closet, but he halted once he seen Desire lift one of his black nylon  bags off of the floor, and start filling it with the guns and ammo that he had placed on his bed.  He didn't know what to say.  He didn't know if he should stop her, if he should send her away, or if he should just allow her to do what she was doing.  He didn't want this for her, he didn't want this to be a part of her life, or a part of their relationship.  He never wanted her to see this side of him, or of his family.  And now that she had, would he feel different about her, he wondered?  Would she now seem tainted?  The innocence that she held in her eyes when she looked at him, would that now be gone?  Would the sparkle be gone from his eyes when he looked at her?  Desire was not Angela, and he didn't want her to be.  If this had been Angela, she would already be gone.  She would have killed half the state by now.  It would be *him*, trying to stop *her*. No, she was not Angela. There would never be another Angela, and his heart was at peace with that. The place that Angela held in his heart would forever belong to her. It was locked, compartmentalized, and forever welded shut. It was their own special place, their own special memories, and he was okay with that. He didn't want Desire to be Angela, or anything like her. He wanted Desire to be Desire. *But what did that mean?*

Desire packed the first black nylon bag, and then lifted a second. She began placing Dante's assault rifles inside of the bag. He started to speak, but stopped cold. He still did not know what to say. He started for his closet, even though there was nothing left for him to retrieve.

"Dante," Desire called out to him.

Dante stopped in his tracks.

"I want you to know..."

"You don't have to say anything," Dante said, cutting her off. He turned and faced her. "I never wanted this for you. I never wanted you to see this, any of this."

"And then life happened," Desire said, continuing his sentence. "Life has a way of ruining plans, doesn't it?"

"Did it?" Dante asked softly. "Did it ruin our plans?"

Desire shook her head.

"I didn't want you to see this," Dante continued. "I didn't want you to be a part of this. I didn't want this to be a part of our relationship."

"It is what it is, Dante. If this is what it has to be from time to time, then so be it. I'd rather see it now, than later. I'd rather know everything up front. I have a right to know everything up front, right? I mean, nobody should entire into a relationship with blinders on. We all have a right to know what we're getting into, so that we can make a conscious decision to stay, or walk away."

"And what is your decision?" Dante asked.

Desire zipped up the nylon bag. "Hand me that other bag over there, will ya?"

Dante smiled. "Are you sure you want this?"

Desire paused and drew in a deep breath. She closed her eyes. "Tell me one thing, Dante. And you can be honest. Promise me, that you'll answer this question truthfully. Promise me."

Dante wasn't one for set-ups, and this question was definitely a set-up. Still, he decided that he would play along. "I promise."

"For real?" Desire asked.

"I swear," Dante said, raising his right hand. "I give you my word."

"Can I walk away?" Desire asked. She examined his face closely, searching for the truth. "Am I really free to chose whether I stay, or whether I walk away?"

Dante tilted his head back and drew in a deep breath. She had just lowered the boom on him. Only moments earlier, he had thought about killing her if she didn't except what he was doing, because she knew too much. She was in too deep to just be able to walk away. But now, he found himself in a different situation. A different mindset. He didn't want to kill her. He wouldn't kill her, he decided. She would be free to go if she so chose.

"Yes," Dante told her. He nodded. "I give you my word, on my Mother, you are free to chose whether or not you stay or walk away."

A smile spread across Desire's face. "Promise me I'll *always* have that freedom? The freedom to walk away."

Dante nodded. "You have it. I promise."

Now, it was Desire's turn to nod. "I'm staying. You couldn't drive me away. I love Lucky more than words could express. And I want you to bring her back home to me. You go out there, and you do whatever you have to do, to bring her home safe, you understand?"

Dante was already planning to do just that, but to have her say it, felt as though a tremendous burden had been lifted off of his shoulders.

"Do you know what you're saying?" Dante asked. "Do you know what that means?"

Desire turned and stared out of the window. She folded her arms. "I'm not stupid, Dante."

"And you're okay with that?" Dante asked.

Desire shook her head. "I'm never going to be okay with that. But, you do what you have to do, to bring that baby home safe. I support you, and I stand behind you in whatever you feel you have to do. If you have to move Heaven and Earth to bring her home, then you move Heaven, and I'll move Earth. I'm with you. I have your back."

Dante walked up behind Desire, and wrapped his arms around her.

19

"What does this mean?"

Desire shook her head. "I don't know."

Deep down, she did. She felt as though she had just jumped in with both feet. She had just taken a blood vow with Dante Reigns, through her acquiescence of murder. She was his wife now, although they hadn't walked down the aisle, or exchanged vows, or rings, they had just taken an oath. He was going to find Lucky, and she was going to support him in all that he had to do. And one of those things, meant that she was forever bound by an oath of silence.

Desire turned inside of his arms and faced him. "It's going to be okay. You're going to find her. And we're going to take her to The Marble Slab, and we're going to eat ice cream until our stomachs hurt. And then we're going to go to the park, and we're going to swing for hours. And then we'll have a picnic, and she'll fall asleep like she always does, and then you'll carry her to the car, and we'll drive her home, where you'll carry her upstairs. I'll put her pajamas on her while she's out like a light, and then we'll sneak off and make out on the couch until we fall asleep."

Dante was almost in tears. His heart was like ice, except when it came to his little girl. He was going to have those days out on the town with his little girl again. He leaned forward and kissed Desire softly.

"You go get her," Desire told him. She patted him on the ass.

Dante turned, lifted his bags of weapons from off of the bed. Desire lifted a couple of the bags herself.

"I got those," Dante said, reaching for the bags.

Desire pushed his hand away. "I got these. You carry those."

Dante smiled. He turned, and walked out of the bedroom, down the hall, and out the back door. Desire followed just behind, lugging two bags filled with weaponry. She was determined to play her role, and to show Dante that she was down with him one hundred percent. Dante stopped just short of the landing pad and turned back toward her.

"I would feel a whole lot better if you stayed here while I'm gone," he told her.

"Why is that?" she asked.

"I don't want to have to worry about you, while I'm out there searching for her. I need to know you're safe."

Desire nodded. She understood completely. She sat the bags she was carrying down on the ground, unzipped one, and pulled out a handgun. She pulled back the slide on the weapon, loading a round into the chamber, and then lowered the hammer and engaged the safety. She then took the weapon and placed it inside of Dante's waistband. He laughed.

"Damn, Bonnie!" Dante said with a smile. "Where'd you learn that from?"

It was her turn to laugh. "Hey, Clyde, my old man taught me."

"I'll remember that when it's time for me to meet Dear Old Dad," Dante said with a smile.

Desire leaned in and kissed Dante passionately. "You go get 'em. And bring my baby back."

Dante nodded. He turned toward his men, who rushed to where he was standing, lifted his bags, and carried them to the waiting helicopter.

"I'll call you later," Dante told her.

Desire shook her head. "No you won't."

She didn't want him to even if he could. She didn't want to know where he was at either. If she saw something particularly gruesome on the news, she didn't want to associate Dante with it. She wanted to be able to rationalize and fool herself into thinking the opposite of what she knew to be true. She needed that plausible denial for her heart.

The helicopter pilot began to power up the massive rotor wing copter, and its blades began to spin. The enormous blades quickly gained power, and the cyclonic blast began to kick up an enormous amount of rotor wash. The extremely loud chopping of the rotor blades made Dante and Desire have to shout in order to be heard.

"You be careful," Desire told him.

Dante nodded. "I will."

He turned, and jogged to the waiting helicopter, and climbed aboard. He had a flight to catch. The helicopter was going to take him out to San Antonio International Airport, where he was going to hop on one of the family's private Gulfstream jets for a quick trip out to New Mexico. He had a meeting with Chacho Hernandez. Chacho had told him that it was important, and that it could be very beneficial for him. Chacho wasn't exactly a friend to the Reigns family, and so he figured that it must be pretty important for Chacho to have interrupted his hunt for his daughter. Dante waved to Desire from the still open door, as the helicopter lifted off into the air. He was going to stop in New Mexico, and then get back on the hunt for his daughter. The bastards couldn't be far. His men were everywhere, and it was only a matter of time before he found them. And when he did, they were going to beg God for mercy, because he would have none.

# Chapter Three

Peaches woke to find herself in a totally unfamiliar environment. Her eyes were filled with days worth of sleep and her retinas were slow to adjust because of lack of use, and as a result were slow to bring things into focus. What she could see, however, was that her environment was white and nearly pristine. The monotonous white was interrupted by the different colored lights from the many monitors and machines throughout the room. And the distinct smell of antiseptic, with a faint tinge of Isopropyl alcohol, permeated the room. Her throat was sore and parched, and her entire body ached like she had just gone ten rounds with Floyd Mayweather. Peaches could feel the sharp stinging pain in her side where the bullets struck, and this brought about some clarity of mind. She now remembered that she had been shot.

The memory of that night slowly flashed through her mind. It came in pictures, surreal almost, as if she were watching a movie of what happened instead of actually living it. But she *had* lived it. It had all been real. The pain throughout her body reminded her that it had all been real. But how she got from there to here, from that night to this afternoon, was beyond her. She knew little, except that she was lying in a hospital bed.

"Hey, beautiful," a voice said softly.

Peaches turned her head in the direction from which it came. Darius was seated by her bedside.

"Glad you decided to rejoin us," Darius continued. He took her hand into his.

Peaches swallowed, but it came with great difficulty. She had an IV hooked up to her arm providing her with the vital sustaining fluids that she needed, but still, she had not swallowed, or spoken, or even opened her mouth in days. Speech came hard.

"What?" she asked weakly.

"We'll talk about that later," Darius told her.

Peaches shook her head. She wasn't going to wait for later. She had many questions, and there was much she needed to know. The fateful events of that night continued to run through her mind, and she thought of one person and one person only.

"V?"

Darius shook his head.

Peaches closed her eyes, and a tear ran down the side of her face. Peaches lifted her hand, and tried to raise up, much of the morphine had left her system, but that which remained reminded her of its presence. Her head swooned, and she was forced to lay back down.

Darius placed his hand on her. "Hey, lay down and rest. What are trying to do?"

"V," Peaches said weakly. "I gotta find V."

"Don't worry about V," Darius told her. "You worry about getting better. We'll get to that other stuff later."

Peaches closed her eyes and shook her head. The thought of V laying out on her lawn dead was too much for her. She needed to get to her. Perhaps she was still alive and just needed help. What about her men? What about Trap? And Joaquin? What had happened? Where was she? How did he get here? How did she get there? But most important, where were her girls? Where was her brother? Where was V?

"V," Peaches said once again.

Darius rose from his seat, took a small paper cup, and poured Peaches some ice water from a pitcher that the nurses left at her bedside. He lifted the cup to her lips, allowing her to sip from it. It felt like Heaven to her. Her careful sips, soon became full gulps.

"V," Peaches said, pushing the cup away. Her throat felt better by leaps and bounds, even though she still sounded a little hoarse when she spoke. "Where is V?"

Darius exhaled. He stared at her and shrugged. "I don't know. I don't know who V is."

Again Peaches closed her eyes. Darius had never met Vendetta, and he would have no idea who she was.  Finding out what happened that night, was going to take some information.  First, she needed to know as much as *he* knew, and then perhaps, she could begin to fill in the blanks.

"What happened?" Peaches asked.

"A massacre," Darius told her.  He shook his head.  "When we got there, they were walking through the estate, executing the men who were still alive.  We engaged in a firefight, took most of them out, the rest fled."

Peaches closed her eyes once again.  "Executing?"

Darius nodded.  "I don't know who else was alive.  We found some, took those who we found to the hospital.  Took you."

"How did you find me?" Peaches asked.

"We're not stupid," he told her.  "One, I had the original plans to your estate.  I pulled them from the city.  And two, when we got there, they were tearing the place apart, and you were no where to be found after we took them out.  That told me that you were still alive.  We looked at the plans, and we realized that something on the plans was off.  I knew instantly that it was a safe room."

"How did you get in?"

"The code wasn't difficult to figure out," Darius told her.

Again, Peaches closed her eyes.

Silence permeated the room for several moments.  The code to get inside of her safe room, was Chesarae's birthday.  Darius had found out about Chesarae.

"You didn't find her?" Peaches asked.  Her mind was on Vendetta.

"I don't know who they found outside," Darius answered.  "I was focused on finding you.  And once I found you, I got you out of there.  I took you to the hospital.  I don't know who else was taken.  But whoever was taken to the hospital, was taken by my men.  The police never showed up.  How can that be?  Who had the power to keep the police from showing up to a massive gun battle?  Who?"

Peaches shook her head.  She didn't have the answer to that question.  Did Kharee have that kind of power?  She doubted it.  Especially in Columbus.

"Is she here?" Peaches asked.

Darius shook his head.  "No one is here, but you.  The rest of the survivors are back in Columbus."

"Back in Columbus?" Peaches peered around the room. "Where am I?"

"You're in Maryland," Darius told her. "Baltimore. As soon as you were stable, I had you airlifted out of there. I needed to get you out of Ohio to some place safe. You're at The Johns Hopkins Medical Center. My cousin Brandon controls Maryland. You're safe here."

Peaches shook her head. She needed to be in Ohio. She needed to be able to find V. She needed to know about Joaquin.

"My brother?"

Darius seated himself in the chair once again. He took her hand into his. "Peach, I was glad to get *you* out of there. It was only by the grace of God that we showed up when we did. I spent every waking hour by your bed in Columbus, and as soon as you were able to travel, Brandon had a doctor sign the papers to have you airlifted to Johns Hopkins. I don't know about anybody else."

"How bad was it?" Peaches asked. "What else got hit that night?"

Darius shrugged. He knew there had been other targets, but he didn't want to tell her. At least not yet. He saw no need to cause her additional stress while she was laying in a hospital bed.

"I need you to find my brother," Peaches told him.

Darius nodded. It was a reasonable request. He still had men in Ohio, lots of men. He would send them out to see if they could find her brother, and to see who was amongst the survivors from the carnage that night. Multiple targets had gotten hit that night, and the body count had been historic. It had made *national* news. But like all incidents involving Black people, the media had labeled it gang violence. In this instance, he was grateful that they had done so. It kept Peaches out of it, and kept The Commission from learning about the true nature of the incident.

"I'll find him," Darius said, patting her hand.

"Don't do that," Peaches told him.

"Do what?"

"Don't patronize me," she told him. "I need you to find him! I need you to find Joaquin."

Darius nodded. "I'll find him. I give you my word."

Peaches turned away from him and grimaced. The pain that she was experiencing was excruciating.

"I need you to find my girl V," Peaches told him. "And Trap. Trap was already in the hospital when this happened. I need to find all my people. I need to know."

Peaches broke down into tears. Darius clasped her hand and kissed it.

"Hey, hey, relax," Darius told her. "Hey, it's going to be all right. It's going to be okay. We'll find everyone. I promise you. I'll get my people on it."

"I need to know, Darius," Peaches told him. "No matter what. Promise me, whether good or bad, you'll tell me. I need to know."

Darius nodded. He knew that the information wouldn't be good. But he would let her know irregardless of his findings. She deserved that much.

"I need for you to get some rest," Darius said softly.

Peaches nodded. She was tired, and the morphine that was still coursing through her veins wasn't going to allow her to stay up for long. Her thoughts were on Ohio, on her brother, on V and Trap, and on what happened. One minute she had been in the house chilling with her girl, and the next minute all hell had broken loose. She had masked men overrunning her estate, coming over her back walls, lobbing grenades at her like they were softballs.  Who had that kind of power, she wondered? Not Kharee. As powerful as he was, he didn't have the manpower or the balls for a straight up assault like that. It would be too bloody for him. He would never risk it, never risk losing so many men. Losing that many people would threaten his grip on what he already had. And then, there was the issue of the police. They *never* came. They never responded to her alarm going off, and according to Darius, they *still* hadn't responded when he and his men arrived. Who had that kind of muscle, those kinds of connections, that kind of power?

Peaches tried to resist the effects of the drugs remaining in her system, but they were too powerful, and she was bone tired. Despite her best efforts at trying to stay awake and to began to think things through, she began to doze off. Soon, she was once again in a deep, medicated sleep.

*****

Vendetta opened her eyes and couldn't believe what she saw. He was still there. He had been there each time she regained consciousness, and apparently hadn't left her bedside. At least not that she could tell. Who was he, she wondered? What was he doing there? Was he a detective? His dress told her that he wasn't, which only increased the mystery surrounding him. She knew where she was, and she even remembered how she got there, but what she didn't know was the who, and why part that concerned the stranger at her beside.

Vendetta figured that today was the day. The day that she would ask him, the day that she was finally able to confront her fears and find out all of the things that she needed to know. She saw the house being over run, and she knew that Peaches had been inside. She saw the explosions, and she remembered clearly all of that night's events. She even remembered briefly coming too, in the arms of the stranger by her bedside. Her strength was up, so she decided to stop playing possum, and open her eyes.

He smiled at her upon seeing that she was awake. Vendetta had to blink. He was beyond beautiful, beyond gorgeous, beyond being drop dead handsome, there were no words that popped into her head that she could use to describe him. Chesarae was cute as hell, Vendetta thought, and her Tavion was gorgeous, but the man sitting by her bedside was on another level. He was flawless.

"Hello," DeMarion said, smiling at her.

"Hi," Vendetta said, meekly. Her thoughts turned to her own looks. She lifted her hand and ran it through her hair.

DeMarion laughed. "C'mon now."

"What?" Vendetta asked, managing a frown.

DeMarion ran his hand through her hair. "You're laying in a hospital bed, don't tell me that you're worried about your hair."

Vendetta blushed. She had been caught, she had been worried about her hair. He didn't understand. He was super fucking fine, and she was laying up in a hospital bed with her hair all jacked up.

"Who are you?" Vendetta asked. After she asked, she hoped that it

28

hadn't come out the wrong way. She didn't want to come off sounding rude.

"D," DeMarion told her. "Everyone calls me D."

"D?" Vendetta asked. "That still doesn't tell me *who* you are."

DeMarion smiled. She was beautiful to him. Lying in the hospital bed with no make-up, she looked gorgeous. It was a natural beauty, one without a painted face, or any kind of adornment, and that meant that it was real.

"My name is DeMarion," he told her.

Vendetta held out her hand. "Pleased to meet you, DeMarion."

DeMarion gently clasped her hand and shook it. "The pleasure is all mines."

Vendetta shook her hand. "I don't think so. I remember you. I remember you from that night. You carried me."

DeMarion smiled. "You do remember."

"Why?"

"Why?" DeMarion asked, lifting an eyebrow. "Well, you looked like you could use a hand."

"That's not funny," Vendetta told him. "Who are you? Why were you there?"

DeMarion lifted his hands in surrender. "Okay, okay, I'm sorry. I didn't mean for it to be funny. But, you did look like you could use a hand. I *was* there that night. And I did lift you up and carry you away."

"Why?"

"Why?" DeMarion asked. "What do you mean, *why*? What was I supposed to do, leave you on the ground to die? Or let them finish walking through the yard, capping off survivors?"

"You killed them," Vendetta said softly, staring off into space. Her memories came to her in bits and pieces. "You shot them. And then you scooped me up into your arms and carried me to safety."

DeMarion smiled. "When you say it like that, it sounds kinda heroic."

"You brought me here?" Vendetta asked.

DeMarion nodded.

"The house?" Vendetta asked. "Was there anyone in the house? Any survivors?"

DeMarion shrugged his shoulders. "I don't know. I didn't go in the house. I took care of the guys who were on the East side of the place. And once I found you, I..."

"You scooped me up, and you left," Vendetta said, finishing his sentence. "Why?"

DeMarion swallowed hard, and stared into Vendetta's face. He wanted to tell her how beautiful she was. He wanted to tell her how he scooped her up into his arms, carried her to a waiting car, and cleaned the dirt off of her face. He wanted to tell her that the moment he rolled her over and saw her face, that his heart fell into his feet and he knew that he wasn't going to leave her side.

"Why not?" DeMarion said, turning away from her.

"Uh-un," Vendetta told him. "Look at me. Don't turn away from me. That was you..."

"What?"

"I felt you rubbing my face, caressing it, telling me to hang on, that everything was going to be okay. It was you."

"So?"

"You don't know me like that."

Again, a smile came to DeMarion's face. She was not only beautiful, but feisty.

"Who are you?" Vendetta asked again.

"I already told you that."

"No," Vendetta said shaking her head. "You told me what your name was, but you never told me who you were. What were you doing there?"

"I came with my cousin," DeMarion explained. "What were *you* doing there?"

"I was visiting a friend."

"Wow, speaking of bad timing."

"That's not funny," Vendetta snapped. "A lot of people died that day, a lot of good men, a lot of people that I knew, people who I considered friends!"

DeMarion hadn't thought of it that way. "I'm sorry."

"I need to know where my friend is," Vendetta continued. "The girl in the house? What happened to her?"

DeMarion shrugged. "I don't know."

Vendetta sat up in bed. "I need to know."

"Hey, calm down," DeMarion told her, resting his hand on her chest. "Lay back down before you pull something, or strain something, or burst something. I'll find out."

"I need to know now!" Vendetta said forcefully.

"I'll find out as soon as I can," DeMarion told her. "Right now, is not the best time to be snooping around. The police, the news, everyone. That place is one big ass crime scene."

Vendetta leaned back and closed her eyes. "Peaches."

"Peaches?" DeMarion repeated. He recognized the name. It was who they came for. He led the team on the Eastern side, while Darius led the team through the main gate. Their cousin DeFranz took more men through the breach on the West side. After he secured his side, and came across Vendetta, he carried her to one of his cars and brought her to the hospital. He hadn't spoken with Darius or DeFranz since. His orders from Brandon were to lay low in Ohio. And that was what he was doing.

"Yeah, Peaches!" Vendetta told him. "Where is she?"

DeMarion shook his head. "I don't know. I can find out for you. I will find out for you. But it's going to take some time. Things are hot right now, even here at the hospital. There are police everywhere."

"Here?"

DeMarion nodded. "Apparently, the gun battle found its way to one of the local hospitals, and now every hospital in the city has been turned into a police encampment."

Vendetta closed her eyes, and her heart sank. "Trap. They went after Trap."

Vendetta shook her head. Ashaad must have been there, she thought. That was where the gun battle part came in. Who was alive, who was not? It was all going to take some sorting out. But one thing was for certain, whoever it was that hit them, had an enormous fucking army, *and* they had balls of steel. To pull something like that off, and to do it in multiple locations? It had to have been Kharee, but to be able to infiltrate that many men into Columbus, without anyone knowing or saying anything, would have been virtually impossible. He didn't have it like that. He just couldn't have. But there were no other suspects, or anyone else remotely possible of being able to pull something like that off. But whoever it was, if they had gone after Trap in the hospital, then they wouldn't hesitate to go after her. She needed to get gone.

"I need to get out of here," Vendetta told him.

"*What?* Are you serious? You're just now starting to heal."

"I need to get out of here before they hit me again," Vendetta told him. "And they will hit me again."

"This place is a police camp!" DeMarion told her. "Plus, I have men scattered all over this hospital. You're safe here."

Vendetta shook her head. "No I'm not. You don't know what's going on here, I do. You don't know anything about Ohio, I do. Whoever hit us, hit us hard, and hit us heavy. If I don't get out of here, then I'm dead. Are you going to help me?"

DeMarion told himself not to do it. He repeated over and over to himself to not look at her, to not look into her eyes. Still, he was drawn to her. One glance into her face, and he knew that he was going to help her.

"I don't know you like that, remember?" DeMarion said, exhaling forcefully.

Vendetta smiled. She knew that he was going to help her. Once she was out, she was going to use him to help her find out what happened to her sisters. She needed to find Peaches and Trap. And then Peaches would want to find Joaquin and Omar and Chesarae. She just hoped that she didn't run into whatever his name was. Oh yeah, she thought, Tavion. Her boyfriend's name was Tavion.

DeMarion smiled at her with his perfect teeth, and million watt smile. His dimples were so deep that they made the Grand Canyon look like a dip in the freeway. Not only was he drop dead gorgeous, but he had men, money, and had domed a couple of guys and then scooped her up into his arms and carried her to safety. She stopped believing in fairy tales a long time ago, she thought. But what was she supposed to do now that she was actually living a real one? Her fucking Prince Charming had killed for her, rescued her, and was now about to whisk her away once again.

"Okay, so how are we going to do this?" Vendetta asked.

"I'll have one of my men grab you something from Saks or Neimans, and then we can get lost," DeMarion told her. "I have Ferrari in the parking lot. That should get us lost pretty quick."

A Ferrari, Vendetta thought?  Pick her up something from Saks or Neimans?  Tavion who?

# Chapter Four

Chacho Hernandez's 5,580 acre ranch, was nestled just above the Sante Fe County's spectacular Galisteo Basin. The massive ranch had panoramic views over the entire basin, allowing it to take in Northern Santa Fe's rugged escarpments, sculpted canyons, dramatic peninsulas, and rich grasslands. In the distance, one could see the areas numerous gentle rolling hills, and lush, green, forested mountains. Chacho had spent millions transforming the ancient landscape into a viable ranching operation, and millions more constructing the nearly 50,000 square foot adobe style mansion that sat in the center of the property. The mansion boasted numerous barns, two massive swimming pools, a tennis court, a basketball court, and even a riding ring for his imported Spanish stallions. The property even had its own private runway. It was on this runway, where he was meeting with his distinguished guest.

The Reigns family's Gulfstream G 650 private jet touched down on the private airstrip, and shortly afterward, rolled to a stop. The pilot maneuvered the jet around to where his guest were waiting, and shut down the jet's massive turbine engines. The door to the massive, black, sixty five million dollar jet slowly opened, and the internal stairs deployed, allowing the jet's occupants to exit from the luxurious cabin. Dante walked down the stairs and was greeted by his host, Chacho Hernandez.

The bright New Mexico sun struck Dante across his face, giving him the first taste of warmth that he had had in the last few hours. The warm rays felt good against his skin, as the interior of the jet had been cool. The brightness of the sunlight caused him to place his hand over his eyes and shield its rays until his eyes could adjust. Chacho extended his hand, and Dante clasped it.

"Dante, que paso?"

"De nada," Dante answered. "Nothing much. What's the deal?"

Chacho placed his arm around Dante, leading him down the flight line. "How are you doing? I mean, *really* doing?"

Dante shrugged. "What do you think?"

Chacho nodded. "I understand. They fucked up. What they did was fucked up. Whoever did this, they crossed the line. They crossed it big time."

Dante nodded. He wasn't here for pleasantries, and he wished Chacho would get on with business. His mind was back in Texas, and that was where he wanted to be. He wanted to be searching for his daughter, and every moment that he wasted in New Mexico, was a moment that he could be spending in the search for his daughter. The clock was ticking.

"I want you to know that I am invoking the charter," Chacho told him.

Dante stopped in his tracks. "The charter?"

"The Commission's charter," Chacho told him. "I am going to call a meeting of the full Commission, and I am going to make a motion to invoke the Commission's charter. An attack on one, is an attack on all. They fucked up when they went after your daughter. Now, they will feel the weight of the entire Commission. We are in this together. They didn't just take your little Lucquita, they took all of our daughter."

Dante was speechless. He had battled with Chacho for many years. They had tried to kill one another many times, and had come pretty close quite a few times. He took territory away from Chacho, and they had pretty much been at a constant state of war since The Commission's inception. And now, Chacho was standing by his side, willing to send men and money to help him in his war, and in his search for his daughter. He hesitated in speaking, because he didn't know if his voice would crack. Lucky was the emotional key to his heart.

"Thank you," Dante said. He extended his hand, and Chacho clasped it.

"I have been on this, since her disappearance," Chacho told him. "I think I have something for you."

Dante looked befuddled.

Chacho placed his hand in the small of Dante's back and guided him toward a small hangar that was sitting just off of the runway. Dante was followed by seven of his men, while Chacho was followed by roughly fifteen of his. Inside of the hangar Dante noticed a man sitting in a chair, with his hands bound behind his back. It was clear that the man had been beaten.

"Right here," Chacho said, guiding Dante up to a metal folding table that had been set up inside of the hangar. Various papers were scattered all over the table. Chacho lifted some documents from off of the table and handed them to Dante.

Dante rifled through the papers. "Passports?"

Chacho nodded.

Dante read through the documents. "What am I missing?"

"How many of them are they?" Chacho asked.

Dante counted the remnants of the documents he held in his hand. "Six?"

Chacho nodded. He handed Dante the remnants of some other documents, and Dante flipped through them.

"What is this?"

"Photo IDs," Chacho answered.

"Passports, photo IDs," Dante said holding up the remnants of the documents. "What are you saying? These belong to the kidnappers?"

"Count the ID's," Chacho told him.

Dante counted the papers in his hand. "Five?"

Again, Chacho nodded. "Five fake ID's, but six fake passports. Five men needed ID's, but they needed six fake passports to leave the country. They're taking someone with them."

Dante closed his eyes.

"And the best passport maker this side of the Rio Grande, is my man, Jesus over there," Chacho said, nodding in the direction of the man tied to the chair. "He's a master at creating false documents. I've used him plenty of times. You need some work, and you need it to look real, you visit Jesus."

And now Dante understood. He understood completely. The man tied up in the chair, the reason for his visit, everything. It all suddenly became clear to him.

"He knows," Dante said, peering over toward Chacho's captive. "He's seen them. He's taken pictures of them."

Chacho nodded. "He may even know how they plan to leave the country."

Dante lifted a pair of scissors from the table and rushed to where the man was sitting. He placed the scissors beneath the man's chin and pressed hard.

"Where are they?" Dante asked, through clenched teeth. "Where the fuck are they going?"

"We were able to get a few things out of him," Chacho said. "But he refused to talk anymore. I know that you could be more persuasive. Even though I hate to admit it, you're a lot better at these types of things than we are."

Dante opened the scissors, and knelt down. He placed the scissors on the hem of the man's trouser, and began to cut. He cut up the man's pants leg, until his thigh was exposed. Dante ripped the pants leg open even further, completely exposing the man's left leg.

"You are going to tell me where they are, or where they were going, or I'm going to cut your leg open, and pull out your femur," Dante told him. "And it's not going to feel good."

"The man stared at Dante. "No speak English."

Dante smiled. He backhanded the document forger across the side of his face. "You wanna play with me? You wanna fucking play with me?"

Dante opened the scissors, and jabbed one of the blades into the mans thigh, and then pulled the blade forward, opening up the mans thigh. Blood poured out of the man's leg by the cup load, as he howled like a wounded animal. Chacho and his men turned away from the gory sight.

"Where were they going?" Dante shouted. "Where? Where are they taking her?"

"No speak English," the man repeated with disdain.

Dante took the scissor blade, and jabbed it deep into the wound that he had just opened up. Again, the man screamed. Dante dug into the man's bone with the scissor blade, like he was trying to carve his initials on it. The man screamed continuously, until he couldn't take the pain any longer. He body shut down, and he passed out.

"Wake him up!" Dante shouted, rubbing the sweat from his brow.

Chacho's men snapped into action. They raced around the hanger trying to find something to revive the man. They found a water cooler with a jug of water in it. They removed the jug and carried it back to where the document forger was sitting. Two of them held the heavy jug, counted, and swung the jug, dashing water on their captive's face and shoulders. The man regained consciousness.

"Don't even think about it," Dante told the man. "It's not going to be that easy. Don't think for one moment, that you're going to be able to escape the pain that I'm about to inflict on you. The good things is, you can stop it. You can avoid the pain that you are about to experience, by telling me one thing. Where were they headed after they took her?"

The document forger shook his head.

"Now you understand what I saying?" Dante asked. "You speak English?"

The man remained silent.

Dante grabbed the man's hair, and pulled his head back. "You speak English now?"

The document forger stayed silent.

Dante released the man's hair, walked around the chair, and again jabbed one of the scissor blades into the man's leg wound. Again, the document forger howled like a wounded banshee.

Chacho and his men turned away. Blood poured from the man's leg like it was a blood fountain. A large puddle was beginning to develop on the floor beneath the chair.

As Dante stepped through the puddle, he was reminded of the man's blood loss. He couldn't keep this up for long, because the man would be dead from loss of blood after a while. He needed to make the forger talk, he thought. He needed something to break the tough son of a bitch.

The distant rumble of a train in the distance gave Dante the answer that he needed. The thought of bleeding and torture didn't move the man to talking, then perhaps certain death would. When men knew that death was imminent, and that it would be excruciatingly painful, their outlook changed somewhat. Perhaps staring death in the face, and watching it slowly chugging toward him would loosen the document forger's tongue. Dante turned to Chacho.

"A train?" Dante asked.

"A train?" Chacho didn't understand what Dante was talking about initially. And then he heard the humming sound of the locomotive nearing his property. He peered at his Rolex. "That's the Burlington Northern Santa Fe."

"When's the next one?" Dante asked.

Chacho thought briefly. He had become so used to the trains roaring by his property transporting goods from one coast to another that he barely noticed them anymore. He had watched them go by, raced them on horseback, threw stones at them with his kids, even camped by the tracks at night. He had even timed them. He knew their schedules like the back of his hand, and could even listen to their sound and tell which one belonged to which company, how many engines it had, and in some instances, what it was carrying. Coal loads had a distinctive sound because of their weight.

"The BNSF is first, and then you have a Union Pacific that goes by thirty minutes later," Chacho told him.

A smile ran across Dante's face. He turned toward Chacho's men. "Bring him."

Dante led the men outside the hanger toward a group of waiting trucks. He climbed inside one of the trucks and waited for Chacho's men, as well as his own, to climb inside of the various vehicles. The document forger was thrown in the back of the truck in which Dante was sitting. Chacho himself climbed into the driver's seat of the truck where Dante was waiting.

"Let's go to the tracks," Dante told him.

Chacho understood. He smiled, started up his GMC Sierra Denali pick up, and headed off toward the railroad tracks.

"You're one wicked motherfucker," Chacho said, while driving across his property.

Dante shook his head. "I'm a father. And I'll do anything to get my little girl back."

Chacho nodded in agreement. He understood where Dante was coming from. He too was a father, and he would walk through hell to keep his children safe. The idea that someone had taken Dante's little girl, was not only repulsive to him, but it shocked him to his core. He imagined what it would be like, if it was his daughter that had been taken. The thought was unbearable. No, he thought, they would all have to take a stand, and stop this shit before it got started. Children were out of bounds. And everyone would have to understand that. You mess with a person's child, then the world was going to come down on you. He had to make this unacceptable, not just because of Dante's daughter, but in order to protect his own. His reasons were selfish, more than anything. He was determined to protect his own children from a similar fate.

Chacho pulled up near the railroad tracks that bordered the northern end of his property. He parked his truck some thirty yards from tracks and climbed out. Dante, and his men climbed out as well. Chacho waved his hand, and his men yanked the document forger from the back of the truck and threw him on the ground near Chacho's feet.

"Find something in the truck to tie him up," Chacho ordered.

His men raced to the back of the pickup trucks and began searching frantically for ropes and cords, or any other material that could be used to secure the forger. He already had bounds on his hands and feet, and they could use those, so they just needed something to secure him to the tracks. They found both rope, *and* bungee cord. The trucks were used on the ranch, so they were pretty well stocked with tools and other materials that were necessary in the day to day operation of a large ranching operation.

The men carried the rope back to where Chacho and Dante were standing.

"Tie this motherfucker to the tracks," Dante told them.

Chacho's men lifted the document forger up, dragged him to the railroad tracks, and then tied him face up across the tracks. Dante and Chacho walked up to the bound man and peered down at him.

"There's nothing out here, amigo," Chacho said, extending his arms. "Nothing. No traffic, no cars, no stop lights, no crossings, no bridges, nothing. When the trains pass through here, they are going full speed. Eighty, ninety, sometimes a hundred miles an hour. And if you get a youngster running it, he'll get it up to one twenty five or more. At that speed, it'll slice you into three pieces."

"You still no speak English?" Dante asked.

Sweat poured down the document forger's face. He could feel the vibration on the track, although none of them could see or hear it. He knew that it was coming.

Dante peered down at his watch. "You still have a little bit of time. Where are they planning to take her?"

Sweat continued to pour down the document forger's face, but he remained silent.

"What are you scared of?" Dante shouted. "What? Tell me! You tell me, and I'll protect you. They won't be able to harm you! Tell me!"

"You can't protect me!" The man shouted. "You can't even protect your own daughter!"

Dante lost it. He began kicking the man in his ribs, and face. "You son of a bitch! You tell me where they're taking her!"

Chacho and his men grabbed Dante and pulled him back.

"Tell me!" Dante shouted. "Tell me!"

The document forger could feel the vibrations on the track growing stronger.

"Jesus!" Chacho shouted to the document forger. "Who sent them here? Who sent them to you? Tell me."

The document forger swallowed hard. He could feel his energy leaving him, his life force was pouring out of him with the blood running out of his leg.

"Who sent them?" Chacho repeated.

"El Paso," Jesus said weakly. "Sheriff..."

"The Sheriff!" Dante shouted. "The Sheriff of El Paso county? He sent them?"

Suddenly, the train could be seen on the horizon. And just as Chacho had foretold, it was moving at breakneck speeds.

"We don't have much time!" Dante told Jesus. "The Sheriff of El Paso county?"

Jesus stared at Dante and smiled. He knew that his time was growing near. And even if he told Dante what he wanted, chances were, Dante would still kill him. And even if Dante did release him, he was dead anyway. He had lost much blood, and would lose much more before he was able to get adequate medical attention. And even if he managed to make it through that, he was a dead man on the streets. No one liked a snitch. Everyone who he'd ever worked for, would now view him as a liability. And he'd worked for some extremely powerful people. He'd be dead within a week. Jesus now resigned himself to his fate. His Catholic school upbringing returned to him, and he began resiting the rosary.

Angered, Dante kicked Jesus in his side once again. "Fuck you! Fuck you! You're not going to Heaven! People who help kidnap little girls don't go to Heaven! There's no forgiveness for you!"

Dante turned toward one of Chacho's men, grabbed him, and reached for the man's weapon. Chacho and the others grabbed Dante.

"No!" Chacho told him. "Wait!"

The train grew larger as it raced closer. The loud rumble of the locomotive's engines could be heard throughout the area. The train saw the grouping of trucks near the tracks, and the engineer began applying the train's massive horn.

"Where were they going, Jesus?" Chacho asked calmly. "There's still time. There's still time to untie you. Tell me. I can protect you. I give you my word."

"I gave my word," Jesus said weakly. "I already said too much."

"Are they taking her back to Mexico?" Chacho asked. "She's a little girl. Innocent. She has nothing to do with any of this. Where are they taking her?"

Jesus peered down the tracks at the oncoming train. He knew that it was too late. He turned back toward Chacho and nodded.

"Mexico?"

The document forger nodded.

"Where are they going to cross the border?" Chacho asked frantically. "Where, Jesus?"

Chacho and Dante's men began backing away from the tracks. The train was barreling down on them fast. There was no way that it would be able to stop in time, even if it had slammed on its breaks miles down the road. Everyone knew that it was all over, and no one wanted to see what was coming. A few of the men climbed back inside of the trucks, so as not to hear nor see what was about to happen.

"Juarez, Laredo, they didn't know themselves," Jesus told them. He turned toward Dante. "She deserves a better father."

With the speed of a cheetah, Dante drew a handgun from one of Chacho's men, who had let his guard down. He aimed it at the document forger.

"And you deserve to feel more pain," Dante told the man. He squeezed the trigger, firing bullet's into the man's legs, and genitals.

Dante peered up at the train as it was passing. He could see horror on the engineer's face, as well as see the man cringing and covering his face at the last moment. Jesus' blood shot all over the area, as did various parts of his body. The massive coal train had sliced Jesus into pieces, easier than a straight razor going through a banana.

"Fuck!" Chacho said, turning away.

"Laredo, El Paso, at least I have someplace to concentrate on now," Dante said. "*If* he was telling the truth. Do you think he was telling the truth?"

Chacho shrugged. "Probably. He knew that he was finished."

Dante nodded. "Thank you."

"Don't you go getting sentimental on me," Chacho told him. "I still hate you. And I still want you dead."

"Ditto," Dante said nodding.

"I just..." Chacho shook his head. "This was way outta line."

Dante nodded.

"Besides, nobody fucks with my niggers but me," Chacho said, smiling. "If there is anyone who is going to bring my niggers to their knees, it's going to be me."

"You're still a cabbage picking, lawn mowing, leaf blowing wetback," Dante told him. "And one day, I'm going to put a bullet in that thick Mongrel, Mesoamerican, Mestizo head of yours."

This time, it was Chacho who smiled. The two men wrapped their arms around one another and embraced tightly.

# Chapter Five

There was luxury, and then there was decadent luxury, and then there was The Plaza Hotel. An iconic landmark on the New York City social scene for more than a century, The Plaza had always been the destination for discerning travelers, important dignitaries, celebrities, and visiting royalty. It was a place of sheer opulence and grandeur, a place where white glove concierge services, Rolls Royce livery, world class spa treatments, and five star restaurants colluded, to provide an unparalleled experience for guest. The Plaza was a place of imported marble, gold fixtures, crystal chandeliers, and Louis XV furnishings. It was a place of $30,000 a night suites, with private champagne bars, and of views Central Park and Fifth Avenue. It was in one such suite where today's meeting of the Old Ones was taking place.

The Royal Plaza suite, was a 4,490 square foot suite that overlooked the legendary Pulitzer Fountain on New York's world famous Fifth Avenue. The suite contained three private bedroom suites, and in-suite gymnasium with state-of-the-art fitness equipment, a gourmet kitchen with stainless steel Viking appliances, a formal living room with its very own grand piano, a private library, a luxurious dining room with seating for twelve, all of which was serviced by the suite's very own private elevator. To say that the Royal Plaza Suite was only for the movers and shakers of society would be a vast understatement. The suite was constantly booked, and only the *extremely* rich and powerful were guaranteed access to it. Today, it belonged to Don Esposito.

The Old Ones were gathered in the living room, seated beneath the massive crystal chandelier, sipping on various glasses of liquor, and puffing on massive imported Cuban cigars.

Don Graziella Biaggio cleared his throat, calling the meeting to order. The butlers and other servants quickly disappeared, retreating into the kitchen and out of the suite.

"My friends, it is wonderful as always to see you all," Biaggio told them. "I don't know how many years, months, days that I have left, so as an old man, anytime I get to see old friends, I consider it a blessing."

"*Centani*," Don Guiseppi De Luca said, lifting his glass. "May you live a hundred more years, my friend."

"*Centani*," Don Amedeo Esposito joined in, also lifting his glass.

"*Centani*, my old friend," Don Tito Bonafacio said, joining in the toast.

"*Centani*," Don Lombardi said, lifting his glass as well.

"Thank you, my friends," Don Biaggio told them. "Time. Time is a precious gift. A gift to be appreciated, valued, and even cherished. But one thing about time, is that despite our most vigorous prayers, it does not stand still. Time moves forward, it changes, and it brings with it a different world. This, this is a strange new world that we are living in my friends. A strange new world. And if this is the direction in which we are going, I am glad that my days in it, will be limited."

"No, no," De Luca said. "Don't say that, my friend. May your days be long."

Don Biaggio waved his hand, dismissing the idea. "I am a dinosaur, and the times have left me behind."

"What is it, that trouble you so much, my old friend," Don Bonafacio asked, leaning forward. Bonafacio was the same age as Biaggio, and the two of them had been members of La Costa Nostra for the same number of years. The wrinkles in their hands and faces told of their years and experiences within the organization. Both men were tired, and both were in their sunset.

"The reason I asked you all to come here, is because I am troubled about what is going on in Texas," Don Biaggio told them. "I'm sure that you are all familiar with the situation."

Don Bonafacio nodded solemnly. "They kidnapped that little Black girl. Such a shame."

"What do we care about that?" Don Esposito asked. "Niggers and Mexicans. Let them kill each other."

Biaggio and Bonafacio exchanged glances. They were no fans of the

46

Reigns family, in fact, they both hated them. But both men understood the implications of the kidnapping, and both had grandchildren roughly the same age, and both of them hated Esposito. The kidnapping of a child, even a little nigger girl, was out of line. They were men of honor.

"It's not that simple, my friend," De Luca said, stepping in, with his extremely thick Jersey accent. "This opens up a whole new can a worms. Kidnapping kids is way over the line."

"Exactly," Don Biaggio said, chiming in. "This thing, is taking what we do, to a different level. It used to be, that a man's family was off limits. In the old days, there was a such thing as honor. Even against the Blacks, we didn't go into their homes, and we didn't kill their women and children. I don't feel good about this."

"I'm not sure that I understand what this has to do with us, Don Biaggio," Esposito told him. "A bunch of Mexicans kidnapped a little nigger girl. That's not a good thing, but why should we care? Isn't it good that they're killing each other? Isn't this our opportunity to grow stronger, while they grow weaker?"

"We should care, my friend, because if this becomes acceptable, then one day, men will come into *my* home, or *your* home, and they will take away your grandchildren or mine," Don Bonafacio explained.

"On that day, the dogs will all die!" Esposito declared with much drama.

"We don't kill kids," De Luca told him. "But I do see your point. I do see this as an opportunity to get stronger, to restore the glory of the families, to take back what rightfully belongs to us."

The fact that it was De Luca saying this, gave the old dons pause. They respected De Luca, and would never offend him. But they did want him to fully understand the implications of what was happening in Texas.

"Those niggers think we don't know about their secret little army in Jersey," Esposito declared. "They got thousands of nigger soldiers all over the place. Just lying in wait. Waiting for the day that our neck is exposed. I say that now is the time to strike. Now is the time to let them, and that upstart Commission of theirs, know who were really are. Now is the time, while they're distracted, to take back Jersey, take back Philly, and run their asses completely out of the Northeast."

Biaggio nodded. "I see your point. And it's not that I'm against it, but what we need to make sure of, is that our play on Jersey doesn't pull us into a wider war with these people. We don't want to be affiliated with kidnappers."

"My father would turn over in his grave if my family were to be associated with kidnapping dogs," Bonafacio told them.

"Of course," Lombardi agreed. "We would never dishonor ourselves with such an association. However, the idea of consolidating our hold on Jersey, and retaking Philly, is very appealing. Of course, we would divide up what was taken?"

"Evenly?" Esposito asked. He was the least affluent of the dons, and needed the revenues that more territory would bring.

Biaggio and Bonafacio exchanged knowing glances. They had been through this many times before. They had been members of La Costa Nostra for fifty years, and their families had sat at the table since the organization's inception. They had seen many wars, and many faces come and go. They had an encyclopedic memory of the organization's history. Leading these new comers along without appearing to lead them was the challenge. They needed them to understand what was real, and what was fool's gold. A war with The Commission, was still a war with The Commission. Whether distracted or not. One day, The Commission would no longer be distracted, and where would that leave them? Were they ready to fight against the full weight of a united Commission? They needed the young dons around the table to understand that the five families were not fly by night entities, and that they planned for the decades ahead, not for the months ahead.

"War, war, war," Biaggio told them. "I've fought many wars in my lifetime. I seen many friends go because of these wars. And once you become an old man, you gain a perspective on war, and what war means. Men die, families are left behind. Wives, children, mothers, brothers, sisters. Why did they die? That is always the question that is left. What was it for, what was gained? We used to go to war to protect our families, to protect our families interest, which is the same thing, and to make sure that the future belonged to our children. War, for the sake of war, or territory, or money, is that a good war? Can I, an old man, look into the eyes of a young woman, a young mother, a young child, and tell them that their father died, so that I could have another avenue somewhere in Jersey that they never even heard of? For money? I don't need money, and I pay my people well, so they don't need it either. So what for? What is the reason I will give for making them an orphan, or a widow? What? You tell me?"

Amedeo Esposito could barely control his contempt of the old man. He was weak. Too weak to sit at the table any longer. When you became afraid of war, then it was time to exit the table. Esposito decided then and there, that he was going to make sure that that was what exactly was going to happen. It was time for the old dons around the living room to go.

Don Lombardi leaned in. "I understand what you are saying, my friend. And I am with you. War is not something to be taken lightly. But a war in Jersey, should not bring us into a full scale war with anyone. Remember, they supposedly gave up Jersey as part of the peace deal. So, why would they go to war over it? Philly is another matter, so maybe we should think carefully about Philly. But Jersey, is open season."

Biaggio understood how this worked. Lombardi had conceded Philly, so now he had to give a little something as well. He would have to acquiesce to the families moving against Jersey. Biaggio nodded, and it was done.

"I still believe that it would be appropriate to send a message to the Reigns family, expressing our sympathies over what has happened," Biaggio told them. "We offer our support, our prayers for this little girls safe return, and we give our blessings to whatever they have to do for her safe return."

"Our blessings?" Bonafacio asked. "I am not sure about offering our blessings to what they are doing. You have heard of their activities, my old friend?"

"The Reigns family has basically invaded Mexico," De Luca declared. "They have sent thousands of men into Mexico, searching for that little girl. The Mexicans have never seen that many niggers before. They are using some pretty heavy handed tactics, and pissing off the locals. People are getting whacked left and right."

"Heavy handed tactics?" Biaggio said, peering down. "Is that what it's called now days? Heavy handed tactics?"

"It is torture," Bonafacio chimed in. "Pure and simple. What they are doing, is evil.  Like the Viet Cong back in my day."

"They are calling it Little Guantanamo," Biaggio added.  "This place where they are taking people.  Some farm, or ranch, or compound near the border.  It is worse than anything our soldiers did in Iraq or Afghanistan or Cuba."

"This Reigns family, is a family of animals," Esposito declared. "And you want to send them a green light?"

Biaggio grabbed his cane from next to him on the sofa, and began tapping it gently on the ground.  It was what he did while thinking.

"We send our sympathies and our blessings, because it disavows any involvement on our part, and it creates a measure of goodwill.  You pat the lion before pulling its tail.  You want to move on Jersey, you smile in their face so they will think nothing of it."

De Luca smiled.  The old man was right.  He had a lot to learn from the old dons arrayed around the room, and he hoped that they were around long enough to give him the benefit of their wisdom and experiences.  His own father had died at the tender age of fifty five, so he had not been able to gain the benefit of his knowledge.  He would began taking the old dons to lunch, and picking their brains.  The old men had survived for fifty years not by being stupid, but by being cunning and treacherous.  He would learn much from them.

"I see the wisdom in this," De Luca said, nodding appreciatively.

Lombardi also nodded in agreement.  "I agree.  We send our sympathies.  Even if we weren't contemplating on moving on Jersey. Kidnapping that little girl, was way outta line."

"We are in agreement then?" Biaggio asked, peering at each of them, in order to gain a consensus.

Bonafacio leaned in.  "I believe that this is the right way to go.  And I, like you, are concerned about the direction this business is going in. The old man predicted that it would one day come to this.  The Blacks and the Mexicans, and there dirty drugs.  And now, they have degenerated even lower.  They are kidnapping children, torturing innocent people, shooting up entire communities.  And this is the business that we chose to join?"

"What they do, is not what *we* do," De Luca said, patting the old man's hand.  "We do our business with honor."

"Let us send a message my friends," Biaggio told them. "We tell all of our families, all of our friends and associates, that no action is to be taken against the Reigns family, or this Commission of theirs. We stay out of what is going on in Texas and Mexico. And I will have my people carrying a message directly to them, extending our sympathies and our prayers for the safe return of their little girl."

Nods went around the room.

"Now, let us discuss strategy," Esposito said. "It's time to turn our attention, and the full weight of our organizations, to getting Jersey back.

"To Jersey!" Bonafacio said, lifting his glass.

"To Jersey!" Biaggio said, joining in.

"To Jersey," De Luca said, lifting his glass.

Lombardi nodded, and slowly lifted his glass in toast, joining the others. "To Jersey."

The vote was unanimous. The five families were now on a path to retake New Jersey, and push out the Reigns family's secret army. The East Coast, was about to get a lot more livelier.

# Chapter Six

El Paso County Sheriff Jimmy Applewhite was sitting on top of the world. He had just won re-election by a landslide, and the federal government had just gave his department an additional fifty million dollar block grant to combat drug trafficking. This was on top of the thirteen million dollar grant he had just received from the government to fight illegal immigration. He was going to transform his department into the envy of every other police organization in the world. He was going to create a massive SWAT team, a High Intensity Drug Trafficking Area Interdiction Task Force, and Immigration and Human Smuggling Task Force, and he was going to expand his regular force by an additional one thousand patrol officers. *And* he was going to buy them all new handguns. He had been wanting to switch his department over from the current issue Glocks, to the new Heckler and Koch forty caliber USP. He also had his eye on a couple a new helicopters with infra red trackers for night time use, as well as more canine units. He had big ideas, and big plans for all of the federal money flowing his way. The war in Mexico was the best thing that could have ever happened to his department. Perhaps even the best thing that could have ever happened to him personally. His expanded department, would give him the largest police force in the country. It would be larger than Chicago's, larger than Los Angeles', and even larger than New York's. Presiding over the largest police force in the nation was going to give him a microphone and a spotlight which he would use to gain national attention. And that national attention was what he was going to use to step into the governor's office.

"Governor Applewhite," he said out loud. It made him smile. He loved the sound of it. "*Governor.*"

Sheriff Applewhite adjusted his tie in the mirror, and walked from his bathroom to his kitchen, where he lifted his gun belt off of the table and fastened it around his enormous waist. It was time to get back to the office. He had ran home for some lunch, and to take a quick dump, and now it was time to get back to the office. He had a mountain of paperwork sitting on his desk. The one thing about federal money, was that it came with mountains of paperwork that needed his signature. And one thing he hated more than anything else, was riding a desk and dealing with a bunch of administrative bullshit. He found himself staying away from the office and going into the field more and more of late. Actual office work, was one of the reasons he wanted to move up to the governorship. Texas governors played golf, raised money, went to parties, and did little else. That was a life he could definitely get used to.

Sheriff Applewhite strolled out of his kitchen and through his front door, not even bothering to stop and lock it. No one was bold enough, or stupid enough, to rob his home. He left his doors unlocked all day, and often all night. If anyone ever got the nuts to rob him, they would be dead within hours. He would have an old fashion Texas posse on their asses so fast that they wouldn't know what hit them. That was '*if*' they managed to get out of his home without getting caught. He had a secret standing order amongst his deputies to shoot all burglars in his jurisdiction. He didn't play that shit. People worked hard for their money, and to have some junkie break in and take their belongings was intolerable to him. He had a reputation for being tough on crime, and it was a reputation that he had worked hard to cultivate. Cleaning up El Paso County was a difficult task, and it required someone with a iron hand. He relished being that person.

Sheriff Applewhite climbed into his patrol car, rolled down the window, and started it up. It was a hot West Texas day, and the inside of his car was blistering hot. The steering wheel, the seats, the dash, he could see heat radiating off of all of them. The heat was the only reason he would be glad to be back inside of his office at the massive El Paso County jail.

Dante stood just behind his technician, peering down at the computer screen. They were sitting in a van across town.

"He's heading back to work now," A voice said, over the radio.

Dante patted the shoulder of the technician sitting at the computer.

"Do it now."

The technician nodded. "I'm isolating his radio now. It's done."

Dante turned to another female sitting inside of the van with them and nodded. She adjusted her headset, and punched a couple of buttons on her computer screen.

"Adam One, we have a situation," the Black woman said, in a deep, country, West Texas accent.

Sheriff Applewhite lifted his walkie-talkie's handset from its mount on his dash. "What is it, Darling?"

"Sheriff, we have ATF on location at a drug stop off of Interstate 180. Deputies are on scene, the feds are requesting your presence," the fake dispatcher told him.

"The feds?" Applewhite shouted into the handset. "In my jurisdiction? In route!"

Sheriff Applewhite slammed the handset back down into its cradle, turned on his emergency lights, and raced off toward Interstate 180. The feds in his jurisdiction, without notifying him? Where the fuck was the professional courtesy, he wondered? He was going to give those federal fuckers a piece of his mind! *Nobody* operated in his territory without telling him! *Nobody!* He didn't care how much money the feds were handing over to him, he wasn't about to become anyone's footstool. He definitely had a few choice words for those ATF boys!

Sheriff Applewhite sped along the highway until he came across a group of cars parked along the side of it. Sure enough, one of his patrol cars was parked in the gravel next to the highway, along with several black Ford Crown Victorias, a few black Chevy Suburbans, and a black Ford Econoline van. It appeared as though the feds had the van pulled over. There were numerous men standing around in dark blue windbreakers, with ATF printed in yellow across the back of their jackets.

Sheriff Applewhite shook his head and huffed at them as he slowly drove past. "Who the fuck wears windbreakers in a hundred degree heat? Fucking federal jackasses!"

The sheriff pulled over behind the last of the federal vehicles, and climbed out of his car. He stormed over to where the ATF agents were gathered, which was at the rear of the black Ford cargo van. The van's cargo doors were open, and the agents were peering inside.

"Who's in charge here?" Sheriff Applewhite huffed.

The Sheriff made his way to the back of the van, and peered inside. He was befuddled, because the agents were all staring inside of an empty cargo van. Had the perpetrators escaped? Had they dumped their cargo? Had the agents already seized it? And what exactly was it? If it was money, and it had been seized in his jurisdiction, then he certainly had a claim to make. And the departments involved in the seizure, were entitled to a portion of whatever was seized. He definitely wanted his share of whatever it was, *especially* if it was money.

"Where's the cargo?" the Sheriff asked, gruffly, staring into the empty cargo bay.

"You're the cargo," one of the agents said smiling.

Sheriff Applewhite turned back toward the smiling agent, just in time to see the agent pull the trigger on the Taser gun he had pointed toward him. The prongs dug into Sheriff Applewhite's leg, and the ATF agent squeezed the trigger, sending 12,000,000 volts throughout the Sheriff's body. The electrical current immediately caused neuromuscular incapacitation, and the Sheriff's ability to resist or control his muscles left completely. He began to fall, and the agents pushed him into the back of the cargo van. Some of them hopped inside, and closed the door. The other agents that had been gathered around, quickly dispersed, climbed inside of their vehicles, and left the scene. The only car that remained, was that of the El Paso County deputy. His body was laying inside of the trunk.

*****

Sheriff Jimmy Applewhite woke to the sound of metal striking metal. He remembered being tasered, he remembered being tossed in the back of a van, and he remembered some strange man injected something in his arm. That was what he remembered. And what he did know, was that whatever he had been given, had put him out like a light, because he remembered nothing afterward. What he also knew, was that it had been an extremely powerful sedative, as he was still a bit groggy.

The Sheriff peered around the room, taking in his surroundings.

There were men in the room with him. They were busy doing various things. There was a table in the room, and a man was preparing instruments on the table. Laying them out carefully, as if he were a surgical technician in an operating room. Another man, was kneeling on the floor, hammering something. Something large, the Sheriff saw. The man was using a large steel mallet to nail gigantic nails into a massive pole. And then there were others. They were on the far side of the room talking amongst themselves. He couldn't hear what they were saying, but surmised that they were talking about him. He was desperate to shake off his grogginess and bring clarity back to his mind.

One of the shadowy figures across the dimly lit room left the consultation, and approached the Sheriff. He snapped his fingers in the Sheriff's face, in order to get his attention. Sheriff Applewhite lifted his head and stared into the man's face.

"Do you know who I am?" Dante asked him.

Sheriff Applewhite focused. His mind was still running in slow motion, but he did recognize the face of the man standing before him. He nodded.

"Do you know why you're here?" Dante asked.

"Do you know who I am?" the Sheriff asked.

"I know precisely who you are," Dante told him. "That's why you're here. I know what you are. I know what you do, I know who you work for, I know all of the little fucked up things you've done over the years."

"If you know who I am, then you know you've fucked up," Sheriff Applewhite told him.

Dante laughed.

"Okay, let's just get something out of the way right now," Dante told him. "That way, we won't waste our time with a bunch of bullshit. You're going to die. Now, how you choose to die, is on you. It can be excruciatingly painful, or it can be as easy as me having the good doctor over there in the corner, inject you with something that will put you to sleep. And while you're sleep, he'll inject you with something that will simply allow you to drift away peacefully. It can easy, or it can be painful beyond your imagination. And whichever way you choose to go, I'm going to get what I need out of this little situation of ours."

"And what is that?" Sheriff Applewhite asked with a look a contempt on his face.

"Information," Dante told him. "I want information. Now, you might be thinking that you're not going to give me shit. That you'll take it with you to your grave, or that you'll trade the information for you life. There have been many men before you, and they were all smart and big and brave and tough. They all thought the same thing, and they were all wrong. There will be no horse trading, no bargaining, no deals. And you will tell me what I want to know, I promise you that. You will break. *All* men break. Some sooner than others. Some have a high tolerance for pain, some have very little, but in the end, *everyone* breaks. There's no dishonor in breaking, and there are no medals for lasting a long time. In the end, there's only death. And in the end, I'll know what I want to know. The only thing you will have accomplished, is prolonging the situation, and causing yourself unnecessary pain. Understand?"

"What is it that you want?" Sheriff Applewhite asked. "Exactly what is it, that you *think* I know?"

"You know what I want," Dante told him. "Let's not play games, let's not insult each other's intelligence. Some men came through El Paso County."

"Lot's of people come through El Paso County!" the Sheriff shouted, interrupting Dante.

Dante waved his finger at the Sheriff. "Ah-ah, these were special men. These men had an audience with the Sheriff. These men were not only given special passage into the country, but they were sent by you, to a document forger in New Mexico. You knew what they were coming into the country for, and you know that they now have my daughter. I want to know, who sent them, and where they are taking her. Are they taking her back across the border? And if they are, where are they going to cross?"

Sheriff Applewhite smiled. The lucidity of his mind was returning by leaps and bounds with each passing moment. Dante had questions, while he had answers. What that meant, was that he was holding all of the cards.

"It appears to me, that we have a dilemma," the Sheriff said with a smile.

"There is no dilemma," Dante told him. "Don't get coy or cute. Your time is running out, and your pain is about to begin."

"It's not my time that's running out, it's that little girl whose time is running out," Sheriff Applewhite told him. "You want to sit here and fuck around, or you want to know where she's at?"

The blood rose up in Dante's face. It took every bit of effort that he could conjure to keep himself from pulling out his pistol, and putting a bullet between the eyes of the man standing before him.

"Where is she?" Dante asked.

"I guess you've rethought your position on negotiating?" the sheriff asked with a smile.

"Where is she?" Dante asked again.

"Can you imagine what those filthy Mexican drug dealers are doing to her right now?" the Sheriff asked with a sadistic smile.

Dante's hands twitched violently. He wanted to draw his weapon. He wanted to shoot the fat fuck that was handcuffed in front of him. But he knew that he needed to find Lucky. He had to remain calm if he were to get his daughter back. He turned toward his men and nodded.

Dante's men walked to where the Sheriff was handcuffed, grabbed him, and drug him to where the guy had been on the floor kneeling and hammering. Once he was close enough to where the man was, he could see what he had been working on. Two massive wooden beams had been fashioned together in the form of a cross. One of Dante's men pulled out a stun gun, placed it against the Sheriff's neck, and sent 60,000 volts throughout his body. The Sheriff went limp instantly.

The Reigns family's soldiers took the Sheriff's wrist, and tied them to the cross, while others took his leg and tied them to the bottom of the cross. The Sheriff's jerking motions slowly began to cease, and the disruption to his central nervous system began to subside. Dante walked to where the Sheriff was lying on the ground, tied to the cross. One of his men handed him a large iron mallet, and a massive railroad spike.

"This is how it feels everyday that my daughter is away from me," Dante said, peering down at the Sheriff. He knelt down, place the spike on the Sheriff's palm, and then pounded the iron mallet down onto the back of the spike, driving it through the Sheriff's hand. Sheriff Applewhite cried out in pain, as blood shot through the air. Dante continued to hammer, until the spike had been driven through the Sheriff's hand and into the wood.

"You ever had a child taken from you?" Dante shouted. "Huh? Ever had something that you love so much, ripped from your arms?"

Sheriff Applewhite's screams were inhuman. They were animal like, guttural, and high pitched at the same time. Sweat poured down his face, and the blood from his hand poured down the wooden cross onto the ground.

"Where is she?" Dante asked. "Where are they taking her?"

"You son-of-a-bitch!" Sheriff Applewhite shouted. "Do you know who I am? Do you?"

"Where is she?" Dante asked again.

"If you ever want to see her again, you'll stop this shit!"

"Where is she?" Dante shouted.

"Fuck you!"

Dante nodded toward his men again, and two of the gripped the Sheriff's other hand, forced it open, and held it down against the wood.

"Stop this shit!" Sheriff Applewhite shouted.

"Where is she?" Dante shouted. He held out his hand, and one of his men placed a railroad spike in his palm. "You can spare yourself a tremendous amount of pain. Just tell me where they are taking her!"

"Let me go!" the Sheriff shouted. "We can deal!"

Dante placed the spike on the Sheriff's palm.

"Wait a minute, dammit!" the Sheriff shouted.

"Where is she?" Dante asked calmly. "Where are they taking her? Where are they crossing the border?"

"Let me take you to them," the Sheriff said, desperately. "Let me take you to where they are at."

"Where are they?" Dante asked. "They're in the state? Where?"

"I take you to them," the Sheriff repeated. "That's the deal."

"I told you before, no deals," Dante told him. He lifted the mallet, and drove the spike into the Sheriff's hand. The Sheriff let out a banshee cry.

Sheriff Applewhite had always been a large man. He had always been one who had a high tolerance for pain. But that was normal pain. What he was experiencing now, was pain on a different level.

"Where is she?" Dante shouted over the Sheriff's cries. "Where?"

"Fuck you!" Sheriff Applewhite shouted. Spittle flew from his mouth as he shouted, while enormous amounts of sweat poured down his furled brow.

"Where is she?" Dante shouted. He kicked the Sheriff in his gut. "Tell me where she is, you fat son-of-a-bitch! Where is she?"

The Sheriff's heart was racing a million miles an hour. He tried to calm himself and control his breathing. His shouting had him out of breath.

"Let me go," the Sheriff told him. "Let me help you find her. Let me help you get her back into your arms."

"She will be back into my arms," Dante told him.

Sheriff Applewhite shook his head. "No. Not without my help. You're running out of time. Use your head, boy! *Use your got damn head!* You can't kill your way outta this one. You can't kill her back into your arms. You have to be smart."

Dante nodded toward his men. Two of them grabbed the Sheriff's feet, place one over the other, and held them down against the wooden crucifix.

"Be smart, Dante!" the Sheriff shouted.

Dante was handed another railroad spike, which he placed against the Sheriff's feet. He peered up at the Sheriff. "Where is she?"

"No," Sheriff Applewhite said shaking his head. "No! Okay, let's talk! Let's talk seriously, let's talk."

"Talk," Dante told him.

The Sheriff broke down into tears. "Give me something! For Christ sake, you gotta give me something!"

"I told you in the beginning, no deals," Dante told him. He lifted the mallet.

"No!" the Sheriff shouted. "Wait! I'll tell you!"

Dante lowered the mallet. "Start talking."

"I want to live!" the Sheriff pleaded. "I want to live. I can clean this up, I can. I swear I can. I'll be yours. I'll do whatever you want. You want to move a truck load of dope through my county, hell, I give you a got damned police escort! I'll do it!"

"Where is my daughter?" Dante asked coldly.

"Rodriguez!" Sheriff Applewhite shouted. "Chief Rodriguez sent them to me.  He gave them safe passage."

"Chief Rodriguez?" Dante asked, lifting an eyebrow.

"Juarez," the Sheriff said, breathing heavily.  "The Chief of Police of Ciudad Juarez.  He sent them.  We do each other favors.  He called this one in.  He wanted them to get through, and my people made sure they got through."

"Where are they now?" Dante asked.

Sheriff Applewhite shook his head.  "I don't know.  I don't know.  I just got them through.  That was it.  He didn't say nothing about letting them *back* through."

"You're lying," Dante said, lifting the mallet.

"No!" Sheriff Applewhite shouted.  "I swear to you!  I swear!  I don't know where they are."

"You just said, that you would lead me to them," Dante told him.

"I just wanted to buy some time," the Sheriff said crying heavily.  "I just wanted time to negotiate.  I swear, I don't know anything else.  I don't know where she is, or where they were taking her."

"Like I told you in the beginning, there would be no deal," Dante told him.  He swung the mallet, striking the hug railroad spike, driving it into the Sheriff's feet.  The Sheriff shrieked like a wounded animal, as Dante drove the spike through his feet, into the wooden cross.  Once Dante was finished, he rose, and stared at the Sheriff.

"You could have saved yourself a lot of pain," Dante told him.  Dante nodded at his men, who made their way around the crucifix.  Together, the lifted the cross off of the ground, and dropped it into a hole they had dug into the ground.  Dante stared up at the Sheriff nailed to the cross.  The Sheriff had passed out, because of the pain.

"Call me when he comes to," Dante told his men.  He thinks his pain is over with.  He doesn't realize, that it's only just begun.

Dante turned, and walked out of the massive barn, leaving his men in the room with the Sheriff.  His men peered at one another, and at the cross alternately.  Many of them had been with the Reigns family for years, and many of the them had done things that they would never be able to talk about.  They had witnessed some of the most brutal killings, and had even participated in many of those killings.  They had witnessed the most vile example's of man's inhumanity to man.  But none of them, had ever seen anything like this. None of them, had ever *witnessed* anything like the things that Dante had been doing lately. They were loyal to the Reigns family, because the Reigns family paid extremely well. But now, they found themselves being loyal to the family for a different reason as well. Dante had put the fear of God back into them. He was once again, as he had been before. Each of them now realized, that the old Dante Reigns was back.

# Chapter Seven

Damian was seated at the head of the table inside of Bio One's main conference room. He was twiddling the pencil he held in his hand, and restlessly shaking his legs beneath the conference table. His mind was elsewhere, as it had been since Lucky's disappearance. He had so many things going on at once, and it was impossible to keep track of all the various operations and businesses that needed his daily attention. There was Energia Oil, and the new Canadian oil sands contract. There was the company's oil discoveries in Kenya, Uganda, Tanzania, Mali, Niger, and Chad. There were negotiations going on with the oil ministries of the various governments, there were environmental terrorist, political terrorist, the risk to his workers, his pipelines, and his production facilities. And that was just Energia Oil.

Bio One still had a massive class action lawsuit that it was fighting. The new HIV and cancer drugs were progressing, and still undergoing tests. The FDA was denying his applications for human trials, because of the debacle from the previous drugs and the ongoing lawsuit. Congress was launching an investigation, and he might be called to Capitol Hill to testify. Those hearings could totally destroy Bio One and everything that he'd built. There was no doubt in his mind, that several congressmen were going to use this to get back at him and to win political points with their constituents. There was Darius, and his refusal to go back to law school. And then, most importantly, there was the search for Lucky.

Dante had every available man spread throughout the state, searching for Lucky. He had called in every political favor that he was owed, in order to get the police to either join in the search, or stay the hell out of the way. He was signing invoices all day, everyday, approving massive amounts of money that was going toward the search. There were police payoffs, helicopter rentals, the hiring of hundreds if not thousands of new soldiers, all of the equipment, the weapons, the night vision goggles, the SUVs, the tracking dogs, and so many other expenses. He would pay whatever it took to get Lucky back, that was not even up for debate or discussion, he just wondered if they were doing it the *smart* way. Throwing money at a problem, was never the smart way, and usually Dante was the one to figure out the smartest way to bring out a desired result, but in this instance, Dante was too close to the issue. Perhaps his brother was so close, so emotionally invested, that he was unable to think clearly and clinically about the issue.

This is the situation Damian found himself in. Dealing with business, legitimate and otherwise, as well as family and financial issues. And this didn't even factor in the stress he was feeling from his family's enormous construction company, or his family's massive entertainment company. All of this was on his plate, and the last thing he wanted to be in on today, was another meeting. Especially this one.

"We have legitimate offers on the table from Merck, Pfizer, Eli Lilly, GlaxoSmith Klein, Bristol-Meyers Squibb, Astra Zeneca, Abbott Laboratories, Roche, and Sanofi-Aventis." Thomas Voight, Damian's business attorney told those gathered around the table. "And then there is the offer from Johnson & Johnson, which dwarfs the other offers by a significant margin."

Kayla Marin, one of Bio One's attorney's leaned back and whistled. "I saw the Johnson & Johnson offer. Those numbers are incredible."

"My only problem with Johnson's offer, is that part of comes in the form of stock options," Diane Malveaux, another Bio One attorney, told them. "There is a significant amount of uncertainty built into the offer."

What do you mean?" Cherin King, Damian's chief personal attorney asked.

"All of the legislation coming down the pipeline is causing a lot of uncertainty in the market," Diane explained. "With the implementation of The Affordable Care Act, pharmaceutical stocks have been on a downward trend. Every new piece of legislation, every new regulation that roles out, every time some politician goes on the news and starts talking about Obama Care, or repeal, or expansion, the market reacts negatively."

"I agree, " Paula Lynch said, nodding. She was the third Bio One attorney. "And then some states are implementing exchanges, and that's driving down prices already. All big pharma stocks are predicted to take a hit."

"So that hefty offer that Johnson put on the table, is really close to the others, once you figure in the real valuation of the stock they're offering," Diane told them.

All eyes turned toward Damian, who was staring off into space, and tapping his pencil against the table.

"Are we boring you, Mr. Reigns?" Paula asked.

"Huh?" Damian asked, snapping out of his day dreaming.

"We are only talking about billions of dollars of *your* money," Paula said with a smile.

"I'm sorry," Damian said, yawning accidentally. "Excuse me."

"Apparently, we are," Diane said, winking at Paula.

"Where are we at?" Damian asked.

"We were talking about all of the offers on the table for the new HIV drugs," Tommy told him. "Damian, any one of these offers, could solve all of our potential financial problems. We could settle every single lawsuit, and still have plenty of cash left over. Maybe we should think about accepting one of them."

Damian was once again, staring off into space.

"Damian, are you okay?" Cherin asked.

"Huh?" Damian asked, peering around the table. "Yeah, I'm good."

"Ah, I'll tell you what, how about we postpone any decision for right now, and we take some time to mull over our options," Cherin told the group. "Damian will take everything that's been said, and evaluate it, and we'll schedule another meeting in a week or so to finalize some of what has been proposed."

Nods went around the table, and the gathered attorneys and scientist began gathering their paperwork.

"Good," Cherin told them. She rose from her seat, and sat on the edge of the large wooden conference table. "Well, we thank you all for coming, and I'll be in touch with each of you in the coming week. Thanks guys."

The meeting's participants slowly filed out of the conference room, leaving a distracted Damian, and his chief attorney alone. Cherin turned toward Damian after the last person had left.

"What's the matter, Damian?"

Damian peered up at her. "What? What do you mean?"

Cherin folded her arms and tilted her head to one side. "C'mon now. How long have we known each other?"

Damian smiled. "Since, forever."

"And you don't think that I wouldn't know when something's wrong?" she asked. "What's bothering you?"

"Besides my niece's kidnapping?" Damian asked, lifting an eyebrow. "The massive lawsuits, the oil finds in North, West, and East Africa, me having to go before a Congressional Committee, and the fact that I'm bleeding money like never before? You really have to ask?"

Cherin rose, walked to where Damian was seated and began to rub his back. "When's the last time you slept?"

Damian shook his head. "Sleep is *not* the problem."

Cherin nodded. "Yes, it is. It's part of the problem. I can look at you and tell you need a good sleep. You look tired as hell. You're no good to anyone like this."

"What am I supposed to do?" Damian asked, exhaling and rubbing his tired eyes.

"Go home, unplug the house phones, turn off your cell phone, climb in bed, and don't get back out of it until tomorrow afternoon."

Damian laughed. "Even if I wanted to..."

"You *have* to."

Damian shook his head. "She's out there."

"And you'll *find* her," Cherin told him. "Trust me, you'll find her."

Again, Damian shook his head. "What am I missing? What stone am I leaving unturned?"

"Right now?" Cherin seated herself on the edge of the table right next to him. "I'd say none. But it's a process. You just have to take your time, and methodically work your way through the state. You've blocked all of the exits. There's a nation wide Amber Alert out for her, and the police are pulling over every car they see with a Black child her age in it. You'll find her, it's just going to take some time. But in the meantime, you're going to have to get some sleep. You're no good to anyone, if you stress yourself into a stroke."

Damian nodded. He knew that she was right. But he also knew that he wouldn't be able to sleep even if he tried.

"I have an Ambien in my purse," Cherin told him. "You want it?"

Damian shook his head. "You trying to turn me into a junkie, Ms. King?"

"I'm trying to make sure that my *only* client stays alive long enough to pay me all my damn money!" she told him.

Damian laughed heartily. It was a laugh that was much needed.

"You also look like you could use a meal," Cherin told him. She nodded toward the door. "C'mon, I'll take you to lunch. My treat."

"Oh, *you're* buying?" Damian asked, lifting an eyebrow.

"Yeah," Cherin said with a grin. "All the lawsuits you're facing, you probably couldn't afford a decent lunch right now anyway."

Again, Damian laughed. "Oh, so you got jokes today?"

"I do," Cherin said, nodding. "I want you to feel better. I want you to take your mind off of your problems."

"Loan me a couple a billion?" Damian asked, peering up at her.

"If I had it, you wouldn't even have to ask." Cherin rose from the table, turned back toward Damian and extended her hand. "C'mon. Up."

Damian rose from the conference table. "Where are we eating at?"

"I hear, that the Bio One cafeteria is off the chain!" Cherin told him.

Damian laughed. "I should have known. Cheap ass!"

Cherin laughed.

The two of them headed out of the conference room for the elevator.

\*\*\*\*\*

Princess was lying back in her hot tub trying to relax. Her body desperately needed the hot, muscle relaxing water, and body massaging jets that the tub had to offer. She had been out and about since her niece's disappearance, and it seemed as though she had been on her feet for at least the last twenty four hours. She was tired, bone tired. And she needed a relaxing dip in the water before getting back on the hunt.

Princess closed her eyes and leaned her head back against the soft pillow that was attached to the hot tub. She wanted to be careful, because she knew that it would be real easy for her to fall asleep in the tub. Sleep was what she needed, but she didn't want to fall asleep just yet. She would power sleep later, perhaps after a quick session with her masseuse. She needed a deep, tissue penetrating massage, and then she would pop a pill and sleep hard. After that, she would be ready to go again. She would be good for a least a couple of days. But it was now a matter of getting to that point. Getting her body ready, and building up her endurance.

Princess' thoughts shifted toward her niece. She wondered how she was doing, what she was doing, and whether or not she was doing okay. She knew that *they* knew, that if they harmed one hair on the child's head, then there would be no place on the planet that they could hide. Dante would hunt them to the ends of the Earth, and furthermore, they would be international pariahs. No country would shelter them, no criminal organization would give them aid, or even deal with them. In fact, they would be hunted by many. This was the one thing that they could count on. And the fact that Lucky was more valuable to them alive, than dead. If they wanted to kill her, they would have done so already. No, they wanted the child alive. They went through great trouble to get her, and now that they had her, they would eventually let their demands be known. The only question that remained, was what those demands were, and would they have to pay too high of a price for Lucky's return? What exactly was *too* high of a price? Giving up California, Florida, or even Texas? Trading Dante's life for the child's? Money? Billions? Hundreds of millions of dollars? How much would they give? How much *could* they give? There were so many questions, and only time would reveal the answers.

"Can I join you?" a voice asked.

She recognized the voice instantly. Princess opened her eyes and smiled.

"What are you doing here?" Princess asked. She peered around. "And where the hell is my security?"

"Your security?" Julian asked. He extended his arms. "This is your brother's house, isn't it?"

"I still have security," Princess said with a smile. "And so does he.

They need to be fired for letting in all the riff-raff."

"Oh, riff-raff!" Julian said laughing. "That's what I am? Riff-raff?"

"What are you doing here?" Princess asked, closing her eyes once again. "Shouldn't you be in Mississippi chasing some little country skirt?"

Julian smiled. "Why would I be doing that, when I could be here with one of the finest sisters to ever walk this planet."

"Oh, Julian, I'll bet you say that to all the girls who could have you killed," Princess told him.

Julian had to laugh.

"So, you never answered my question," he told her.

"And what question is that?"

"Can I join you?"

Princess waved her hand toward the empty side of the hot tub. "It's a free a hot tub."

Julian walked to the other side and stepped down into the hot tub. "Feels good."

"It did," Princess told him.

"Oh, so why it got to be like that?" Julian asked again. He had the slick smile of a Cheshire cat spread across his face.

"What do you want, Julian?" Princess asked.

Julian clasped her foot, and Princess jerked it away.

"Hey!" Princess exclaimed.

"Ahhh, ticklish, are we?" Julian asked with a smile.

"Keep your hands to yourself, before I chop them muthafuckers off."

Julian laughed. "Why so touchy?"

"My question, exactly."

Julian nodded. "Why are we playing games?"

"Games, Julian?" Princess asked, lifting any eyebrow. "The only game being played is the one you're playing, and it's a dangerous one. Trust me. You want what you can't have. You want to see if you can achieve the ultimate conquest, is that right? Well, you can't. Move on to your next target."

"Why can't I just be a man, who likes a woman?" Julian asked, turning up his palms. "You do remember those days don't you? The days when a man pursued a woman that he liked?"

"Why now?" Princess asked. "Why all of a sudden? Is it because I'm now with Emil? Is that what this is? You have some secret beef with Emil, so now you want to fuck his girl?"

"Emil is a non muthafuckin factor," Julian said , shaking his head. "I wish you would realize that. The only consideration I have with regards to him, is to make sure you don't make the mistake of a lifetime."

Princess laughed. "I don't make lifetime mistakes. But I have made mistakes, and a big one, would be to fall for any of your bullshit."

"Don't marry him."

"Why not?" Princess asked. "What? You want to marry me? Is that it?"

Julian nodded.

Again, Princess laughed. "Boy, please! You know what? You know what I do remember? I remember you collecting comics back when you and Damian were at Harvard. And I remember you collecting sea shells at Martha's Vineyard. And then I remember you went through you Versace phase, were you were collecting Versace housewares. And then I remember you collecting African art. And then it was exotic cars. You've always had a passion for collecting. You won't get to add me to one of your little collections."

Princess' cell phone rang. She had completely forgotten to turn it off. Subconsciously, she thought, perhaps she really didn't want to turn it off. Otherwise, why would she have set it next to her on the deck near the spa tub? She grabbed it, pressed the answer button, and placed it to her ear.

"Talk to me."

"Hey, sis, I need you to do me a favor," Dante said, on the line.

"What's up?"

"I have a friend in Nuevo Laredo that I need you to go see," Dante told her. "He has some information about Lucky."

Princess sat up.

"Who is it?"

"The chief of police," Dante told her. "I'm told, he's dying to tell us what we need to know to get her back."

Princess smiled. "I'm on it."

"Thanks."

"Dante."

"Yeah, sis?"

"How are you doing?"

"I'm fucking fabo," Dante told her. "I'm on the hunt."

"Have you slept?"

"I'll sleep when I'm dead."

"Dante."

"What?"

"I need you to get some sleep," Princess told him. "I need you to get some rest. And I need you to eat. Stop, eat, and get you a few winks, okay?"

There was a long pause on the phone. Finally, Dante spoke.

"I can't. I... I... I can't. Not until she's back in my arms."

Princess closed her eyes and leaned her head back. She could actually feel a tear welling up in her left eye.

"Don't worry about Nuevo Laredo," she said softly. "I'm on it."

"Thanks, sis."

"Happy hunting, Baby Boy."

Princess disconnected the call, sat her phone down on the deck, and exhaled. She wanted some sleep, and even before Dante's call, she knew that she would be hard pressed to actually get some. And now, she knew that there was no way she would be able to rest. She had a plane to catch. Places to go, and people to see, she told herself. The Chief of Police of Nuevo Laredo was dying to talk to her. And she would make she that he did just that. He was going to die, but first, he was going to talk to her.

# Chapter Eight

The Reigns family's cabin in Idlewild, Michigan was really more of an estate, than a traditional log cabin. It was more than ten thousand square feet, and was nestled deep in the woods, with a long winding driveway, and a rear view of the massive lake. The rustic cabin contained more than eight bedrooms, a massive two story great room with a real wood burning fireplace, a large well equipped chef's kitchen, a massive dining area, and even a movie theater. The twenty eight acre lake front property also contained a covered boat dock, an additional guest quarters, and a large caretaker's quarters. The main home itself hadn't been used for years, but remained in immaculate condition because of the property's dedicated caretakers. Inside of the great room, a shirtless DeMarion began stacking logs in the fireplace in order to get a fire started.

Vendetta peered around the massive great room, taking in the rustic decor, and the old pictures of Reigns family members. Some of the pictures went back so many decades, that they were in black and white. She didn't know who they were, but she did know that there appeared to be a lot of them.

"And this is your grandmother's place?" Vendetta asked, peering at DeMarion.

DeMarion rose, lit a match, and set one of the logs on fire, getting the fireplace going. he turned to her.

"It was. Now, it just belongs to the family. Nobody ever uses it anymore. In fact, no one in the family has been here in at least fifteen or twenty years."

"Are you serious?" Vendetta asked, peering around the massive log home. "You have a mansion on the lake, and you don't even use it?"

DeMarion smiled. "We have plenty of mansions on plenty of lakes all over the country. The world for that matter. This is just one more piece of lost history."

DeMarion walked to the sofa, and seated himself. He nodded toward the fireplace. "C'mon over here and get warm."

"I'm not that cold," Vendetta told him. There was a chill outside, but the drive up to the cabin in DeMarion's Ferrari had her adrenaline going. He was handsome, sexy, rich, and even sounded educated. And he had saved her life, and then whisked her away from the hospital to a damn log cabin on a lake. What fucking rabbit hole had she fallen into, she wondered? This was definitely some Alice in Wonderland type of shit. Niggas weren't that pretty, and rich, and fine, and smart. Not all in one sexy ass package. And he wasn't soft either. He had killed men. In fact, he had killed men in order to save her. Something just wasn't right. Something just wasn't adding up, she thought. Again, her suspicions were elevated. Who was he, she wondered? Where had he come from? And why the hell did he save her, and why was he so interested in her well being? She wasn't well enough to overtake him and get his weapon away from him. She wasn't well enough to run and escape from the place he had spirited her to. She needed to bide her time, and she needed time to heal. The cabin was well away from the violent drug worlds of Columbus and Detroit, and so she felt semi-safe there. It was a place where she could sojourn until her health returned, and so she decided that she would spend the time learning more about her mystery host.

"So, why do you say that?" Vendetta asked.

The question took DeMarion by surprise. "Huh?"

"You called this place another piece of lost history," Vendetta told him. "Why?"

"Oh," DeMarion said, sitting back of the sofa and relaxing. "Because, that's what it is. That's what this whole place is. Idlewild. Just another lost piece of history. My grandmother used to tell us stories about this place, you know, back in its heyday. According to her, it was the only place in the Midwest where Blacks could come and vacation, and relax, and own property away from prejudice Whites. Her mother used to bring her here to vacation when she was young. Well, you see what it is now?"

Vendetta walked to where DeMarion was sitting, and sat down next to him. She was intrigued. Intrigued by this place, a place that she had never heard about. Intrigued by a man who had been told stories by his grandmother, a man who knew something of his family's history. He definitely wasn't a hood cat, that much was for sure. Most cats from the hood could tell you about there Big Mama, but little else. And that's because it was Big Momma who raised them, while Mom's was out partying, doing drugs, or working her ass off. She wanted to know more.

"Some Black people could come here and buy land, and vacation and shit?" Vendetta asked. "So these was some rich as negroes we talking about?"

DeMarion smiled and nodded. "Yeah, for the most part. They were professional people. This place is where they summered. They came from Chicago, Detroit, and all over the Midwest. This was prior to the Civil Rights Movement of course. After that, after Blacks had the right to vacation in other places, that was when this place began its long decline."

Vendetta nodded. The thought of Blacks *summering* somewhere brought a smile to her. Who the fuck used words like *'summered'*, she thought? Where they do that at? Niggaz in the hood *summered* in the hood, and at the city park where they played basketball and swam in a dirty ass municipal swimming pool. Niggaz in the hood *summered* at the muthafucking fire hydrant when the city cut them on to test the pressure.

DeMarion rose, walked to a hall closet and pulled out a patch work quilt. He brought it back to her and spread it over her.

"What are you doing?" Vendetta asked.

"Making sure you're warm."

"I'm okay!" Vendetta told him. Instantly her thoughts turned to Tavion. He wouldn't have gave two fucks about her welfare. He loved her, that was for sure. But he was just a different type of dude. He was hood through and through. He didn't open doors for her, or pull out chairs, or even think about pulling off any type of romantic shit. That just wasn't him. This dude was different. She wasn't sure how she felt about *'different'*.

The timer went off in the kitchen, letting them know that their hot water was ready. DeMarion rose, walked into the kitchen, and began fixing them some hot cocoa. Vendetta took the opportunity to rise, and walk to the massive windows in the front of the mansion. She peered out over the vast front yard. DeMarion's red Ferrari was parked in the front.

"Your car is out front," Vendetta told him. "Since we're hiding out, shouldn't you pull it into the garage or something?"

"I am," he shouted from the kitchen. "I just wanted to get you straight first."

Again, she was taken aback. A guy who was putting her first.

DeMarion walked up behind Vendetta, and handed her a mug of hot cocoa.

"This reminds me," Vendetta told him. "Exactly how much food did you buy from that little convenience store on the way here?"

Her question made him smile.

"Enough to last a couple of days. I can always run out and buy more."

"And who is going to do the cooking?" Vendetta asked.

DeMarion extended his arms. "I can burn, baby."

Vendetta laughed. "I don't eat hot dogs."

"Oh, you got jokes!" DeMarion told her. "Don't worry, I got this. I got the food."

"Um-hum," Vendetta said nodding. "And how many bedrooms does this place have? Ain't nobody died up in here or nothing, have they?"

DeMarion tilted his head to one side. "Naw, girl! Ain't nobody died up in here. We got plenty of rooms. But I figured we would camp out down here next to the fireplace. At least for tonight. Tomorrow, I can get with the caretaker, and make sure that the heat works, and make sure that everything else with the house is straight."

Vendetta nodded. "Oh, that's a good one. And a new one. I'll give you an A for originality."

DeMarion laughed. "See, it ain't even that type of party. You think somebody trying to get into your drawers and it ain't even like that."

"Um-hum," Vendetta said, rolling her eyes.

"Girl, ain't nobody trying to hump you!" DeMarion told her. "Hell, you just got outta the hospital, you aint' ready to get sent back."

Vendetta burst out laughing. "Oh, please! You ain't even cut like that! You know what they say about niggaz who talk about they size. They really ain't packing shit!"

"I don't know what *they* say, or who *they* are, but *they* obviously ain't had none of *this*."

Again, Vendetta cracked a smile. She loved his confidence and his arrogance. It only served to make him even sexier.

DeMarion lifted the quilt, and wrapped it around her shoulders.

"Thank you," Vendetta said, smiling.

"You're welcome."

"So, you never answered my question," Vendetta told him. "Who *are* you? I mean, for real? Why were you there, and what were you doing there? And who are you, that you would come with soldiers? And why would you bring soldiers to Peaches' house? I need to know, for real."

DeMarion exhaled. She deserved to know. She needed to know, especially if she was to trust him.

"My name is DeMarion Reigns, and I came up to Ohio with my cousin, Darius Reigns. Darius fucks with your sister, or home girl Peaches. We had people watching. We knew they were assembling for the hit, *before* they actually hit. We got our ass there as soon as possible. It was too late of course. They had already overrun the whole place. It was bad."

Vendetta closed her eyes. The memories of that night caused shivers throughout her body.

"You weren't too late," she said, opening her eyes and staring at him. "Every breath I take right now, is because of you. In case I haven't said it before, or even if I have, I'm saying it again. Thank you."

DeMarion nodded.

"I need you to get in touch with your cousin," Vendetta told him. "I need to find my sister."

Again, DeMarion nodded. He understood.

"I will get in touch with him, I give you my word. I just wanted to make sure that you were safe first. I'll try to call him tomorrow."

Vendetta nodded. She inhaled deeply. Just by giving her his full name, he had explained so much. He was a Reigns. That told her everything that she needed to know. That explained the soldiers, that explained why he had no problem putting those other muthafuckers to sleep, it explained the money, the fancy cars, the unused mansion, everything."

"So, you're a Reigns?" Vendetta asked.

DeMarion nodded. He didn't know if that was a good thing, or a bad thing in her eyes.

"Where does that leave us?" Vendetta asked.

DeMarion shrugged. "Us, as in the Reigns family? I don't know. Us, as in you and I? I hope that leaves us where we left off."

"And where is that?" Vendetta asked.

"With you thanking me," DeMarion told her. He leaned in, and kissed her on her lips.

Vendetta's hand rose to the back on DeMarion's head. She found herself closing her eyes, opening her lips, and kissing him back passionately. She found herself moaning, her blood rising, and her blood flowing to places it shouldn't be flowing. After a moment, she pushed him away.

"I thought you said you weren't trying to go there?" she asked, breathing heavily.

"I'm not," DeMarion told her. "It was kiss. Nothing more, nothing less."

Vendetta nodded. She had a man, but she also had this man whom she found herself extremely attracted to. He was a good man, or at least he'd treated her well thus far. It was a deep physical attraction, of that there was no doubt. But was there more to it, she wondered? He had saved her, and then probably saved her again by getting her out of that hospital. And now that she knew who he was, and why he was there that night, she found herself in a very unfamiliar place; she found herself trusting a man whom she just met. And yet, she felt comfortable doing so, she felt comfortable with him.

It was a weird feeling, Vendetta thought. Before her, stood a man who she could do absolutely nothing for, and who wanted nothing from her. But he continued to give and give and give without a price. It only served to make her want him even more.

\*\*\*\*\*

Chief Javier Rodriguez had been on the Nuevo Laredo Police Department for the better part of twenty five years. He started on the force straight out of his tour of duty with the Mexican Army, where he cut his teeth battling cartels near the Belizean border. After returning home to Nuevo Laredo, he found a town decimated by violence, run by the cartels, and racked by corruption. It was in this environment that he pledged to his family, his neighbors, his entire community, that he would do all that he could to make life better for them. Those were the days where some of the biggest, wealthiest, most violent and powerful cartels ruled the landscape. Things had surely changed since then. At least the names had. But some things never changed. Some things were as certain as the setting sun. People grew older, wiser, and more cynical as the years went by, and bills always needed to be paid. And it was for those last two reasons, that Chief Rodriguez's life had changed. He did what he could to make things better, and a big part of doing what he could involved cutting a deal with the very same drug lords that he had once vowed to put away. If they agreed to tamp down the violence in his city, he would agree to look the other way. And looking the other way eventually gave way to acquiescence, and acquiescence eventually gave way to assistance, and assistance grew until he and his department were fully in the pockets of the cartel. And that was where he found himself today. Disappointed with life, disappointed with the way his life had changed, disappointed in himself for the hard choices that he made over the years. But he was resigned with having to live with those choices.

Chief Rodriguez put on his coat, straightened his tie using his reflection in the window, and then walked out of his office where he paused to lock the door. He had a big evening planned. His daughter's piano recital was today, and afterward, he had dinner reservations at the finest restaurant in town. His daughter's recital was going to go a long way toward her gaining admission into The Julliard School in New York City. And after Julliard, would come a life as a world renowned concert pianist. His daughter's success, would go a long way toward the restoration of his conscience, and his good name. It would virtually wipe the slate clean of the many underhanded dealings that he had to involve himself in with the various cartels. It was the cleansing that he needed, it was the cleansing that his mind needed, it was the cleansing that his soul was desperate for.

Chief Rodriguez took the stairs down to the first floor, and then hurried out into the parking lot. He was running a little behind, and wanted to make sure that Nuevo Laredo's notorious traffic didn't cause him to be late. He didn't want to miss one second of his daughter's performance.

The Chief arrived at his Mercedes at the same time the Black van did. The van pulled behind him blocking him in. The side of the van had *Policia* stenciled across it big yellow letters, and the seal of the Nuevo Laredo Police Department on the door. It was one of his department's vans.

"What are you doing?" the chief shouted. "Move your ass!"

The rear door to the van slid open, and several masked men jumped out of it. One of them hit the chief with a Taser, sending millions of volts through his body. The chief went limp instantly, and fell into the arms of more masked men. They quickly drug the chief into the van and pulled away.

*****

Chief Rodriguez awoke to find himself naked, spread eagle, with his hands and feet handcuffed to the four corners of a wooden poster bed. There were others inside of the room with him. Niggers. All of them. Instantly, he knew what this was about, and why they were there. Still, his mind was on his daughter's recital. They needed to get it over with, ask him what they needed to ask, and send him on his way.

"I am the chief of police!" Rodriguez shouted. "Release me, or feel the wraith of the Mexican government!"

Princess laughed.

"I know who you are!" Rodriguez said, staring at her in contempt. "I know who all of you are! And all of you, had better release me, or you'll spend the rest of your miserable lives in the worst federal prison in Mexico. I'll make sure of that!"

Princess walked to the side of the bed, and stared down at the chief. "I have some questions."

"I have little time for you questions!" the chief told her.

""Guadalupe's eyes," Princess started. "They are as blue as the Sea of Cortez. And her hair. Her hair is like a beautiful sun bathed field of honey golden wheat, is it not? Guadalupe. That *is* your daughter's name, isn't it?"

The chief turned as red as the insides of a ripe watermelon. "My daughter! Don't you dare speak of her! Don't you even say her name!"

"And her tiny fingers," Princess continued. "So small, so delicate. And the ways she strikes the keys. Her piano playing is divine."

Chief Rodriguez closed his eyes. Princess had struck deep. She knew about his daughter, she knew of his daughter's talents, perhaps even of her concert that evening. And that scared him more than anything. His daughter was out there defenseless against these Black monsters.

"The questions that I have are about Mozart, Brahms, Beethoven, and Bach," Princess continued with a smile. "She plays Mozart as if she had composed his Concerto Number Five herself. And as for Brahms, well, I don't think that she should play him as often. His music is so... masculine, so powerful, so Teutonic. She should leave the German composers alone, and focus more on the more harmonic and less bassy compositions. That's her key into Julliard."

Tears ran down Chief Rodriguez's face. They knew too much. They must have tapped his phone, and perhaps been following him and his family for days, or evening longer. His precious Guadalupe was in danger, and he was handcuffed to a bed, helpless to save her. The chief began to struggle against his restraints, shaking the bed violently in the process.

"Also, she should leave the Steinway Pianos alone," Princess continued. "Since she seems to have an affinity for Germanic composers, she should be playing and practicing on a Boesendorfer. Personally, I prefer to play on a Fazioli, because of the extraordinary range of the F308. In fact, it's the one I keep at my home in Florida. I have a Boesendorfer 290 Imperial as well, and I play that when I'm in the mood for something a little more Teutonic. She's playing a piece by Wagner tonight, is she not?"

"What is it that you want to know?" the chief asked quietly. Princess had broken him. She had broken him without a single blow of physical torture.

"Wow, this was absolutely no fun at all," Princess said with a smile. "I thought you would at least last through the first ten to fifteen minutes of torture."

"What you have been saying, is even worse than your physical torture," the chief said, sounding defeated.

Princess nodded. "Going after a man's child, is going directly for his heart. It's worse than torture. This is how my brother has felt, every waking hour since his daughter was taken from him. Now, what we must do, is work together to ensure her safe return. Like a team, you understand? Of course you do. You like being a team player, that's why you're here right now. The only problem is, you chose to roll with the wrong team."

Princess seated her on the edge of the bed next to the chief. "I could talk music, and pianos, and composers all day long, but alas, I find my time very constricted at the moment. So, how about we talk about a beautiful little girl, who would very much like to return to the arms of her father. Or better yet, let's talk about two little girls, who would very much love to see their fathers again. Once in Mexico, and one in the United States. I am correct, am I not? One is still in the United States?"

The chief closed his eyes and nodded.

"Good, good," Princess said in a soft, calming, reassuring voice. "Now, where is my little princess, where were they taking her, and what are their plans?"

# Chapter Nine

Emil's chauffeur driven, custom colored, Moonstone Pearl White, Rolls Royce Extended Wheelbase Phantom pulled up to Damian's estate, and instantly his mood changed. He spied a Nero Pegaso Black colored Lamborghini sitting in the driveway, and knew instantly whose vehicle it was. He may have been born at night, but not last night. He wasn't stupid.

Emil's chauffeur pulled the car up to the front, climbed out, and opened up the rear coach doors for his boss. Emil climbed out, peered around the estate, and then smoothed out his dark gray, custom tailored, William Fioravanti suit. He headed inside to find his future brother-in-law.

Julian was inside of Damian's billiard room, fixing himself a drink. Emil stuck his head inside.

"Julian," Emil said, greeting his fellow commission member.

"Emil!" Julian said, surprised to see Emil. He was hoping to see Princess, and surprised that Emil was in town. "When did you get into town?"

"Half an hour ago," Emil said, stepping inside of the parlor. "Where is Damian?"

"Gone," Julian told him. He turned, and held up a second drink. "Scotch?"

Emil walked into the billiard room, took the drink, and turned toward the massive plasma Damian had on his wall. "Thank you. I see you have the game on."

"Spurs are playing," Julian told him.

"I didn't take you for a Spurs fan," Emil told him.

Julian shrugged. "Mississippi doesn't have a team."

"So, you go for someone else's," Emil told him. "A lot of that going on lately."

"What's that?" Julian asked.

"People latching on to other people's things," Emil said with a smile. "Or at least trying to."

Julian nodded. He knew what Emil was getting at. How he had found out was a mystery. He knew that Princess hadn't told him. The last thing she wanted, was conflict between the two of them. Perhaps Emil had his own little spies inside of the Reigns household.

"Well, you know how that is, if you don't have a team of your own, you root for a good one, and hope that one day it might relocate to your city. NBA teams upgrade to better cities all the time," Julian told him. "Nothing wrong with upgrading, huh?"

Emil let out a half smile. "Yeah, but it's against the rules to pursue another city's franchise, if that franchise is not up for relocation. If that team is happy where it's at, you *leave it alone.*"

Julian laughed. "Happiness, like beauty, is in the eye of the beholder."

"You are absolutely right about that," Emil said, swirling the ice around in his drink. "It's all about how a person sees things. Some people see beauty, where there is none. Some see treachery and betrayal, where it doesn't exist. While some refuse to see it, when it's right in front of their face. Me, I'm not like that. I don't have that problem at all. My eyes are wide open, and I see everything."

"That's a good quality," Julian told him.

"Oh, yeah, the ability to see everything, and see *through* everything, helps out a lot," Emil told him. "It allows you to see who your friends are, and who's really out to stab you in the back."

"I'm sure you don't have that problem, Emil," Julian said, jovially slapping Emil across his back. "No one's out to get you."

"Me, maybe not," Emil said, sipping from his glass. "My woman, that's another question."

"What?" Julian asked, trying to look serious. "Someone's out to get Princess? Good thing she rolls deep and has a lot of bodyguards."

"Guys are always out to get her, and in more ways than one," Emil told him. "With some of them she need bodyguards, while with others, it's up to me to guard her body."

This time is was Julian who sipped. "Princess is strong. No one can touch her, unless she wants to be touched. I guess that's pretty much true with any woman, huh? They can't be touched, unless they want to be touched."

"Women see with their emotions," Emil replied. "Sometimes they can't see when something's bad for them. Especially when they're distracted. Women will walk over a snake in the grass without paying any attention. They won't recognized it for being a snake until it bites them."

"I guess that's where having a strong man comes into play," Julian said with a smile. "Having a man who came protect them, defend them, fight for them. A man whose arms they can run to."

"I agree," Emil told him. "But sometimes, when their man's away, that's when all of the creepy crawly, underhanded slugs come out and try to take advantage of them. Some bad things even sneak into the house pretending to be friendly."

"Well, it's a good thing that I'm around when you're busy," Julian said, with smile. "She can lean on me, when you're not around. She know's that I'll take good care of her."

"That's the problem," Emil said dryly.

"Huh?"

"Let's cut the bullshit, Julian!" Emil told him. "I don't know who the fuck you think you are, or who the fuck you think I am, but you are playing a dangerous game."

"And what game is that?"

"Don't fuck with another man's wife!"

"I'm not fucking with another man's wife!"

"Touch what belongs to another man, and you could easily find your hands being chopped off!"

"Emil, I think your imagination hasn't gotten the better of you," Julian told him.

"Don't insult my intelligence!" Emil shouted. "You stay the fuck away from my fiancee! This is your first and *last* warning! You want to try me, you keep it up!"

Julian turned his palms up. "What, Emil? What are you going to do?

Georgia is going to go to war with Mississippi, because you can't keep your woman? You going to send hundreds of men to die, because of your own personal failings and insecurities? Is that where we're at?"

"Stay the fuck away from my woman!"

"She's a grown woman, and no one can do anything other than what she allows them to do."

"Julian, I think you have me confused with some other muthafucka!" Emil said. "I will kill for mine. Do not get it twisted, I will go to war over mine."

"Wow, I didn't know you were so *hood*," Julian said laughing.

"Try me if you want to," Emil told him.

"Am I interrupting something?"

Both Emil and Julian turned toward the entrance into billiard room. Chavo Martinez, Princess's loyal under boss from Florida, was standing in the doorway.

"Who the fuck are you?" Julian asked.

"Julian, this is Chavo," Emil told him. "He's one of Princess's men from Florida. He's here to speak to Princess."

"She's not here," Julian told them.

"Damian?" Emil asked.

"Not here either," Julian told them. "And neither is Dante."

Emil and Chavo exchanged glances.

"What's this about?" Julian asked.

"It's a matter concerning my fiance," Emil told him.

"Well, seeing as how she's not here, and seeing as how I'm the only one who has the ability to get in touch with any of them, maybe you should think about telling me," Julian said with a smile.

"No one has time for your bullshit, Julian!" Emil told him. "Where's Damian?"

"Like I said, he's gone," Julian said. He seated himself at Damian's bar, and took a drink from his glass of Scotch. "If it's an emergency, I can get in touch with him. Other than that, they are busy, and don't want to be disturbed. They do have a child to find."

Emil and Chavo exchanged glances once again.

"Princess needs to get to Florida immediately," Chavo told him.

"Immediately?" Julian asked.

"Yesterday," Chavo said, walking into the billiards room. He walked up to the bar, and began fixing himself a drink. "She needs to get to Florida yesterday. The state is slipping away. Despite my best efforts, I am only one man. I can't save the state alone. She needs to get there, and she needs to get her house in order. Everyday that she's away, more and more of her people are defecting. I can consolidate her hold in the north, if she can come back and re-take the south. But as it stands now, the state is not only pulling away, but a civil war is brewing between the north and south. You're going to have Miami and Tampa, battling Jacksonville, Orlando, and Tallahassee. It's going to be a blood bath. Only *she* can stop it."

"Jesus!" Julian said, tossing back a significant amount of Scotch.

Chavo nodded. "It's worse than you can imagine. Her bosses are conspiring left and right. People are cutting independent deals with the Colombians, the Cubans are getting strong again in Miami, they even have some new players on the scene. The Puerto Ricans are making noise in Orlando, and we even have some new Colombians making moves throughout the state. The shit is bad."

Emil turned toward Julian. "You wanna call Damian now?"

Julian nodded slowly. "What do you need?"

"Muscle," Chavo told him. "And leadership. It's her state, she took it, now she needs to be there to run it. It can't be done from Texas."

"Yeah, but her brothers need her here," Julian told him. "And as far as muscle goes, every soldier they have, is spread throughout Texas, or is in Northern Mexico searching for Dante's child."

"Then she's going to lose Florida," Chavo shrugged.

"She just doesn't have the manpower!" Julian told him. He faced Emil. "What about your people? You don't have men to send her?"

"I've sent men to Florida," Emil told him. He hated being questioned by Julian, like Julian was his boss. "I've sent hundreds of men to Florida. And I've sent hundreds of men to Mexico. I don't even have enough men left in my state, to make sure that it stays copasetic. If someone wanted to make a move against Georgia right now, I'd be shit out of luck. I have no more men to spare."

Julian exhaled. He knew exactly where Emil was coming from. He was in the same position. He had sent most of his men to Texas and

Mexico to help out in the search for Dante's daughter as well. That was the price of being a friend to the Reigns family. The closer you were to them, the greater the danger was to you. But also, on the flip side, the greater the reward. The Reigns family was a family with deep memory, and they never forgot, one way or the other. And it was better to have them never forget that you were a friend, than to have them never forget that when they needed you, you weren't there for them. Something needed to be done.

"I'll call Damian and fill him in," Julian told them. "I'll call Dajon as well, as see if he and Anjounette have any men they can spare. I doubt it. I'm sure Dante has pulled all of their soldiers into the hunt as well. But I'll see. In the meantime, I suggest that you chill. Once Damian is back, he may want to meet with you and assess the situation for himself. So, get comfy at your hotel."

Chavo nodded. He turned, and left the room. Emil turned back toward Julian.

"So, you're a Reigns now?" Emil asked.

"I'm a friend of the family," Julian told him. "Damian left me here to man the phones."

"Well, I just hope you remember that," Emil told him.

"And what is that?"

"That you're the help," Emil told him. "Princess is my wife, Damian is my brother-in-law, Dante is my brother-in-law, and this is *my* family. Don't mess with a man's family. Don't mess with a man's wife. And don't forget what I told you. This is your first, and *last* warning."

Emil turned and left the room. Julian smiled, and tossed back a drink. Emil had him fucked up, if he thought that this was the end of it. He was weak, and Princess would eat his weak ass alive. She needed a *real* man, a man like him. And he needed a strong woman, a woman like her. Together, they could dominate the world in which they lived. She would rule over Florida, while he would rule over Mississippi, and they could split Georgia between the two of them. Why sit on a Commission with a bunch of idiots and assholes dictating to them what they could or should do, when the whole thing could be just one big family affair. Dante and Damian in Texas and California, Dajon in Louisiana, and he and Princess ruling over the rest of the Gulf States, they could have a virtual monopoly on all of the entrance points for the nation's drug trade. That was after they had gotten rid of Chacho and Ceasario and taken over Arizona and New Mexico of course. But it could be done.

Julian had bigger plans in the works. Plans that were bigger than Emil, and even larger than his relationship with Princess. He wanted to become a billionaire. He wanted to make the Forbes list. He had an entire state's drug trade on lock down, and he was a graduate of Harvard, and Harvard Business school. There should be nothing stopping him from joining that list. If Oprah, Janet, and Jay Z could be on it, then why the hell couldn't he?

Julian tossed back the last remaining corner of Scotch in his glass, and rose from the bar. He pulled out his cellphone, and dialed up Damian. He would inform him of the situation in Florida, and then offer to send in men to help out. He had sent hundreds of men to help out with the search for Lucky, but what they didn't know, was that he had hundreds more waiting in the wings to take out Emil's ass. He had been recruiting and getting big for the longest. And he had kept those men in reserve just in case. And now, he would use them. He would use them to earn Damian's gratitude, and Princess's love. He would send them with her to Florida, to help her save her state. He would show her what a *real man* was capable of. He would show her what a man with power was able to do. She couldn't turn to that weakling fiancee of hers, but she *could* turn to him, and that was one thing that he wanted to put in her head. Julian was strong, and was able to help her, while Emil wasn't. When in need, Damian calls Julian to come and hang out, and talk to, Dante calls up Julian to send some men to help, and now she was able to get muscle from Julian to save her state. Julian, Julian, Julian, the savior of the Reigns family, time and time again. That was what he wanted flowing through her mind.

Julian turned back to the bar, and poured himself another drink. He took a swig from the glass of straight Scotch, and relished the burn rolling down his throat. He was going to have Princess. And it was going to be Princess that was going to put a bullet in the side of Emil's head. She had a reputation for doing just that. Once she was done with you, and you were no longer of use to her, she simply ended your existence. Yes, it was going to be his little black widow, who was going to make the choice, the only logical choice, and put Emil out of his misery and then jump into *his* arms. He was going to make that happen. His first call would be to Damian, his second would be to his underbosses. It was time, to assemble his troops.

# Chapter Ten

Earl Brenner had been the police chief of El Paso, Texas for the last twenty years. He saw mayors and city councilmen come and go. Having been a police officer for the last forty years, he had witnessed the rise and fall of many a politician, the election of many governors and presidents, and saw the world change before his eyes. Texas had gone from being a solidly democratic state, to a solid republican one. He had witnessed the rise, the fall, and the re-emergence of many cartels and drug lords over his forty year history on the force, and so had the people of his city. But the one constant they had through all of the turbulent times, was seeing Earl Brenner at the ballot box, and knowing that his re-election was the one certainty that they could count on. He was the calm, in the rough and rocky seas of life.

"Fuck me, *Papi*!" Conchita shouted, as she road the chief's cock like a champion bull rider in a rodeo. "*Aye, Papi!*"

The out-of-shape chief peered down the length of his sweaty, rotund belly at the young, tender senorita gyrating her hips on top of him. Conchita was his favorite prostitute, and the one he found himself visiting with exclusively as of late. She understood his needs as a man, as an *aging* man, in particular. He knew that his vigor wasn't what it used to be, and his once proud penis no longer stood at one o'clock when fully erect, but now only rose to about three thirty. And his stamina had taken a significant hit as well. Back in the day, he used to be able to stay up all night at the whorehouse and service a multitude of woman before the sun rose to usher in a new day. Now, he was down to about twenty minutes of great sex, and about twenty minutes of stop and go sex, while trying hard not to cum. And she understood that. She wasn't judgmental when his soldier ran out of steam a little early, and she acted like his sex was the greatest sex in the world. She screamed and shouted, like he was killing her, although he knew that those days were long gone. But like guitarist and bluesman Jonny Lang's hit song *'Lie To Me'*, he was more than happy to be lied to.

"That's it, right there, baby!" the chief shouted.

"*Aye, Papi*," Conchita cried out, as she worked her hips faster and faster, bringing the chief to a quick climax. He cried out, and clasped her hips, as he orgasm. She could feel him throbbing inside of her. She leaned forward and kissed him. "*Mi policia* was full of energy today."

Chief Brenner slapped Conchita across her ass. "You bring it outta me, Sweety."

"Get ready for round two, *Papi*," she said, kissing him on his lips.

"Not today, Darling," the chief told her. He was spent. Going two rounds back to back was no longer in him. Of late, he liked to get it and go. It wasn't just the fact that he was busy, it was just that he found that he could no longer regenerate like he once could. Already, he was popping Viagra like Tic-Tacs. "I'm gonna have to grab me something to eat."

"You want me to wait on you to come back?" she purred.

"No," the chief said, kissing her back. "How about you just be ready to rock and roll again tomorrow."

"I have to wait that long to see *mi Papi* again?" she moaned. "I can't wait that long."

He loved her, because she catered to his ego like no other woman. He was a widower, with children that had left the nest long ago. And so, Conchita provided all of his nocturnal recreation and sexual relief. She was all he had, and he appreciated her kindness greatly. It was even to the point where he would ask her grab something to eat with him. Not a dinner at a restaurant of course, because he was the chief of police and she was a prostitute, but a stop on the outskirts to grab something to go and take back with them to his place, or to an out of the way motel. That was about as far as they could go right now, at least until he finally retired and headed for Belize, or some small fishing village in Costa Rica. Then he would be free to love her openly. Would she go with him, he wondered? What more did she have? What woman wouldn't want an easy, leisurely life strolling the beaches, or lying out on a fishing yacht most of the day?  He could give her a much better life than she had now, and she could give him the companionship that he required.  It would be a pretty good match of convenience.  Of course she would go with him, he thought.

Chief Brenner tapped Conchita on her ass, telling her to get off of him so that he could get up.  He was done for the evening.  She had relieved the tension that he felt from having a rough and busy day.  A good meal, a glass of booze, and it would be another good day behind him.  It was how he counted his days now.  Another day's work was more money in his bank and more money going toward his pension.  It had been another day without losing an officer an work, and  another day of good sex, being capped off by some good food, and great booze.  Those were the four things that made his day a good day.  And today was one such day.

Conchita rose from off of the chief, walked to her purse, opened it, and pulled out a stun gun.  She pulled the trigger, causing blue sparks to light the dark room, along with a rolling cackle from the electric charge.

"What the hell is that?" Brenner asked.

Conchita shrugged.  "I'm sorry."

"What?" the chief asked, now sitting up.

"They have my family," Conchita said sadly.  She quickly placed the prongs of the stun gun against the chief's leg and pulled the trigger, sending high voltage throughout his body.  The stun gun caused the chief to fly back on the bed and jerk uncontrollably.  Conchita walked to the door, and unlocked it.  Several dark suited men entered into the room.  One grabbed the chief's holstered gun and clothing.  Dante walked in behind them.

The chief slowly began to come out of his central nervous system interruption.

"Hello, Fat Boy," Dante told him.

"How could you..." the chief asked.

"Don't worry about her," Dante told him.  "It's not her fault, so don't you go to your grave blaming anything on her.  In fact, she resisted quite determinedly.  We had to grab her grandmother in order to get her to cooperate, so don't blame her."

"I'm sorry," Conchita said, now covering the lower half of her face and sobbing.

"Hey, you did what you had to do," Dante told her. "Don't you worry about him. You take your family, you take the money we gave you, and you run. You go deep into Mexico, and you start a new life, with a new name, do you hear me?"

Conchita nodded, wiping away her tears.

Dante clasped her arm to make her focus and look into his eyes. "Do not try to stay in the United States, do you hear me? If they figure out that you two were here together, they will give you the death penalty, understand? Do you know what DNA is?"

Conchita nodded.

"Good," Dante told her. "Take the money, and go and start a new life. Open your restaurant. Go back to school. Do whatever it is you always dreamed of doing."

Again, Conchita nodded.

Dante nodded toward the door. "Now, go!"

Conchita grabbed her clothing, and ran out of the room.

"You son of a bitch!" the chief shouted.

"Me?" Dante asked, pressing his hand against his chest. "I'm the son-of-a-bitch? You, you were the one taking advantage of a young immigrant."

"It was consensual," the chief told him.

"She was fucking you to feed her grandmother!" Dante shouted. "And her son."

The chief's eyes flew wide.

"Yeah," Dante said nodding. "She has a son. You didn't know that did you? She's twenty two, with a seven year old son."

The chief shook his head. He shifted his gaze from Dante, to each of the men in the room, before focusing on Dante again. "So, what happens now?"

Dante smiled. "I hear you love to go fishing?"

*****

The chief woke to find himself on a large ship. He was tied with his hands behind his back, and his legs were bound. Her peered around, and could see ocean for miles. A lone bodyguard lifted a walkie-talkie.

"He's awake," the bodyguard said into the walkie-talkie.

After a couple of moments, Dante arrived, with several others in tow. He walked up to the chief with a grin as wide as a kid walking through the gates of Disney World.

"Good, morning," Dante told him.

The chief struggled with his bonds. "What are you doing?"

Dante waved his hand around the ship. "You remember my man giving you the shot to knock you out. And that's probably the last thing you remember, so let me update you. You were carried out to a waiting ambulance, where you were taken to a hospital. We used a life flight helicopter to lift you to the airport, where you were transferred to my jet. From there, we flew out here together to San Diego, and from the San Diego airport, we were flown by helicopter out to this wonderful ship. She's called *The Mystery Breaker,* and she belongs to Bio One. She's a research vessel. You know how my braniac brother is, always funding crazy science projects and experiments all over the world. Well, in all honestly, I actually thought that this one was pretty cool. You know what this vessel is doing?"

The chief remained silent. He had no idea what was going through Dante's twisted mind, and he wasn't going to play whatever silly little game Dante wanted to play with him.

"You mentioned DNA," the chief told him. "Mine is back at the motel room. And so is Conchita's, so is yours, and all of your men's. They will find you, and when they do, the State of Texas is going to put you to death."

"I bought that motel," Dante told him. I had my people go over that room with a fine tooth comb. We disposed of your car. It will never be found. We wiped clear any trace of your last steps. The last anyone saw of you, was when you left work. And that is where the trail goes cold, and that is where the trail will end. You bought two tickets to Cuba. Well, at least your credit card did. And you left a note. You ran to Mexico, got on a plane, and went to live out the rest of your life your young homosexual lover."

"Fuck you!" the chief shouted, trying to get after Dante.

Dante laughed. "That's the trail that we created for you. You're a laughing stock, a disgrace to the department and to the city. They're not going to spend a dime looking for you. That's the way your twenty years of service as the chief of police, and your forty years of service as a crooked pig is going to end. In disgrace. Like it should."

"Who are you to judge me?" the chief asked, staring at Dante in disgust. "It was consensual!"

Dante peered over the side of the ship into the ocean. "You like fresh meat? I'm going to give you the opportunity to *be* the fresh meat."

And now the chief had an idea of what Dante had in store for him.

"Seal Island is that way," Dante said pointing. "You know what that is?"

The chief rolled his eyes at Dante.

Dante nodded. "You do. You're a fisherman, with a love of the sea. You know what Seal Island is. You know who frequents Seal Island this time of the year? You know why? White sharks patrol the island this time of the year, because it's breeding season for the seals. Plenty of fresh, young, naive seal pups to feast on."

"I'm supposed to swim for it, is that it?" the chief asked, through gritted teeth.

The salty, fishy smell of the ocean, was slowly giving way to a horrendous stench that was growing strong and stronger.

"No," Dante said, shaking his head. "The white sharks aren't patrolling the island today. They're here. Right here, right next to us. You know how I know that?"

Dante lifted his arms and spun slowly. "Because of this wonderful ship that my brother paid an arm and a leg for. This research vessel's big project, is to tag great white sharks. And according to the feedback from the tags mounted to their dorsal fins, the satellites have them here. A whole shit load of them."

Dante's men began covering the lower half of their faces, in an effort to shield their mouths and noses from the horrendous stench that was hanging in the air.

"What you are smelling now, is the reason all of those big hungry sharks are here, and not feeding on tender young seal pups," Dante continued. "A dead humpback whale carcass."

Dante broke into an evil laugh. His laughter was such, that his own men eyed him strangely.

"It's fucking beautiful, Man!" Dante shouted. "Fucking beautiful!  I was going to have them take you back to the farm, so I could torture you by hanging you from a fucking cross, but then I got a call from Steve, the captain of this ship, saying that they found a dead whale carcass out here near Seal Island. Steve doesn't know about my daughter being taken, so he didn't know not to disturb me. He was just following the last instructions he was given, which were to call me so that I could fly out and check out some great white breaches. So, you can imagine the fucking surprise when I got that call. Immediately, I knew, how you were going to die."

"For what?"" the chief asked nervously. Sweat began pouring down his face.

"I don't even want to ask you any questions," Dante said calmly. "I'll let you decide if you have anything you think that I should know."

"Look, I had nothing to do with your little girl getting kidnapped!" Chief Brenner shouted.

"Ahhhh," Dante said nodding. "See, we're already on topic, and I haven't even asked you a single question." Dante nodded toward his men.

Chief Brenner now realized that he was latched to a cable that was a part of the ship's crane that was used to recover small boats, jet skis, supplies, etc... The crane lifted him into the air, and swung him over the side of the ship. Slowly, the cable was lowered so that he was almost eye to eye with Dante. He peered down, and for the first time, he could see the massive whale carcass below him. He was suspended nearly thirty six feet in the air.

"Don't do this!" the chief shouted. "Please, don't do this! I'll tell you whatever you want to know. Please!"

Dante pointed toward the giant carcass. "See how it shakes violently. Each time it shakes, that's a white shark shaking its head, tearing off chunks of blubber."

The chief was shaking his head constantly now. "Don't do this!"

"Where is she?" Dante asked calmly.

"I don't know!" the chief shouted.

"Who does?"

"I don't know!"

Dante nodded. And the screaming chief was lowered into the water, next to the horrendous smelling whale carcass. Dante stared at his watch, waited twenty seconds, and then nodded. The chief was lifted out of the water. He gasped for air.

"Awww, they didn't even take a bite!" Dante told him.

"Please!" the chief shouted. "Please! Don't do this! Please!"

"Okay, I wasn't going to tell you this, because I didn't want to scare you," Dante said smiling. "But, one of the white sharks down there, is Big Bertha. She's the largest recorded white shark ever tagged. They believe she's an Australian great white. She's been recorded traveling to South Africa, back to Australia, and up the South American coast to Seal Island. Satellites have even tagged her off the coast of Cuba. She a roamer. And a fighter. She has bite marks and scars all over her body. She's twenty two feet long, and she weighs seven thousand pounds. A record breaker. I can't believe she didn't take a bite out of you. Hmmm. How about we give her another crack at you?"

"No!"

Dante cupped his hand behind his ear. "What? I can't hear you. She's where?"

"I don't know where she is!" the chief shouted.

Dante waved his hand, and the chief was lowered back into the water. Again, Dante peered down at his watch, counting to twenty five seconds this time, before nodding for the chief to be pulled back up.

The chief gasped for the sweet taste of oxygen as he came up from the putrid waters. This time, he actually got a close up glimpse of several of the massive monsters swimming in the water all around him.

"Help me!" he shouted. "Help me! Stop it! Please, stop! I'll tell you everything!"

"That's what I'm talking about," Dante smiled.

"Chief Lopez!" Brenner shouted. "He called in a favor. The Juarez Cartel pulled the strings!"

"Lopez?" Dante asked.

"Laredo Chief of Police!" Brenner shouted.

Dante nodded. It made sense. He was in the pocket of the Juarez Cartel. And if it was the Juarez Cartel, that meant Nuni Nunez was behind it. Everything was crystal clear. Galindo wanted the Reigns family and The Commission to wait and to not get their supplies from their rivals on the Yucatan Peninsula. It was why they needed her alive. She was no good to them dead, and that gave him some hope.

"I don't need to know who or why," Dante shouted. "I can figure that out later. Right now, I only want to know one thing. Where is she?"

"I don't know!" the chief said, shaking his head.

"Where are they taking her?" Dante shouted. "I need to intercept them before they get her across the border!"

Chief Brenner shook his head frantically. "I don't know!"

"Where are they going to cross?" Dante shouted.

"I don't know!"

Dante waved his hand, and the crane operater dropped the chief down into the water, causing a hug splash. Unfortunately for the chief, this time, the splash caused unwanted attention. While a fat human was not as rich in blubber as an enormous whale carcass, he still deserved an exploratory bite. A great white hit him the the force of a locomotive, and took an enormous bite out of his side. The bite was so powerful, and the shark so massive, that the tug on the cable caused the boat to shake.

"Jesus!" one of Dante's men cried out.

Dante waved his hand, and the crane operator lifted the chief out of the water. Half of him was missing. He had a bite the ran from his right knee, all the way up to his shoulder. Blood was pouring from the chief's mouth.

"He's finished," Dante said, shaking his head.

One of Dante's men pulled out a handgun and aimed it at the chief's head. Dante grabbed the gun and lowered it.

"What the fuck are you doing?" Dante asked.

The man shrugged. "He's finished, he's through, I mean... I was just going to put the poor bastard out of his misery."

"You feel mercy for him?" Dante asked. "He helped those bastards kidnap my daughter, and you feel sorry for him?"

"No, I mean, I was just going to..."

"We all have a choice to make," Dante told the man. "And you just chose the wrong team."

"What?" the man asked, turning up his palms. "Dante, I'm loyal. I'm with you."

Dante peered at the men behind the pleading man and nodded toward the ocean. The other bodyguards lifted the man off of his feet, and tossed him into the shark filled waters. Dante peered at the chief, who had just about bled out.

"Cut that piece of shit down, and toss it into the water. Let the sharks finish the job." He peered at his men. They could hear the screams of the other bodyguard in the water. "Anyone else want to choose the wrong team? Decide right now! I don't have time for half dedicated muthafuckas! Either you're with me, or against me! And if you're against me, have a nice swim back to the shore!"

Dante turned and stormed off. His men peered at one another in fear. Quickly, they all got to work cutting the chief down so that they could toss his body into the shark filled waters.

# Chapter Eleven

Damian was seated inside of his home office, checking various
spreadsheets and going over various financial numbers. The numbers
were astronomical, and his family's various accounts were bleeding
money like they had a massive open wound. Dante was spending, and
spending, and spending. The cost in men, material, and bribes to law
enforcement and other officials was staggering. There was the cost in jet
fuel, the cost in gasoline, the hotel cost to house thousands of men all
across the state and in Mexico, and then the cost to feed this massive
army three times a day. The car rentals alone were unbelievable. And
then there were the damages to homes and motel rooms, and vehicles, and
the other ridiculous cost that he was facing. Dante had purchased
ranches, helicopters, entire motels, and was burning through cash like he
was throwing it into a massive bonfire. Damian had promised his brother
the world, and there was no cost that he wouldn't incur to get his niece
back, but the money had to be spent more judiciously. The family had
just turned the water back on, and got the dope flowing again. And now,
it seemed, that every single dollar that was coming in, was being spent in
the search. And that left him where he was in the beginning; surviving on
the money that his entertainment company was bringing in. And that
wasn't enough.

Bio One was facing a massive class action lawsuit, and the new
drugs that it had in the pipeline were on hold until the FDA's concerns
could be alleviated. The Food and Drug Administration was on his ass,
and from here on out, every single 't' would have to be crossed, and every
single 'i' would have to be dotted. Bio One's other drugs were still doing
okay. They had taken a hit because the company's reputation had suffered
in the process. So those past drugs, were simply maintaining Bio One as

103

an entity. Energia Oil was all tied up because of over investing in Africa. And now that oil was dropping like a damn hot rock, the company was feeling the pinch. An enormous pinch to be exact. America's own oil industry was once again surging due to new technologies, the old oil fields were productive again, and new sources of oil were popping up all over the place. Wyoming was producing. Hell, even San Antonio was now producing oil because of the massive Eagle Ford Shale Project just to the south of the city. Throw in North Dakota, and Canada, and the North American oil market was going to be brimming over with excess production. Even China's insatiable appetite for oil was now being met. And despite his best efforts at trying to delay the massive Keystone Oil Pipeline, that project was now about to go through as well. It would be decades before Energia Oil would even begin to recoup all of the money it had invested in Africa. And so, that left him heavily dependent on the revenues from the family's construction company, and the family's entertainment corporation. Something needed to break. And if nothing broke, then soon, his family would be.

A knock came to the door of Damian's office. His office door was open, and he peered up to find his brother Dajon peering in at him.

"Hey!" Damian said, rising. Dajon walked in, and the two of them embraced. "What are you doing here?"

"Hey, man," Dajon said, embracing his brother. "Just stopping by to see you."

"Sit down," Damian told him, pointing to a chair on the other side of his desk. "Is Anjounette here?"

"No, no," Dajon said, shaking his head. "She's still in West Texas."

"Oh," Damian said nodding. He understood what that meant. "And the kids? How are my niece and nephew?"

Dajon shrugged. "Man, your guess is as good as mine. I haven't seen them since the day of the wedding."

Again, Damian knew what Dajon meant. His brother hadn't seen his children, since Lucky's kidnapping. Dajon had been on the hunt since day one. And like all of them, he looked tired and aged. Damian could see the red in his brother's eyes, and the fatigue on his face.

"Go home," Damian told him. "Get some rest. Hug your kids. We'll take it from here."

Dajon let out a half smile. "You know there's no way on Earth I'm doing that."

"I know," Damian said nodding. Again, he understood. There was no way he was going to abandon the search either. They were all going to weather through this crisis as best as they could. "So, you were in?"

"Dallas," Dajon told him. "Tearing Dallas upside down, inside out." Dajon paused, and then shook his head. "Nothing. Not a trace. They may not have made it that far. And then, I went to the border to help out there. Nothing."

"Like they just vanished into thin air," Damian said, exhaling.

"How's Dante?" Dajon asked, leaning back in his chair.

Damian paused, staring blankly at the wall behind his brother. He was trying to find the most accurate words to describe Dante's condition. None came. He resorted to the general.

"Not good," Damian finally said, shaking his head. "He's taking it hard, of course. Hasn't slept."

"And you?"

Damian shook his head.

"Slept?" Dajon asked.

Again, Damian shook his head. "I can look at you and tell that you haven't."

Dajon smiled. "Sleep is for the weak."

Damian laughed. "Sleep is for the weary."

"Where is Dante?" Dajon asked.

Damian lifted an invoice from off of his desk. "According to this, he was last headed to San Diego."

"San Diego?" Dajon reached for the document Damian was holding. "A refueling bill?"

"Apparently, he took one of the Gulfstreams to San Diego," Damian said, leaning back and straightening his tie. "Why? I don't have the slightest idea."

"I'm worried," Dajon told him.

"About?"

"About Dante," Dajon told him. He lifted the bill. "About this. About all of this. It's too much."

"You're telling me," Damian said, letting out a half smile.

"No," Dajon said, sitting up, and leaning in. "Damian, I'm serious. It's too much. All of it, it's way too much. Too much noise, too much static, too overt. Too much money. Everything is being done in excess."

"What do you want me to do?" Damian asked, turning up his palms. "What? She's our niece, and he's our brother."

"Reel it in," Dajon said flatly. "For his sake, for Lucky's sake, reel it in. Get control of the situation. It's out of control. I wish that I could say that it was spiraling out of control, but it's already out of control. All moderation, all strategy, all perspective, all rationality is gone. I don't know, maybe we're all too close to the situation. But I *do* know, that we're not using our heads. We're pounding the ground with thousands of soldiers, we're kicking in doors, we're torturing people, we're throwing tons of money at it, and none of it is working. Damian, we're using a sledgehammer, when maybe we should be using a scalpel."

"How is pulling back going to help the situation?" Damian asked.

"We need to gain some perspective," Dajon told him. "Bring in someone who isn't so close to the situation to run it, sit back, reassess the situation, get a view of the entire situation, and think smart."

Damian shook his head, instantly dismissing the suggestion. "Dante would never go for that. If it had been Cheyenne, would you? No, you wouldn't. Nothing in the world would pull you off of the hunt, and let you rely on someone else to lead the search to find her. Let's keep it real."

"Keep it real?" Dajon asked, leaning in even more. "You wanna know what keeping it real is? Damian, we are going to lose all of our political protection if this goes on any longer. And if we lose that, then we lose everything we've built. How's that for keeping it real? The tactics are *too* heavy handed. Pull it back."

"How? At this point, how?"

"Find a way," Dajon told him. And do it, before it's too late. Damian, I went to the border. I talked to our men. They talked to me in confidence, and what they had to say was not good. For all intents and purposes, the Reigns family has invaded Mexico."

Damian let out a half smile.

"Seriously!" Dajon told him. "We have thousands of men in Northern Mexico and along the Texas-Mexican border. I saw a ranch,

Damian. And on this ranch, Dante had set up his own private air force. There were helicopters with night vision and infra red cameras. There were small drones with night vision and infra red cameras attached to them. We have so many drones flying over Mexico, that the Mexican government has lodged an official complaint with our embassy. Did you know that? Dante has set up a high tech search facility, with a computerized grid, and he's checking off each grid after the men have gone over it with a fine tooth comb. He's buying up satellite time from private companies who traditionally do mapping and weather monitoring. Companies are complaining that all of the satellite time is being bought up! Our drones are bumping into the Border Patrol's drones, the Coast Guard's drones, Homeland Security's drones, the Department of Defense's drones, Immigration and Customs Enforcement drones, DEA drones, and the Mexican Army's drones. It's too much."

Damian let out a half laugh, but nodded in agreement.

"And then, there's the other issue," Dajon continued.

"What's that?"

"We've pulled soldiers from all over Texas, California, Louisiana, and Florida," Dajon told him. "Emil's sent us soldiers from Georgia, Julian has sent men from Mississippi, and even James has sent us people from Virginia. We're all stretched bone thin, Damian. Bone fucking thin. And unless we cut this thing back significantly, we're going to lose Florida. Those men need to get back to Florida. And you already know that Emil is always on shaking ground with his underbosses. He needs his men, even though he would never admit it."

"Florida?" Damian asked, lifting an eyebrow.

Dajon nodded. "Florida. Have you talked to Emil?"

Damian shook his head. "Not yet."

"He's going to tell you how bad it is," Dajon told him. "Princess is on the verge of losing Florida. She needs to get there, and she needs soldiers, lot's of them."

"It's that bad?"

"No, bro, it's worse."

Damian leaned back, and placed his finger beneath his chin, thinking about what he had been told. After a few moments, he peered up at Dajon.

"Give me some time to think about this," Damian told him.

"We don't have much time," Dajon replied.

Damian nodded solemnly. "I know. Let me sleep on it. Or at least, try to sleep on it."

Dajon exhaled. He hesitated momentarily, but then continued. Damian should know, he thought.

"Damian, there are rumors," Dajon told him. "Rumors of another place. Another ranch that Dante has. It's not good."

"It never is," Damian told him. "Let me sleep on it, bro. Do what you can to buy us some time. I just need a moment to figure this out, and plot a course for us. I agree with everything that you said. In fact, I had similar thoughts the other day. We do need to reassess the situation. Give me time to do that."

Dajon nodded. "Get some sleep."

"You too," Damian smiled.

Dajon rose, and Damian did the same. Damian walked around his desk and embraced his brother.

"You be careful out there," Damian told him.

"I will," Dajon said. "You have a guest waiting for you in the living room. I wanted to speak to you first. You want me to send him in on the way out?"

Damian's stare was a question. "Who is it?"

"A representative from New York," Dajon told him.

Damian understood. From New York, meant the Old Ones. He wondered what they wanted.

"No, don't send him in," Damian said, exhaling forcibly. "I'll meet him in there."

"Okay, bro," Dajon said, again hugging his brother. "I'll get with you again before I leave."

"Where to?" Damian asked.

Dajon shrugged. "I guess, I'm headed back to the border."

Damian nodded. "We'll grab something to eat before you leave."

Dajon nodded, and waved, as he exited the room.

*****

Damian strolled into his living room to find his guest staring at his pictures on the wall. The guest paused in front of one massive painting in particular, taking it in.

"It's an original Rembrandt," Damian said, startling his guest.

"Mr. Reigns," the man said turning. "How are you?"

"I'm well," Damian told him, walking gingerly into the room. "Thank you for asking. And your name is?"

"Giuseppe," the man said, bowing slightly. His accent was thick, and distinctly Old Sicilian. "Thank you for allowing me into your home."

Damian nodded, and waved toward a nearby sofa. "Please."

"No, thank you," Giuseppe told him. "I will not be intruding for long."

"No intrusion," Damian told him. "Can I offer you a drink?"

Giuseppe shook his head. "No, thank you. Again, I will be here only a very brief time."

"I take it that you had a pleasant flight?"

"*Si*," Giuseppe said, nodding. "Thank you for asking."

"And our friends in New York," Damian asked. "They are well?"

Giuseppe smiled and nodded. "They send you the best wishes, and good tidings."

"And a message?" Damian asked.

Giuseppe nodded, and peered around the room, insuring that they were alone. "They have asked me to convey their deepest and most heart felt sympathies for the kidnapping of your niece. And they would like for me to inform you, that you have their full and utmost support in this matter, and they support whatever actions you deem necessary for the blessed child's safe return."

Damian smiled. "That is most kind of them. Please convey my most sincerest and heart felt thanks to the dons. Our eternal friendship is strengthened by the comfort they have conveyed."

"The dons would like you to know, that whatever you need, you have to simply ask, and it will be done," Giuseppe continued.

"Really?" Damian asked, lifting an eyebrow.

Giuseppe bowed slightly and nodded in the affirmative.

"Please convey to the dons, that their friendship is more than enough, and that their message has brought joy and hope to my heart."

Giuseppe again nodded.

Damian laughed on the inside. Having to use the language and terms of the old mafia always tickled him. But it was the language that the old school dons spoke, and observing such niceties were a part of diplomacy.

"If there is nothing else, I must get back to my work," Damian told his guest.

Giuseppe nodded, and peered at Damian's hand. There was no ring for him to kiss. Embarrassed at the awkwardness of the situation, Damian quickly called for one of his men.

"Senor Giuseppe, this is my man, Jake," Damian said, introducing one of his bodyguards. "Jake will take you to the airport, and he will make sure that you have everything that you need."

"Thank you, *Senor*," Giuseppe said, nodding and bowing slightly.

Damian turned, and hurried out of the room, before Giuseppe saw the smile on his face. In the hallway, he burst into laughter. The old ones, and their old ways. He would never understand it, but it was who they were. They were the *real mafia*, not the flashy ones, the ones who wanted to be stars. These were not the Sammy the Bulls, nor the John Giotti's of the underworld, they were the men way above them. The real families, they were the *old ones*. The ones who truly guarded the old ways, and the old traditions. They were the ones who would die, rather than snitch. They were the ones who would go to prison for life, rather than betray anyone, or bring disgrace to their families. Some of their old ways were funny to him, but he admired the hell out of them for their code of *Omertia*.

# Chapter Twelve

Laredo police chief Daniel 'Danny' Lopez pulled up to the hostage scene with his tires screeching to a halt. He leaped out of his patrol car, and raced up to a group of waiting officers. One of them was a lieutenant he recognized.

"What's the situation?" Chief Lopez asked.

"Not good," the lieutenant said, shaking his head. "It's a barricaded hostage situation, with multiple hostages. The gunman is inside, and he's taking pot shots at the officers with a high caliber assault rifle. He's threatening bloodshed if anyone goes near the house."

"Shit!" the chief said, shaking his head. "Where's the fucking media? Are they here yet?"

The lieutenant pointed down the street toward a police barricade, that had been cordoned off using yellow police tape. All of the locals channels were there, with cameras already filming.

"Keep them at bay!" the chief commanded. Get a negotiator here, and get SWAT on the scene."

"On the way, Chief," the lieutenant told him. "Also, the mobile command vehicle is parked around the corner."

"Good!" the chief said gruffly. "I'll be in the command center. Let me know when SWAT gets here, and send the negotiator over to the command center."

The chief turned and stormed off towards the giant recreational vehicle that the city had equipped to operate as a mobile police command center. The vehicle was parked some one hundred yards away from the scene, hoping to be a safe distance away from the barricaded suspect's rifle fire. They had to protect the hundreds of thousands of dollars in communication equipment inside of the vehicle.

The chief walked as fast as his legs would allow, as age and gout were now creeping up on him. An arthritic knee also reminded him of his age every once in a while. He had been a police officer for nearly thirty years, and had seen it all and done it all. And now, his body was paying for him having been there and done that. Chief Lopez had joined the force straight out of the Army. He saw action in Grenada as a U.S. Army Ranger, and had even done a brief tour as part of the Army's elite Delta Force unit. But after Panama, and a host of jungle tours conducting secret and legally questionable missions in South America, he decided that it was time to call it quits. He would still fight the bad guys, he thought, but it would be on a more manageable and less global scale. He would return home and combat the drug violence that was racking his hometown.

Chief Lopez often thought fondly of those days back on patrol. He was young, idealistic, and despite his tours of duty in the military, naive even. He actually believed back then, that he could make a difference. And then, he ran into the cartels from Juarez, Sinaloa, Michoacan, Nuevo Leon, and Tamaulipas. They came first, in waves that hit like Hurricane Sandy. And then came the boys from Zacatecas, Jalisco, and Guanajuato. They hit like Hurricane Katrina. And the worst of all, were the cartels composed of ex-rebels and the former Mexican Special Forces units that fought against them. They came from deep within Mexico, they were the boys from Chiapas. The ex-Chiapas rebels turned dope dealers were the worst. They were the ones who didn't give a fuck. They were from the jungle, and had been at war for years. They were battle hardened, raw, and ruthless. They were the beheaders of women and children. He had weathered all of those storms, and had even gotten caught up in them. He found himself with a choice between two evils, and he had to chose the lesser of them. He jumped in bed with the boys from Monterrey, Mexico in order to get rid of those fucking monsters from Chiapas, Tamaulipas, and Zacatecas. And once Monterrey got rid of them, they lost *their* power to the boys from Juarez, who he then started doing business with by default. The deal was simple, I'll look the other way, but you keep the shit to shoe level, and that was it. And that was where he found himself today. Just managing one crisis to the next, biding his time until retirement. His hope was that someone young, and new, someone idealistic, someone who still believed that he or she could make a difference, would step into his shoes. It was what the community desperately needed.

Chief Lopez climbed up the steps into the massive command center RV, and to his surprise, found several of the U.S. Marshal Services Fugitive Task Force inside. The blue windbreakers were clearly marked, and the command center was a bee hive of activity.

"What's going on in here?" Chief Lopez asked. His neutral expression changed to a frown. Federal agents on his turf, without his knowledge? That was a big no-no. Professional courtesy dictated that he be informed.

"Hi, I'm Agent Michaels, and I'm the lead agent here," one of the men said, introducing himself. "My apologies for the unannounced intrusion, and for using your command center."

"Why are you here?" the chief asked coldly.

"Well, your hostage taker is a fugitive that we've been tracking for months," Agent Michaels explained. One of the reasons he's holed up."

"So, you're the reason why he's taken hostages and not wanting to surrender?" the chief asked.

The agents inside of the command vehicle all stared at one another in silence.

"Now let me get this straight," the chief said, making his way through the gaggle of agents to a coffee pot on a counter, where he poured himself a steaming hot cup of java. "You all have tracked a dangerous fugitive to my city, and not had the professional courtesy to stop by the station and let us know, is that right, Agent Michaels?"

"Yes, sir," the agent said, smiling sheepishly. "Again, my apologies. The situation developed rather rapidly. Way before we could get a handle on things."

"I see," the chief said, allowing his words to trail off slowly. "You know we do have telephones way down here by the border, don't you?"

Again, the agents all peered at one another.

The chief drank from his cup of coffee, relishing the full bodied flavor of the dark liquid. Strong coffee, was the real life blood of the policeman, he would often say. It had gotten him through many a night of long boring patrols, and intense criminal investigations while serving as a detective. He penchant for drinking coffee twenty four hours a day, was well known. The other officers on the force even joked about him having a coffee IV machine hooked up to his veins, so that he could shoot the caffeine directly into his system.

The chief took a second deep gulp of the tasty brew, and that was when it hit him. His head swooned, and everything around him began to spin. He turned and gripped the table behind him, trying to balance himself.

"You okay, Chief?" Agent Michaels asked with a smile.

Chief Lopez shook his head. He didn't know whether he was experiencing a heart attack or a stroke. All he knew was that he was about to hit the deck.

The agents standing inside of the command center caught the chief, and gently laid him down on the floor. Another agent, laid an enormous crate down on the floor near the chief's head, and opened it up. The crate was marked weapons on the side. It was six feet long, and looked as thought it housed numerous assault rifles. Two agents grabbed the chief by his arms, while another grabbed his feet. They lifted him up, and placed him inside of the massive, black, metal, gun carry crate, and then locked the top on it. Once this was done, four agents, two on each side, lifted the massive crate, and carried it out of the command center, and placed it inside of the back of a black U.S. Marshal's van. The chief would sleep soundly for the duration of his trip to 'The Farm'.

Inside, Agent Michaels lifted his walkie-talkie, and spoke into it. "The canary's in the coal mine."

Inside of the house that the police had surrounded, one of the men lifted his walkie-talkie and replied. "Roger that. Canary's in the coal mine. Fourth of July commencing."

The men inside of the house, all made their way into the basement, and then through a secret smuggling tunnel that led to another house several blocks away. Once the men were all a safe distance from the house that they had just left, one of them turned, and dialed a number on his cell phone. The number that he dialed, caused another cell phone inside of the home to ring, and that ringing set off the charge that it was attached to, which in turn, detonated the massive fertilizer bomb that they had brought with them and placed inside of the garage. The house went up in a massive explosion that sent a fireball hundreds of feet into the air. Dirt, debris, and glass flew everywhere, and the entire area immediately surrounding the house was devoid of oxygen for several moments. The explosion had been built so the it channeled its force skyward, away from the other homes and the surrounding area, but it had also been built to suck the oxygen from the air. The officers in the immediate vicinity found the oxygen being sucked from their lungs as they were tossed backwards by the sheer force of the blast. It hadn't been designed to kill them, but it had been designed to scare the shit out of them, and send most of them to the hospital. The scene was one of utter chaos. And it was through this chaos, that the U.S, Marshal's vans pulled away with their cargo, and picked up their comrades several blocks away. Everything had gone perfect.

*****

Chief Lopez woke in a dark room that smelled of death. It smelled of rotting flesh, unburied corpses, shit, piss, sweat, and fear. It took his eyes some time to adjust to the darkness, but there was no doubt about the pungent smell that was stinging his olfactory senses, and causing his stomach's regurgitation system to act reflexively. He was drying heaving uncontrollably, trying to vomit.

"You will get used to the smell," the voice from the shadows told him.

"Who are you?" the chief asked.

Dante stepped from the shadows into a sliver of light that was coming through a hole in the dilapidated metal roof of the structure. The moonlight poured in, bathing the entire room in a eerie yellow light, that caused dancing shadows to appear against the four walls.

"You!" the chief said, after making out Dante's face in the dim lighting of the room. "What have you done?"

The chief knew about about the disappearance of some of his counterparts. The disappearance of one Sheriff was a big thing, the disappearance of two, along with several chiefs of police along the border was something big enough to grab the world's attention. He knew those men, they were colleagues, and friends even. And deep down inside, he

115

had a gut feeling that he was on someone's list as well. He had suspected the cartels involvement, and not the Reigns family. But now things made sense to him. They were searching for that little girl, and they were rounding up the people who they thought knew something, or who they felt was directly involved. Despite all of his years of investigatory experience on the force, he had never made the connection between those two events until this moment. He knew what his involvement in the kidnapping was, it was acting as a middle man. He had done nothing more than what he usually did, which was to put people together. He was not responsible for what those animals did.

"I can't help you," the chief said feebly.

"I don't need your help," Dante said softly. "I'm not asking for your help. I just want you to help yourself."

"And how can I do that?" the chief asked.

"You can help yourself by telling me where my daughter is," Dante told him.

"I was afraid you were going to say that," Chief Lopez told him. "I can't tell you, what I don't know."

"You'd be surprised at how much you can actually remember," Dante told him.

"I didn't say that I forgot," the chief told him. "I said that I didn't know."

"Know what?" Dante asked.

"Where you little girl is," the chief told him.

"You hooked some people up, and those people came into this country, and they kidnapped my daughter," Dante told him.

"And you think that if I wouldn't have put them together, they wouldn't have found another way?" Chief Lopez asked.

"Perhaps," Dante said, nodding slowly. "But you made it easy for them. Real easy. And just like they went to you in order to find a secure way in, I'm sure they asked you to help them find a secure way out. It's not easy for a bunch of grown ass Mexican men to get across the border with a little Black girl. No, they are going to need even more help crossing back over, than they needed coming into the U.S. My question is, where are they going to cross?"

"I don't know," the chief said softly. "And just for the record, if I would have known why they wanted into this country, I would have never helped them."

"I would have never helped them," Dante repeated. "But you did. And you know things. Lots of things. I have a lot of men searching this border. But so far, they've been unlucky. I want you to help their luck change."

"I can't tell you what I don't know."

"What you do know, is where they are going to cross," Dante told him.

"How am I supposed to know that!" the chief shouted.

"Because, you know this area like the back of your hand," Dante reminded him. "You know every rat hole, every tunnel, every passage way, every smuggling trail this side of the border. You know how they are going to get back to Mexico."

"And what makes you think that they are going back into Mexico?" the chief asked.

"Because they have no where else to run and hide," Dante answered.

"What makes you think that even if they were going to cross back over into Mexico, that they were going to do it in my territory?"

"It's the quickest route," Dante told him. "It's the route that will take them straight into Nuevo Leon, or Tamaulipas. They are heading for Matamoros. That's what my gut tells me."

"Then why are you here, and not there?" the chief asked.

"I am there," Dante told him. "I am everywhere. I have men spread out all along the border. But they don't know the trails, the smuggling houses, the tunnels. You do. And just like I can guess where they are going, you've been doing this long enough to know which route they are using, which safe houses they are staying in, which tunnels they are taking. You know."

Chief Lopez shook his head. "I don't know."

Dante waved for his man to come over. Out of the shadows one of Dante's men emerged. He was pushing a steel cart, with utensils spread out on it, like they were in a hospital operating room.

The chief peered down at the instruments of torture and shook his head. "That's not going to make me tell you what I don't know."

"Maybe not," Dante said with a smile. "But they will help you to make an educated guess."

Dante lifted a razor sharp scalpel from the metal tray.

"Don't!" the chief told him.

Dante ran the scalpel across the man's arm, and then down the center of it. The chief cried out in pain.

"I told you, I don't know!" the chief shouted, after his wails.

Dante sat the scalpel down, took his has and placed them on the chief's arm. He them began to pull the skin off of the chief's arms. The chief howled like an animal. In the shadows, one of Dante's men could be heard throwing up.

The chief struggled against his bonds, but to no avail. He was slightly suspended off of the ground, with his arms chained behind his back. His clothing was no where in sight, and he was completely naked. Dante peeled the skin off of his left arm as far as he could, and left it hanging near the bottom of the chief's forearm. He lifted his scalpel and walked to the chief's other arm.

"Where are they going to cross?"

"I don't know!" the chief shouted.

"What route would they use to smuggle her from San Antonio, to Matamoros?" Dante asked. "Where are the safe houses?"

"I don't know!" the chief shouted.

Dante went to work on the chief's other arm, cutting a circle around the top near the chief shoulder, and then creating a long incision down the side of the chief's arm. Again, the chief wailed in pain. Dante sat the scalpel down, and peeled the skin off of the chief's right arm, all the way down to his wrist. His hands kept slipping because of all the blood that was pouring from the chief arms.

"What route are they taking?" Dante shouted. "Tell me! What route are they taking to the border, you fat fuck!"

The chief was growing weak from the blood loss. He had blood pouring from both of his arms, and he was not a young man anymore.

Dante lifted the scalpel, and ran the blade down the center of the chief's chest, all the way down his belly, to his navel. He then ran the blade sideways, carving a nice crosscut into the chief's body. Dante place the scalpel on the tray, took his finger, and peeled the skin off of the chief's chest. More of his men could be heard vomiting in the shadows.

The chief's wails sounded inhuman. The pain, had become unbearable.

"Where is she?" Dante shouted. "Where is she?" He lifted the blade once again, and went to work on the chief's back. He peeled all of the skin from the man's back, and this time, there was no reaction from the chief.

"Where is she?" Dante shouted.

No response.

Dante punched to chief's skinless stomach.

"Where is she?" she shouted. "Where? Where the fuck is she?"

Dante clasped his head for a brief moment, and then began stabbing the chief in his legs with the scalpel. The noise had become too much for him to deal with. He could hear her. He could hear her laughter, he could see her smiles. He could hear her calling him Daddy, and he could see her tucking away her favorite teddy bear. His mind spun round and round. It was confusing. A jumbled mess. He hadn't eaten anything in the last twenty hours, and hadn't slept in the last forty eight. Alternately he covered his ears, and then stabbed, covered his ears, and then began stabbing again.

"Where is she?" he shouted continuously. Never mind that he had been shouting at a man, who had now been dead for the last five minutes. He kept stabbing and asking.

# Chapter Thirteen

Darius strolled into one of the many guest bedrooms that his cousin Brandon maintained at his enormous Maryland mansion. This particular estate, was really a family one, although Brandon's presence in Maryland pretty much gave him defacto control over it. It was the Reigns family's Montgomery Maryland estate, nestled along the banks of the historic Potomac River.

The estate itself was of the Georgian variety, which meant that it boasted a red brick facade, with enormous, white, two story columns at the entrance. The estate was nestled on fourteen prime acres, and boasted some twenty thousand square feet, some thirteen bedrooms, and numerous entertainment and gathering rooms. Inside of the aforementioned guest bedroom, Darius found the person he was looking for. Peaches was standing next to the bed, packing a suitcase.

"What are you doing?" Darius asked.

"What does it look like I'm doing?" Peaches replied. "I'm packing."

"I see that," Darius told her. "Why?"

Peaches stopped and turned toward him. "Why do people pack? Because they are leaving!"

"Leaving!" Darius exclaimed. "Why?"

"Because, it's time," Peaches told him. She caressed the side of Darius' face. "I'll never forget what you've done for me. Never. I can never repay you for all of the stuff. For saving me, for the bringing me here to safety, for allowing me to stay here and recover, for the clothes..."

"What the fuck are you talking about?" Darius asked, exploding. "Where is this coming from?"

Peaches exhaled, turned and began packing again.

"Why are you leaving?" Darius asked again.

"Because, I have to find my peeps," Peaches told him. "That's the main thing on my mind. But first, I have to go to this stupid ass commission meeting in Texas."

"A commission meeting?" Darius asked. "You're in no condition to travel. Why are you even thinking about going to some bullshit like that?"

"Because I have to!" Peaches told him. "I'm on the commission, have you forgot?"

"No, but you just got shot, have you forgot?" Darius asked. "Why would you risk re-opening your wounds, just to go to a damn commission meeting?"

"Because, I have to!" Peaches repeated. "They've called a mandatory full meeting of the commission. They are invoking the commissions charter because of your niece. They are calling it an attack against the entire commission. I have to be there."

Darius shook his head. "No you don't!"

"Yes, I do!"

"So they can see that you're wounded?" Darius asked. "So they can see the bruises? See you limping? That'll get them to asking questions. Questions that you don't want them to ask!"

"And by me *not* showing up, that'll get them to asking even more questions!" Peaches told him. "I'm new, remember? Why would I *not* show up? I was sponsored by the Reigns family, now what the hell would it look like, if I didn't show up to give my support to the people who are responsible for me gaining my seat?"

"It'll look like you're doing what you're supposed to be doing, which is consolidating your hold on Ohio," Darius explained.

"It'll look like I don't have shit under control, if I can't leave the state for single weekend," Peaches told him.

"And how are you going to explain your wounds?" Darius asked.

"By telling any nosy muthafucka who asked, that it's none of they got damned business!"

"And get them suspicious?"

"Look, D, I'm damned if I do, and damned if I don't!" Peaches said, snapping at him. "So, I might as well go and get this shit over with, and then get back to Ohio and find my girls!"

"Ohio?" Darius asked, crossing his arms. "The place where they damn near killed you?"

"Yep, that the place."

"Why? Why do you need to go back there?"

"Because that's my home!"

"What home?" Darius shouted. "You don't have a fucking home anymore, remember? The only thing left, is a burnt out, bullet riddled piece of rubble!"

"I'm not talking about that place," Peaches told him. "That was my *house*. Ohio is my *home*. And I'm going home. I have to find my brother, and I have to find my sisters. It's that simple."

Darius clasped her arm. Peaches stopped cold and stared at his hand on her forearm, until he removed it.

"Look, if you go back there, they will kill you!" Darius told her.

"That's the chance I'm going to have to take," Peaches told him.

"Why?" Darius asked, throwing his hands up in frustration. "Why are you being so fucking stupid? So fucking hard headed? They are going to kill you!"

"I have to go back!" Peaches shouted. "*This is not my life!* My life is in *Columbus*! My family is in *Columbus*! My businesses are in *Columbus*! I have to go back and rebuild!"

"Rebuild what?" Darius asked. "How can you rebuild if you're dead?"

Peaches shook her head. "I wish you would understand."

"Make me," Darius told her. "Please help me to understand. I'm trying hard, but I just can't seem to understand why you are determined to go back to a place where someone just sent hundreds of men to kill you. And they damn near succeeded. Are you in a hurry to die?"

"I'm not going to die," Peaches told him.

"I'm sure you thought that before they started coming over your walls with machine guns."

Peaches lowered her head and nodded. "Why can't you support me?"

"I *more* than support you," Darius said. He didn't use the word love, but both of them knew what he meant. "I don't want to see you get killed."

"If I can get in touch with Chi Chi, I can see what's going on,"

Peaches told him. "She has soldiers. I can stay with her. I'll be safe there."

"*If* she's still alive," Darius told her. "Peaches, you don't understand what happened that night. It wasn't just your house that was hit. Someone with a lot of money, and a lot of manpower, took your whole organization off the map. They tried to wipe you out, and they pretty much did."

"You have men in Columbus?" she asked, staring into his eyes.

Darius exhaled. "My cousin has men in Columbus. And he's under a lot of pressure right now. They can't stay. He has to pull them out and send them to Texas. Dante is pulling every available man the family has, and sending them to search for my niece. No one has men to spare. He's turned Texas into an armed encampment, with thousands of soldiers from all our families territories from across the country. He's pulled so many men from California and Florida, that rumor has it, we're going to lose both of those states. And now, he has Brandon pulling men from Philly and Maryland. We're even pulling men out of Hampton Roads in Virginia, which is leaving us vulnerable there, and we're pulling men out of places where nobody even knew we had men."

"How long can he keep them there?" Peaches asked.

"In Columbus?" Darius asked. He shook his head. "Not long. In fact, he's already started pulling men from the state."

"Damn," Peaches said, turning away. "I need enough to get me back into the state, and to keep me safe while I move around, and see who's still alive. If Chi Chi made it, then I'll be okay. If Fat Momma made it, or Zeus, then they'll have some men I can borrow."

"*If* they made it, and that's a big *if*, that doesn't men they'll have men to spare," Darius told her. "I'm sure they got hit pretty hard, and lost plenty of men. And what they have left, will be too busy protecting *them* while they try to put their *own* shit back together."

Peaches lifted her hands to her face and rubbed her tired eyes. She had been bed ridden for the last week and was not physically exhausted, but mentally exhausted. Her mind had been consumed with thoughts of her brother, and Trap, and V. Thoughts of her grandmother, and of rebuilding. She had thousands of kilos sitting in warehouses all across the city. Were they still there, she wondered? And then there was

Melvin, and Get Money, how did they fit into the equation? There were so many factors to consider. She needed soldiers, she needed her peeps. She needed to get back to the basics in order to rebuild, which meant she would need to hit the hood and get with people that she trusted. The problem is, she had tried to run from that life in order to find her independence. She felt as though she had outgrown her roots, outgrown the hood, outgrown the fools she had grown up with. And now she found herself needing them again. She found herself having to run back into the arms of Young and Holding, a group she had tried for years to run from.

"I need to get back with my peeps," Peaches told him. "If I can have enough time to get things together, I can get with my peeps, and I'll be all right."

"Your peeps?" Darius asked, lifting and eyebrow. He was suspicious of her terminology. "What does that mean?"

"It means just that," she told him. "I have to get with my peeps. I'm from the hood, Darius. It's who I am, it's where I'm from."

"Back to the hood?" Darius asked. It was part dismissive, and she caught his tone.

"Yeah, back to the hood!" she said. "Is that a problem for you?"

"That depends," he shot back.

"Depends on what?"

"Depends of what that means," he told her. "Back to the hood? Getting with your peeps? What does that mean? I mean, is that code for getting with your boys again?"

"Oh, okay!" Peaches said, throwing up her hands. "Here we go. Now it's all coming out. I was wondering when you were going to bring this up."

"What?" Darius asked, turning up his palms. "I'm supposed to be a fucking ostrich and bury my fucking head in the sand? Is that what you think?"

"What, Darius?" Peaches said, throwing her hands up. "What? Ask me? Go ahead and ask me?"

"Ask you what?"

"Ask me about him!"

"Do I need to?"

"You want to!"

"I know all that I need to know about him," Darius told her.

"Well, that's good then," Peaches said, growing uneasy. "Did you little spies tell you that he's been in Detroit? Did they tell you that?"

"You'd be surprised what they told me," he said coldly.

"What?"

"Forget about that!" Darius shouted. "M y question is, when were *you* going to tell me about him?"

"Tell you what?" Peaches asked, turning up her palms. "There was nothing to tell."

"If there was nothing to tell, then it should have been easy for you."

"Easy for me to do what?  To tell you nothing?"

"Why didn't you tell me he was out?" Darius asked.

"Because it didn't matter!"

"It didn't matter that the man who you were in love with, the man who you were practically married to, got out of prison after all of those years?" Darius asked. "That didn't matter?"

"No, it didn't!"

"Why didn't it matter?" Darius asked. "It didn't matter because of *me*, or because of *him*?"

"What?"

"It didn't matter because what we have didn't matter, or because what you two have no longer matters?" Darius asked, staring into her eyes. "Which one is it?"

Peaches shook her head and turned away.

"That's what I thought," Darius told her.

"What?" she snapped, turning back towards him. "You thought what? Say it! I dare your black ass to say it! Say it doesn't matter between us! Say it! I sweat that I'll fuck you up!"

Darius smiled, but Peaches was dead serious.

"So, the love of your life gets out of prison, comes to you, and what?" Darius asked. "You no longer have feelings for him? Is that what you're saying?"

"I didn't say that," Peaches said, shaking her head. "But I'm a grown ass woman. I decide who I want to be with, and what type of relationship I want to have, and *who* I want to have it with. I control *me*, not you, and not Chesarae!"

126

"Chesarae," Darius sneered. It was the first time he had heard her speak his name. He didn't like it.

"He's out, okay?" Peaches continued. "Nothing I can do about that. Me and Ches have a past together. But that don't have nothing to do with me and you."

"Apparently you thought it did, because you never mentioned him."

"Darius, did you think that I just popped out of my Momma's pussy the day before I met you?" Peaches asked. "I've had boyfriends! Who do you think I am?"

It was a question that she hated she had asked, as soon as she asked it. She didn't want Darius to contemplate her past, or question the woman he was with. One of the things she loved about him, is the way he loved her. He made her whole, and treated her like she was somebody. And now, he had heard about the damaged side of her, he had dug into her past, and she now wondered how much he now knew. And that made her uncomfortable. Would he still look at her like she was perfect? Or would he see something else when he looked at her?

"I know you've had boyfriends, but they weren't the hubby, and they aren't fresh out, and the code to your safe room, wasn't their birthday!"

He had her on that one, she thought. She had no justification for that. Yeah, Ches' birthday was the code she used for her safe room. Why? She had no idea. Ches had been in prison when she had that house built. And his birthday, and social security number, made up plenty of codes and passwords in her life. What did that tell her about herself? Had she really let go? She had issues, and she would have to work through those issues. She had always known that, and she had planned on working through her situation, but she never thought that she would have to face them so soon, and under those circumstances.

"You still love him?" Darius asked.

Peaches closed her eyes. "Darius..."

"It's a simple question."

"I will always have feelings for Chesarae, because of what we went through," she told him. "We were young, and dumb, and we came up from the hood, and we have so many memories. Living that life, you know, going from the projects and then living the glamorous life, and then having it all taken from you, and having to go through a trial, and sit in a courtroom, and go and visit the jail and the prison, and so many other things. I mean, unless you've been through it, you wouldn't understand. We've been through a lot together, and so yeah, I still have something deep down inside of me that cares about what happens to him."

"Do you know how many times I've heard that bullshit?" Darius asked. "I don't love him, but I care about what happens to him? That's a ghetto cop out! Some straight up bullshit! It's a simple question! Do you love him?"

Peaches turned and started packing again.

"I guess that answers my question," Darius told her.

"So now, does that mean you don't give a shit if I go or stay?" Peaches asked.

"I care about what happens to you," Darius told her, turning her words against her.

Peaches closed her eyes.

"You go to Texas, and the commission members see you're injured, they are going to have questions," Darius told her. "You go back to Ohio, they are going to try to finish the job. I'll see what I can do to keep some soldiers there for you. I can't guarantee how long they'll be able to stay, but I'll do the best that I can. As for your brother, and your girls, I'll try my best to find out what happened to them."

"Thank you," Peaches said, without turning to face him. She kept her gaze on the clothing that he had bought for her, that she was now packing to take with her.

"No problem," Darius told her. "That's what friends are for right? I care about what happens to you."

Darius turned and walked out. Peaches bit down on her bottom lip, and forced herself to keep her tears inside. She wasn't a soft bitch, and she was never going to allow herself to cry over another nigga. Never again, she had promised herself. Never. She would lock her feelings away, and concentrate on the task at hand. She had a trip to take, and then she had a state to get back to, and an organization to rebuild. She just hoped that she wouldn't have to do it alone. She prayed that she wouldn't be burying a brother, and two friends once she got back.

# Chapter Fourteen

Princess strolled into the family room of Damian's mansion, and found her guest waiting for her near the fireplace. She opened her arms wide, and rushed into his arms.

"Honey, Baby, Boo-Boo!" she shouted playfully, wrapping her arms around her fiancee.

Emil reciprocated. He pulled her close to his person, hugging her tight. "Hey, Baby! I missed you."

Princess kissed Emil on his lips. "I missed you too."

Emil's hands ran down her back to her butt. "Naw, Baby, I *really* missed you."

Princess laughed, and brought his hands back up to her back. "Yeah, I'll bet you did. You been behaving yourself."

"As best as I can," Emil shrugged.

"You better be!"

"Hey," Emil said, shrugging again. "I'm only human. You know, a man's got needs."

"Yeah, like needing to keep his penis attached to his body," Princess told him. "You fuck around on me, I'm a cut that mother fucker off."

Emil laughed. "You're going all Loren Bobbitt on me."

Princess clinched her teeth. "I'll cut that mother fucker off, and toss it in the San Antonio River."

Emil laughed. He kissed his fiancee once more. "Damn, I've missed you."

Princess rubbed his chest, running her hand across the lapel of his finely tailored Ascot Chang suit. "You missed me?"

"Like a fat kid misses cake."

Princess threw her head back in laughter.

"We'll see if we can spend a little time together tonight," she said, seductively.

"Oh, that would be nice," Emil told her. "So nice."

"So, what did you need to talk to me about?" Princess asked.

"Florida," Emil said flatly.

"What about it?"

"It's gone."

Princess recoiled. "What do you mean, *it's gone*?"

Emil shrugged. "I mean, if you don't go to Florida in the next few days, and take enough men with you, you're going to lose the state."

"Lose Florida?" Princess pulled away from him. "Aren't you being a little hyperbolic?"

Emil shook his head. "Not at all. The situation is serious."

"Serious?"

Emil nodded. "Dire."

Princess turned, and contemplated what she was being told. *Losing Florida?* That was so far out of her mind and so far fetched that she couldn't believe what he was saying. He had to be kidding. She turned back to him.

"You're joking right? Tell me this is a joke."

"I wish that it was," Emil said, exhaling. "But it's not. Things have changed. A lot of things have changed."

"Changed? How? In what way? How could this happen? You're right next door, and you were supposed to be keeping an eye on things for me!"

"Princess, I *was* keeping an eye on things!" Emil said forcefully. "I did the best that I could do, but I live in Atlanta, not Miami! I can't be there twenty four-seven, when I have a state of my own to run, and problems of my *own* to deal with. Florida spiraled out of control fast. The whole thing took everyone by surprise."

"What?" Princess asked, turning up her palms. "What's going on? What are we talking about here? Some underbosses going rogue? A few idiots in Miami kicking up some noise? What?"

"We're talking all of the above and a whole lot more," Emil told her. "You have new players on the scene in Miami, and they are making some big time moves. They are bringing in their own product, using their own connections, and they are gaining the loyalty of your people."

"*What?*"

Emil nodded. "I'm not done."

"There's more?"

Emil nodded. "Those are the Cubans. You also have a Dominican problem in Orlando. They've taken Orlando, and have been making moves in the north. The underbosses who are loyal to you, are *overwhelmed* trying to fight the Cubans in the south, and the Dominicans in the north, as well as the underbosses that have gone bad. The underbosses that *have* gone bad, have split into two factions, one in the north, and one in the south. So, you also have a north-south civil war going on in the state. It's bad."

"And all of this shit just happened over night?" Princess said, snapping at him. "Are you serious? Are you really fucking trying to tell me that?"

Emil shrugged. "I'm afraid so."

Princess shook her head. "I don't believe this shit. And of all the times that this could have happened, it happens now. I can't leave Texas, I can't. My brothers *need* me. Dante *needs* me. Lucky *needs* me. I'm not leaving until she's found. No way, uh-un. No fucking way!"

"Princess..."

"*I'm not leaving, Emil!*" she shouted. "Florida is just going to have to take care of itself for now. I'll deal with that shit later."

"*There's not going to be a later!*" Emil shouted. "Why can't you understand that? The longer you wait, the more men you lose, and the more your people go over to the other side. Go now, while you still have some soldiers left. You wait, you won't be able to raise an army, because they'll all be working for someone else. And then how much blood will it cost to retake the state? How much money will it cost in bribes for the politicians and the police to look the other way while you engage in a full blown war? The days where we could just engage in open warfare on the street, and blame it on gang violence, are over! Times have changed. The politicians like their streets nice and quiet, and they aren't going to put up with a bunch of bullshit. Every time someone is shot, people are screaming terrorist, or mass shooter, and the FBI has to look into it! Times have change, Baby. You have to *hold it*, because it'll be impossible to *re-take it.*"

Princess cuffed her hand around her forehead. "What am I supposed to do? Am I supposed to just walk away and abandon my brother, abandon my niece? They need me! They need me now more than ever!"

"Dante will understand," Emil told her. "He'll understand. You *cannot* lose Florida. The cost is too high. Not to mention, it's an entrance point, and these people are bringing in dope from their own supplier. They do that, and they are allowed to continue unchecked, they will gain in money, they will gain in power, and the next thing you know, they are rolling into Georgia, South Carolina, North Carolina, Alabama, Mississippi, Virginia, Tennessee, Louisiana, Arkansas, and *eventually* Texas. You have to take them out now."

Princess exhaled.

"He's right."

Emil and Princess both turned in the direction from which the voice came. Damian was standing in the doorway.

"Dante..."

"Will be fine," Damian told her. "You have to go back to Florida."

Princess shook her head and exhaled.

"Princess, *I'm* here, Anjounette's here, Dajon is here, Mina's here, we're all here helping in the search," Emil told her. "We will find her. You go and make sure that Florida is safe and secure, and that it stays in your hands."

"You don't have a choice," Damian told her.

"I don't have the soldiers right now!" Princess said forcefully.

"Pull them," Damian told her.

"Pull them from the search?" Princess snapped. "Are you *kidding?* Dante needs those men!"

"*I* need those men!" Damian shouted. "*You need those men!* I need them and you, in Florida!"

Damian walked into the room, and hugged his sister.

"Damian, I can't leave him like this," Princess said softly.

"He'll be okay," Damian said softly. "Pull as many men as you need to re-take the areas that have defected."

"That could be hundreds of men," Princess said.

Damian nodded. "He has thousands. He's pulled men from

Louisiana, California, Florida. He's pulling Brandon's men from
Pennsylvania, D.C., and Maryland.  Emil has sent men from Georgia,
Julian has sent men from Mississippi, Dajon has sent just about every
man he could spare from Louisiana."

"And if I pull hundreds out, that'll blow a hole in the net that we've
cast," Princess told him.

"Don't worry about that," Damian told her.  "We're going to revamp
this strategy anyway.  Going in heavy like this, is not working, and it's
scaring our political and police protection."

Damian, the net is *closing*!" Princess told him.

"We have to revise the strategy anyway!" Damian told her.  "Florida
isn't the only state we're losing!"

"*What?*" Princess asked.  She turned to Emil for answers.  He had
none.

"California is in danger as well," Damian told her.  "I'm not just
pulling out men to send to Florida, I'm pulling out men to save California
as well.  We have no choice but to revamp our strategy."

"Jesus!" Princess said, placing her hand against her forehead.

The Reigns' families most loyal, and trusted henchman made an
appearance at the living room door.

"Hey, there you guys are," Nicanor Costa Mendez said, walking into
the room.

Princess hugged Nicanor.  He had been with the family for years, and
had even married an older cousin.  She kissed him on the cheek.

"Hey, Nick."

"Hey, Princess."

"What's up, Nick?" Emil said, greeting him.

"Hey, Emil," Nicanor told him.  The two exchanged handshakes.

"What you got for me?" Damian asked.

"Good, or not good, depending on how you look at it," Nicanor told
them.

Damian exhaled.  "Give me the news."

"Found the housekeeper's car," Nicanor told them.

"Are you serious?" Damian asked.

"Where?" Princess asked.

"Get this, is was parked at fucking Dominguez State Jail," Nicanor told them.

"What?" Damian asked.

"Get the fuck outta here!" Princess shouted.

"Good news, Lucky was not in the car," Nicanor told them."

"How is that good news?" Emil asked.

"Because the housekeeper was," Nicanor told them. "They found her in the trunk. You guys eat yet?"

Damian, Princess, and Emil exchanged glances, and all of them shook their heads.

"Good," Nicanor told them. He pulled the manila envelope that he had tucked beneath his arm, and pulled from it, several large 8x10 pictures. Damian, Princess, and Emil gathered behind him and stared over his shoulder at the graphic pictures.

"She was found in the trunk," Nicanor continued. "They cut her throat from ear to ear."

Nicanor showed the the police photo of the dead housekeeper's bloody, slightly bloated, and decomposing body, with a deep slash all the way across her throat. Her body was already showing discoloration in the photos.

"Of course, rigor had already set in," Nicanor told them, flipping to the next gruesome photo. "Which means, they probably killed her the same day she took Lucky."

"Cold blooded," Emil said, shaking his head.

"No, it makes sense," Nicanor told him. "She's the housekeeper, her photo was going to be  everywhere within hours, so you get rid of her, you tie up that loose end right away."

"Dominguez Unit," Damian said. "Damn!"

"What's the matter?" Emil asked.

"Dominguez is right on the fucking outskirts of town!" Damian explained. "*It gives us nothing! It tells us nothing!* It doesn't give us any type of hint about which direction they were heading in!"

"The prison parking lot has to have cameras," Princess told them.

"It does, and I'm already on it," Nicanor told them. "I've got a guy on the inside, but he needs to gain access to the control room that monitors the cameras. Also, I'm sure the police are going to grab a copy, so I'm working that end as well. I'd love to get a copy and run it through editing and see what these assholes look like."

"The police are going to do it," Damian told him. "They'll do the same thing, clean up the images, and put it out on the news to see if the public has seen these guys. I imagine we'll get to see the images soon enough."

"I still want my own copy," Nicanor told him.

Damian nodded. "Of course."

"I'll give the news to Dante," Princess said, starting for the door.

"Nice try," Damian told her. "I want you on a plane to Dallas, tonight. Pull your men, and as many extras as you need. I want you back in Florida tomorrow."

"I have a meeting to attend as a member of The Commission, remember?" Princess said with a smile.

Damian nodded. "Get to Dallas, get your men ready, and start sending them in to the state. After the commission meeting, I want you in Florida."

"My own brother, kicking me out of Texas," Princess said with a smile.

Damian turned to Nicanor. "You tell Dante about the housekeeper. I want you to check him out, see what he looks like. I want you to personally assess his condition, and report back to me. I've hardly slept, so he probably hasn't slept at all. I need to make sure he's okay."

Nicanor nodded, turned, and headed out of the room.

"Emil, how's Georgia?" Damian asked.

Emil shrugged. "Same as always."

"I could use your help," Damian told him.

Again, Emil shrugged. "Sure."

"Came you spare the time away from Georgia?"

Emil nodded. He could spare a little time away. His state was relatively peaceful at the moment.

"Good, I want you to take over the Dallas search from Princess," Damian told him. "Keep the squeeze on the area, using the men you have left."

Emil nodded. "Sure, I'll do that."

"Good," Damian told him. Princess in Florida, Dante's at the border, Anjounette is in West Texas, and Dajon is in East Texas. We should be okay."

You forgot something," Emil said with a smile.

"What's that?" Damian asked.

"California?" Emil told him. "You said it's in trouble, and you're pulling men to send to California. "Who's going to go and lead the effort to re-take that state."

Damian smiled. "I'm sending the one person I got left."

"Who's that?" Princess asked.

Again, Damian smiled. "The best person I've got. Me."

Princess and Emil exchanged glances. Neither knew what that meant, or if Damian was kidding. He hadn't been in the field running operations in years. He wasn't an operator, he was a thinker, a strategy guy. And he sure in the hell wasn't ruthless enough to deal with a state like California.

"You're kidding right?" Princess asked.

Damian stared at his sister. He gave her a look that she hadn't seen since the two of them were at war with each other for the control of the family. She hadn't seen this Damian in years. He had been so fixated on pulling the family out of the drug world, and expanding the family's legitimate businesses, that she had forgotten that Damian could in fact be ruthless. He had fought her ass to a draw. Of course, it was two against one, she told herself, but still, Damian could be a ruthless mother fucker if he wanted to be.

Princess stared into her brother's face, trying to gauge him. Had the cartel's in Mexico fucked up severely with their latest move? Had they brought back something that none of them could deal with, or wanted to deal with? Was the old Damian back, she wondered? Heaven help those fools in California if he was. Dante enjoyed killing, and he had turned it into an art form. Damian, on the other hand, was cold, calculating, and efficient. He was a machine, like a fucking computer with a machine gun. As as we all know, computers have no soul, no conscious, no humanity, no feelings, no nothing. It was about X's and O's. Who needed to be moved from the chess board, in order to win the game. That was the Damian that they would now be facing. A chess master of life and death.

# Chapter Fifteen

Pedro Gomez was sitting on his couch watching television, when his door was kicked in. Instantly, he reached for his big, black, menacing semi-automatic shotgun that he kept near him at all times. But it was too late. Like all small ranch houses built in that era, the front door led directly into the living room, and the intruders were upon him in seconds. They too, had big, black, menacing looking shotguns, as well as a variety of other weapons. Some of which he had never seen the likes of before. A couple of which were pointed at his head.

"Don't even think about it!" one of the men told him.

Pedro slowly released his shotgun, and another one of the men snatched it away from him. He knew who they were, and who they worked for, and why they were in his home. All of the men were Black, well dressed, and well groomed. That meant they worked for the Reigns family.

"Well, well, well," Dante said, strolling through the front door, peering around the living room. "Nice remodel. Ninety-two inch T.V., brand new leather sofas, updated light fixtures. I see you've done well for yourself, Pedro."

Pedro shook his head and exhaled forcefully. "What is it, Dante? I don't know where she is, I don't know where they are, and I had nothing to do with that shit. I don't roll with operations like that, man. I don't kidnap no kids."

"Of course not," Dante said smiling. He rifled through Pedro's hair in a playful manner, like a father ruffling his kid's hair for doing good in sports. "You're much too honorable for something like that. No, Pedro, I want to talk to you for a different reason."

"What is that?" Pedro asked.

Dante continued to walked around Pedro's living room, taking in the decor, lifting little statues, vases, and figurines, and checking out the workmanship of Pedro's living room remodel.

"I want to talk to you about goats and worms," Dante told him. "Goats and worms."

"Goats and worms?" Pedro let out a half laugh, and peered at Dante's men. He was confused.

"Yeah, Pedro, goats and worms," Dante told him. "You see, you are without a doubt, the best smuggler to have ever walked this planet. The *absolute* best. Whether it was human cargo, or drugs, or whatever, you always got it through. And you've never lost a single cargo, or a single person in what? Twenty years? Thirty years?"

Pedro nodded. He was proud of his record.

"You know every single path, every single smuggling trail, as if you were a fucking goat," Dante told him. "Back when you were working with us, I swear, I used to tell Damian that you were half goat."

Pedro smiled and let out a half laugh.

"And you know every fucking tunnel from San Antonio, down to Matamoros, Brownsville, Lajitas, Laredo, the entire fucking border," Dante continued. "Hell, some of them you burrowed yourself. It was as if you were part worm. And so, that's why I needed to talk to you, because you know this shit like that back of your hand. If a single leaf was broken off on a trail, you could tell if the trail had been discovered. If some stupid ass border patrol agent had taken a leak next to one of your trails, you knew it because of the smell. The best! *The absolute fucking best!*"

Pedro turned his palms toward Dante. "But hey, man, I didn't have nothing to do with this one."

Dante turned back toward him and wagged his finger at him. "Ahhh, you may think that you weren't involved, and you may not have been *directly*. But we are all interconnected in the events around us, one way or another. Sometimes foreseen, and most of the time, in ways unforeseen. Every person that you brought over into the U.S., did you kill them afterward?"

"No!" Pedro said, shaking his head.

"Every person that you smuggled back into Mexico, did you kill them afterward?" Dante asked.

Again, Pedro shook his head. "No."

"Funny thing about people," Dante said with a smile. "We remember. And it's always the little things we remember. Ever bring the same people over more than once?"

"Of course," Pedro told him.

"Multiple times?" Dante asked.

"Yeah," Pedro nodded.

"Ever take the same people back multiple times?"

"Yeah."

"And so, they learned your paths, they learned your routes, they learned when and where to hide," Dante explained. "They learned which houses were safe, they learned when the border patrols would pass, and in what areas. They learned their schedules, how they operate, and so many other things. We teach one another every single day, and do so, without consciously knowing it. Like a child observing his or her parents. Daughter learning to cook, or clean, or that men in general ain't shit, because she's heard her mother say it a thousand times. Boys learning how to throw a ball, or mow a lawn, or wash a car, because they've seen their father do it hundreds of times. You were taking them back and forth, and they were learning from you, learning from the great master himself."

Pedro closed his eyes and swallowed hard.

"I want to know the location of every single trail, path, safe house, and tunnel from San Antonio, to the Mexican border," Dante told him. "I want you to draw it out for me, write it out for me, diagram it. I want to know every contact, connection, informant, and crooked cop on your payroll. I want all of the dummy accounts, the document forgers, the gas stations that you use, the truck stops, the restaurants, everything. I want it all."

"Dante, you're breaking my back," Pedro told him. "This is my *business*. I have sources to protect. I still have to make a living."

"Trust me, dying ain't a living," Dante told him.

"Dante..."

"You're going to give me what I need, or I'm going to consider us not friends anymore," Dante told him.

"This is my *business*," Pedro said again. "I promise you, I had *nothing* to do with this.  I would never have done anything like this, or helped out anyone who was.  I'll do what I can, but let me protect my sources, my contacts, my people.  I still have to use those places to make a living.  C'mon, man, be reasonable!"

"Come with me, Pedro," Dante told him.  "Let's go for a drive.  I want to show you my new farm."

Dante nodded toward the front door.  His men lifted Pedro off the sofa and carried him outside to a waiting car.  On the way to the car, Pedro was hit with an injection in his buttocks.  He was out like a light before the car made it down the street.

*****

Pedro woke to a smell that was indescribable.  He peered around the room, focusing his eyes on his environment.  He tried to wipe his eyes, but found that he was chained.  Chained to something.  A chair he realized.  He was seated in metal chair, and his arms were chained tightly to the armrest.  There were men in the room.  Dante was there, and so were others.  He knew that he had been kidnapped, and brought to this place for a reason.  Dante was about to torture him.

Nicanor walked up to Dante.  He had arrived at 'The Farm' while Dante was away, and he had taken a tour of the place.  He kept his comments to himself about what he saw, and wanted to keep his conversation and stay at the farm as brief as possible.  He was there to give Dante a message.

"Hey, Nick," Dante said greeting him.

Nicanor wrapped his arms around Dante, pulled him close, and embraced him tightly.  "How are you?"

"I'm good," Dante said, patting Nicanor on his back.

"You look like shit," Nicanor told him.  "When's the last time you ate?"

"I ate this morning," Dante told him.

"When's the last time you slept?" Nicanor asked.

140

Dante shrugged. He couldn't remember. He fell asleep in the car and on the plane in between trips, but that was about it. A full night's sleep was a distant memory. He couldn't sleep, he had to keep going, he had to keep moving, he felt as if time was against him.

"You need to sleep," Nicanor told him. "You hear me? You're no good to her if you can't think straight. A brain that's fatigued, is a brain that makes mistakes, and a brain that makes mistakes, is a brain that misses things, you understand?"

Dante nodded.

"Get some sleep, and eat something."

"My sister tell you to tell me that?" Dante asked with a smile.

"She did," Nicanor said, returning his smile. "And your brother did too. And they're right. You don't want to get caught slipping, you don't want to make careless mistakes that turn out to be big mistakes, and you don't want to miss something important. Sleeping is strategic at this point."

Dante nodded. He knew that Nicanor was right. "How's the search going?"

"We found the car," Nicanor told him. "Lucky was not in it, the housekeeper's body was found in the trunk. They cut her throat from ear to ear."

"Lucky bitch," Dante told him. "That was a lot better than what she was going to get if I found her first."

Nicanor nodded. "They found the car, get this, at Dominguez State Jail."

"Get the fuck outta here!" Dante shouted.

Again, Nicanor nodded. "We have the photos from the crime scene unit, and the autopsy. We're trying to get the camera footage from the jail's parking lot. I'm working on it."

"Can we get the car?" Dante asked.

"No time soon," Nicanor told him. "It's part of the crime scene, and since it's a part of the kidnapping, the FBI has taken custody of it."

Dante nodded. "I wish our people could dust it for prints."

"I'll see about getting the FBI's results from the forensics."

"Thanks," Dante said, patting Nicanor on his shoulder. He knew that Nicanor knew his shit, and that he would leave no stone unturned. He didn't need to make any suggestions, or give any instructions, as Nicanor would have already thought of it, or done it. He turned his attention to Pedro.

Nicanor followed just behind Dante, as he approached the chained up smuggler.

"You're awake now, Sleepy Head," Dante said, again rubbing Pedro's head like a proud father does his child. "Good. Because I have some questions to ask you."

"Dante, I already told you, I didn't have anything to do with this," Pedro told him. "I don't know who they are, where they are, where they are going, or even how they got in. I had nothing to do with it."

"I know you didn't, Pedro," Dante told him. "I already told you that. What I want, are your paths, your safe houses, your document forgers, your crooked cops and border patrol officers, I want your gas stations, your restaurants, your tunnels, your entire infrastructure."

One of Dante's men, walked up with a massive jug from a water cooler, and he had a couple of thick bath towels hanging over his shoulder. Two others walked to where Pedro was seated, and stood on each side of his chair.

"Dante, don't do this," Pedro pleaded. "Let me hit the streets. Let me help you find them."

Dante nodded. One of his men wrapped a thick towel around Pedro's face, while the other two tilted his chair back and held it. Dante took the water jug, and poured it over the towel that was wrapped around Pedro's face, water boarding him and causing him to feel like he was drowning. Pedro gasped for air.

Dante nodded, and his men brought Pedro's chair back to its normal position, and pulled the towel from around his face. Pedro's eyes were bulging out of their sockets, and he was gasping for sweet air. His face was bloodshot red, and he was coughing, wheezing, and choking, while spitting out water.

"I need your routes," Dante told him. "I need your contacts, your safe houses, you infrastructure."

"*Dante, please!*"

Dante nodded again, and again, his men wrapped the wet towel around Pedro's face and tilted his chair back. Dante poured more water over Pedro's face, causing him to choke, and cough, and struggle to breath. The water ran through the towel, into his nose and mouth, causing a burning sensation in his nostrils and throat. The simulated drowning experience was horrifying. It caused his stimuli in his brain to supercharge, and caused him to have a panic attack. Dante nodded, and his men brought Pedro back up again.

The towel was removed from Pedro's face, and he coughed up large amounts of water. He didn't look well at all, and not just because of the fact that he was being water boarded.

"Give me your infrastructure," Dante said softly.

Pedro was too busy coughing and hacking to answer. Snot was pouring from his irritated nose, and tears were flowing from his bloodshot eyes.

"We don't have to keep this up," Dante told him. "Give me what I want, and this can all be over with."

"Dante, please..." Pedro said, between bouts of coughing. He wasn't feeling well, and it wasn't just from the simulated drowning.

"Ready to talk?" Dante asked.

"Dante, let me help you," Pedro told him. "I can help you. I can hit all of the places along the way, and I can see if they've been through. I can, you know I can. I can track them."

"Wrong answer." Dante nodded, and his men sprang into action.

Pedro was tilted back once again, and the wet towel was wrapped around his face. He screamed like never before. Dante poured the water over the towel that was covering his face, and Pedro began choking and kicking once again. And then it stopped. Watery red drops began spilling into the catch basin beneath Pedro's head. Dante stopped, and nodded to his men, who brought Pedro back up. The towel wrapped around his face quickly began to turn red. The men removed it. Blood poured from Pedro's nose, mouth, and ears, and his eyes were rolled to the back of his head.

"Fuck!" Dante screamed. He kicked the metal catch basin on the floor, sending it across the room.

"He burst a blood vessel in his brain," Nicanor told them calmly. *Fucking amateurs*, he thought.

"Motherfucker!" Dante shouted. "What the fuck is wrong with you people? *Just tell me what the fuck I need to know!*"

Dante turned to Nicanor. "They won't fucking talk! They'd rather *die*, than talk! Fuck!"

Dante pulled out his pistol, and pumped two bullets into Pedro's chest, and then headed for the door. He shouted back to his men while pointing his pistol toward Pedro's body. "Get rid of that piece of shit!"

# Chapter Sixteen

Nicanor found Damian sitting behind the desk in his home office. He was going over paperwork, invoices, and spreadsheets. Nicanor knocked on the door to the office, despite the door being open.

Damian looked up and saw Nicanor. "Come in."

Nicanor stepped into the office, and waved his hand toward one of the chairs in front of the desk. "Got a minute?"

"Sure," Damian told him. "I wanted to get with you as soon as you got back, so I'm glad that you stopped by. What's on your mind?"

Nicanor seated himself, and straightened his tie. He took in a deep breath. Damian sensed his friend's hesitation.

"What's the matter?" Damian asked. "How's Dante."

"That's what I want to talk to you about," Nicanor told him.

"What?"

"I gave Dante the news about the car, and about the housekeeper," Nicanor told him.

"He didn't take it well?" Damian asked.

"He didn't give a shit," Nicanor told him.

"Really?" Damian asked, lifting an eyebrow. "Hmmm."

"He had other business to attend to," Nicanor told him.

"I imagine he's busy."

"Yeah, he's been pretty busy."

"How's he look?" Damian asked. "Has he been eating, or getting any sleep?"

"No," Nicanor answered. "But that's not the problem. Well, it is the problem, but it's the least of them."

"So, what *is* the problem?" Damian asked, still rifling through his paperwork.

"He's either losing it, or he's already lost it," Nicanor said bluntly.

Damian let out a half laugh.

"I'm not laughing," Nicanor told him.

"C'mon, Nick. You know Dante, and you know how he feels about Lucky. She's all he has. Cut him a little slack."

Nicanor shook his head. "No, I can't. Not on this one. This one isn't just about *cutting him a little slack*. This one is about his mental state."

Damian peered up at his guest. "*His mental state?*"

Nicanor shrugged. "He needs help."

"Nick, think about this," Damian told him. "What if it were your daughter who had been kidnapped? How would you react? Something like that, is enough to drive us all a little mad."

"*A little*, perhaps, but what I saw?" Nicanor shook his head. "Dante was gone when I arrived. I took a tour of this place, this *farm*, as they call it. It's not a farm, it's a fucking house of horrors. The men are calling it, *Little Guantanamo*, and Damian, it's ten times worse than the *real* Guantanamo."

Damian lowered his paperwork, leaned back in his chair and stared at Nicanor. "What are you saying?"

"Damian, I stood in a room, while he water boarded a guy to death," Nicanor told him. "He was drowning the guy, I mean, literally drowning the guy. Fortunately for the poor son-of-a-bitch, he popped a blood vessel in his brain and died before Dante could drown him."

"Nick..."

"Damian, he has heads on fucking pikes *lining a wall!*" Nicanor shouted. "He had men nailed to giant crosses, lining the inside walls of a giant barn! He's impaled dozens of men and he still has their corpses hanging up and rotting. The stench of that place is indescribable. The entire area smells like death!"

"C'mon, Nick," Damian said, shifting his head to one side. "Aren't you exaggerating a little bit?"

"*Exaggerating?* Damian, *pull your fucking head out of your ass and get down there!* Go and see it for yourself! He's has *crucified* people! I mean literally nailed men with rail road spikes to crosses! He has men living in dog cages, he has torture rooms, he's locking people into steel pits and leaving them out in the sun for days at a time with no water!

Damian, I fought in every got damned war in Central America in the Eighties. I helped the Contras fight the Sandinistas, I helped the Salvadoran government fight the FMLN rebels, I helped the Battalion 316 destroy the leftist rebels in Honduras. I fought with the CIA in Colombia, I fought *with* the Cubans in Angola, and I fought *against* the Cubans in Namibia. I fought against the Russians all over Africa, and I'm telling you, I have never seen any of them do the shit that your brother is doing at his *'farm'* near the border. And I saw the Honduran military, as well as the Contras and Sandinistas do some pretty fucked up shit! It needs to stop! Dante needs to be stopped. You need to shut that place down, you need to take over the search, and you need to have him placed somewhere where he can rest and put himself back together. That's *if*, he can be put back together."

"Nick..."

"Damian, how long have you known me?"

"A long time."

"Then you know I'm not one to engage in histrionics," Nicanor told him. "This is serious. You're going to lose your brother. You have to save him. You have to talk to him, you have to pull him back, and you have to take charge of this thing. He needs rest. And I'm not just talking about some sleep. He needs to go away, he needs to talk to someone, he needs to gain perspective. I've seen many men who have come back from a war zone, and they can't put things back together. And slowly, the things that they did in the war began to sink in, and it eats them up from the inside."

"This is Dante we're talking about," Damian told him. "He wasn't exactly an angel *before* Lucky was kidnapped."

"What he's doing now, he'll never be the same even once she's home. The things he's doing to get her home, leaves me to question what type of mind he will have once he finds her. What happens then? You can't turn off horror like a light switch. You can't go from this far, this deep into *that* world, and then just go back to normal. You have to help him. See if there is anything behind his eyes left to salvage."

Damian stared at Nicanor for several moments, before finally lifting his telephone and calling up his personal secretary. "Call the airport, and get the jet ready. We're taking a trip."

*****

Damian was seated in his backyard, staring past the pool into his lush flower garden. He had much on his mind, and even more to think about. What exactly had Nicanor told him earlier about his brother, he wondered? What *exactly* was he saying? That Dante needed to be committed? Was that what he had been trying to say? Damian knew that Nicanor was a man of very few words, and was not given to hyperbole. If what he had said was true, then things were much worse than he thought. Did he mean it *literally* when he said that Dante had been crucifying people? Heads on a pike? It was too much for anyone, even for Dante. He knew his brother, and he knew what his brother was capable of doing. But if what Nicanor was saying was true, then Dante was in trouble. Had his brother in fact lost his mental faculties?

He would head down to this ranch, this so-called *'Little Guantanamo'*, and see what was going on for himself. And while he was there, he would check on his brother, see if he could get him to rest a little bit, perhaps eat a really big meal. They could all use some rest, and they could all use something to eat, that much was certain. And then, once this was all over with, they all needed a vacation. A long one, somewhere out of the country, where they could unwind Afterward, it would be back to work.

The search for Lucky couldn't have come at a worse time. The family's financial situation was precarious to say the least. Bio One was barely able to support itself. Energia Oil was supporting itself, but had drastically over invested in new fields throughout Africa and The Gulf. The cocaine had just recently began flowing into the country again, and even that was not coming in anywhere near the amounts that he needed it to be. And the operation to find Lucky, was bleeding the family's savings. And if Bio One was hit with a massive fine on top of the massive settlement that they were facing, the family's finances would be in dire condition. He needed this operation to be over with, and he needed to focus on getting the drugs flowing again at acceptable levels. And then

148

he needed to handle the Florida and California situations.

Losing California was not an option. California brought in way too much money to allow it to fall into another person's hands, and the amount of manpower that they could pull from California pretty much matched the manpower that they could pull from Texas. And allowing another person to have that kind of money and manpower just wasn't going to happen. They were going to keep California, and they were going to do it at all cost. That was going to cost more money of course. Money in bribes, money for manpower, money for police protection, money, money, money. And then add the cost of keeping Florida. The numbers to do both of those things were staggering.

Florida would be more expensive than California, despite the fact that they had a more extensive infrastructure already in state. Florida was in the process of a complete meltdown, with a full blown revolt, combined with a full blown war involving multiple players, each with their own agendas. The Cubans and Colombians were once again gaining power in Miami, the Dominicans were gaining power in Orlando and Jacksonville, and Princess's underbosses were going there own way, and fighting each other in their own wars for control of the state. And the crazy part about that, was while they fought amongst themselves, the Cubans, Dominicans, and Colombians were all getting stronger. Princess would need help. She was going to need Dante, and perhaps even Nicanor and some others to go in and help her. It was a one big ass mess. And he was going to have to foot the bill to clean all of that shit up. It was all too much for him, and everything felt as if it were spiraling out of control.

"Hey, Cuzzo," a voice called out from behind. Damian felt a gentle hand rub him across the top of his back. He peered up to find his cousin DaMina smiling at him.

"Hey, Mina," Damian said, returning her smile.

"What are you doing back here all alone?" Mina asked.

"Just thinking," Damian told her.

Mina took the seat next to him. She was the younger cousin, but she had grown up with Princess, Damian, Dante, Dajon, and Damian, and she was more like a sister to them, than a cousin. She knew what each of them were thinking, and she could tell that something was bothering her older cousin.

"A penny for your thoughts," Mina said with a smile.

"How about a billion?" Damian asked.

Mina nodded. If he was worried about billions, she knew exactly where his thoughts were. "Bio One?"

Damian nodded. "Among other things."

"Like ?"

"Money, finding Lucky, Dante's sanity, Princess losing Florida, and the family losing California," he told her. "Those things, on top of the family bleeding money because of the search, Energia Oil is barely maintaining, Bio One is about to take a major hit, and the water is flowing again, but not enough."

Mina nodded. "Princess is not going to lose Florida, she's strong. She going to do whatever it takes to make sure that doesn't happen. As for Lucky, we're going to find her, don't worry about that. As for Dante, he's always been insane, so that's nothing new. Bio One will work itself out, and so will the oil company. Oil prices fluctuate, so don't worry. Some tanker will crash somewhere, or some refinery will catch fire, or Israel will bomb someone, or something will happen in the Middle East to drive the prices back up. You can *always* count on crazy. Now, as for you, don't you sit here and drive *yourself* crazy worrying about things that you can't control. Everything takes time, Damian, you know that. Things will work themselves out. You just have to be patient, plan, stick to your plan, and things will happen."

Damian nodded. "Impressive."

Mina laughed.

"But you forgot something," Damian told her.

"What's that?"

"California," Damian told her. "Try to make me feel good about that."

"I will personally go to California, and I will *personally* raise enough men, to squash any foolishness in the state," Mina said with a smile. "How's that?"

Damian caressed the side of DaMina's face. "You look more and more like your mother everyday. And you're becoming more and more like her."

Again, Mina laughed. "Is that a good thing or a bad one? Are you saying I'm getting old?"

"We're all getting old," Damian said, with a laugh. "And, it's a good thing. You have her strength."

"Hey, I'm a Reigns woman," Mina said, patting Damian's leg. "You know we bring 'em up strong in this family. In fact, we need a few more Reigns women. When are you going to give me another cousin-in-law?"

Damian laughed. "I don't know about that. The last ones haven't exactly worked out too well."

"Well, then, maybe you should think about making an honest woman out of that Stacia Hess," Damina told him.

"Stacia Rogers, remember?"

"She's divorced now," Damina reminded him. "It's Hess again. And all she needs to do is change her name to what it always should have been."

"Which is?" Damian asked, although he already knew the answer.

"To the same last name as all of her children, and the father of her children, Mr. Reigns," Mina said, rising from her chair. "C'mon in here and eat. I'm going to fix you something. And I don't want to hear anything about you not being hungry. *And stop worrying!*"

Damina patted Damian's shoulder as she walked past and headed into the house. Damian turned his attention back to the flowers in his garden. Mina was definitely on to something. He needed to stop worrying, and baring that, he needed someone to share his worries with, someone to talk to, someone to confide in. Finding a wife would be a dream, but his luck with woman was horrible. Either they knew exactly who he was, and had dollar signs in their eyes, or once they found out who he was, they *got* dollar signs in their eyes. Finding a good woman, who just wanted him for him, would definitely be a dream.

# Chapter Seventeen

Dante's massive caravan of black Infiniti QX 56 SUVs motored down the highway at illegal speeds. The caravan consisted of more than twenty of the massive seven passenger vehicles, and every seat, in every vehicle, was occupied. And each of the occupants inside of the vehicles, was armed to the teeth.

The caravan rolled down Texas Interstate 10 toward Houston to meet up with someone whom Dante never expected to meet with in a million years. They were meeting Special Agent in Charge of the Houston, Texas FBI field office, Grace Moore. Her phone call to Dante had come out of the blue, but she told him that she had something for him, something that would be of use in his search. He dropped everything, gathered some men, and raced to meet her.

The meeting was to take place at a rest stop half way between Houston and San Antonio. The spot had been chosen for convenience more than anything else. Dante's motorcade pulled in to the stop, and dozens upon dozens of Black men in expensive suits leaped out of the vehicles and spread out, forming a massive security perimeter. The sight of so many menacing looking Black men scared the devil out of all of the travelers that had stopped to use the restroom and stretch their legs. The rest stop emptied in record time.

A lone E Class Mercedes Benz motored into the rest stop, parked on the side of the line of Infiniti SUVs and Grace Moore climbed out and peered around. Dante was standing in the middle of a crowd of suits. She spied him instantly.

Dante made his way in between two of the behemoth SUVs and met Grace at the front of her car. The two stood face to face, gauging one another in awkward silence for a few moments, with each one not knowing what to say. She wanted to express her condolences about the kidnapping of his daughter, but couldn't find the right words. He on the other hand still hated her and wanted her dead, and was anxious to get down to business. Grace spoke first.

"Thank you for meeting me," she told him.

"You said that you had something that would help me," Dante replied.

Grace nodded. "How is the search?"

Dante shrugged. "It's going."

"Any leads?" Grace asked.

"None in particular."

"Where are you at with this thing?"

"You and I both know that I'm not much for small talk," Dante told her. "Especially since I'm a little busy of late, and *especially* with you. I'd just as soon put a bullet in your skull and dump your body inside of one of those filthy bathroom stalls than talk to you."

"And I feel as though I should have been hiding in that field across the highway with a sniper rifle, so that I could have put a bullet in your head as soon as you climbed out of your vehicle," Grace shot back.

Dante smiled.

"I don't like you, and you don't like me, Dante," Grace continued. "We never have, and never will. I know who you are, and I know what you've done. But this thing, it's bigger than the both of us. It's about a little girl, and *innocent* little girl, who shouldn't have to be made to pay for the sins of her father. *That's* why I'm here. Not for you, not for Damian, but for a beautiful little girl who's already been through so much in life. She's already lost her mother, and now, her life has been put in the hands of complete strangers. Strangers who I'm sure, are just as filthy and vile as her father. So, let's not get it twisted."

"What do you have?" Dante asked.

Grace stepped to the driver's side of her vehicle and reached inside. She pulled out a manila envelope, reached inside of the envelope, and pulled out some documents. She laid the documents on top of the hood of her car, and Dante stepped up next to her to review the documents with her.

"What is this?" Dante asked.

"Highly classified," Grace told him. "You never, ever, *ever* saw this, do you hear me?"

Dante nodded. "Okay, what is it?"

"NSA communications intercepts," Grace told him.

"Really?" Dante asked, lifting any eyebrow. "Of what?"

"Nuni Nunez," Grace told him.

The hairs were raised on the back on Dante's neck,. The National Security Agency was intercepting communications from drug lords now. The United States government was turning its high powered spy network on drug dealers. It almost caused him to reel slightly. He knew that the government spied on people, and that the FBI and DEA could go to a court and get a warrant to intercept communications. He had built up the Reigns families communication network to defeat their capabilities. But the capabilities of the NSA was way beyond his ability to counter. He could hire the best computer and communications geeks, former Russian spies, and all of the slickest computer hackers that Europe and the United States had to offer, it would still take the NSA a matter of seconds to burst through his encryption network and figure out his family's codes. The idea that the NSA was now in the game, was scary. He would have to go back and start using messengers, and not talking on the phone.

"Why is the NSA targeting Nuni Nunez?" Dante asked.

"They're not," Grace told him. "He was caught in the net of a wider communications operation. They were monitoring an Al Qaeda operation to get terrorist into this country by disguising them as Mexican nationals, and using the smuggling trails."

"Are you fucking kidding me?" Dante asked.

"I wish that I was," Grace told him. "Homeland Security sent this out to the Texas, New Mexico, Arizona, and California field offices. I requested more information from the Joint Terrorist Operations Center, and got tons of raw data. Included in that raw data, was this."

"Nuni is helping terrorist get into the country?" Dante asked.

"*No!*" Grace said, dismissing his question out right. She eyed Dante like he was stupid. "He was talking to a contact from Chiapas, Mexico, who *does* have Middle Eastern connections. Nuni was trying to pull men from Southern Mexico to help Galindo in his little war. Where better to get hardened soldiers than from Chiapas? And it just so happens that the former Chiapas rebel factions are also looking for a little Middle Eastern money to fund *their* operations."

Dante nodded. He now understood. "And in exchange for this money, they would help terrorist get into the United States. Nuni got caught up because he was talking to the wrong muthafuckas."

Grace nodded. "*Exactly.*"

"So, the NSA is not spying on drug dealers?" Dante asked, allowing a sigh of relief to creep into his voice.

Grace smiled. "No, you can relax. The United States government doesn't give a fuck about drugs anymore. The only way to get funding from Congress, or any attention from The Administration, is to pretend like you're helping to fight terrorist, or stopping illegal immigrants from crossing the border."

It was Dante turn to smile. "You scared the shit out of me."

Grace turned his attention back to the top secret documents she had spread out on her vehicle. "Nuni's communications started getting monitored, just in case the Chiapas boys were going to use him as *their* conduit into the country. And while the NSA was listening in, they picked up some pretty interesting stuff."

Dante's smiled widened even more. "Like what?"

"Like his strategy for dealing with the other cartels," Grace said, allowing her own smile to creep across her face. She knew Nuni and Galindo's playbook.

For the first time ever, Dante wanted to grab Grace and hug her. He knew what she was saying, and what she had. She had the battle plan for Galindo's cartel, and she was offering it to him on a silver platter. With that information, he would be able to destroy Galindo, or at the very least, counter his moves in Northern Mexico. It was completely life changing. With the information that she had, he could alter the outcome of the war between the cartels. But he would have to play it right. He didn't want to tip the scales and cause the war to prolong itself, no, he needed to use the information to destroy Galindo's cartel and end the war in favor of the other cartels. But what would that mean? Would he be getting rid of one monster, and creating an even worse monster? Galindo's cartel had been about business before the latest bullshit, and they had done good business with them for years. But the kidnapping of Lucky had destroyed that, and destroyed any possibility of them ever working together again. So, the answer was pretty much a given. He would have to destroy Galindo's organization, and just deal with whatever came next. But even then, he had already established a relationship with the powerful, no nonsense cartels on the Yucatan Peninsula. So really, whatever came after Galindo and Nuni, matter little.

"I need that," Dante told her.

"I know you do," Grace told him.

"Any mention of Lucky?"

Grace shook her head. "Yes and no. No direct mention. They're talking in code, but we're pretty sure what they were talking about. Dante, there's no doubt in my mind, that Nuni Nunez is responsible for the kidnapping of your daughter."

Dante knew it, but hearing it stated with so much authority and factual evidence to back it up was something else entirely.

"I knew that," Dante told her. "I've always known it."

"Why?"

"Because they wanted us to wait," Dante told her. It felt weird talking to Grace about these things. He never, in a million years, could have foreseen himself telling the Special Agent in Charge of the FBI's Houston, Texas field office that he was a part of a vast drug organization with ties to a large and powerful Mexican drug cartel. Everything in his life seemed to have crossed into the surreal.

"To wait?"

Dante nodded. "Their war, the border closing, all of it. They wanted us to wait until the border re-opened, and they were able to wrap up their wars against the other Mexican cartels."

"And so they kidnapped Lucky in order to get you to wait?" Grace asked. She couldn't believe what she was hearing. Incredibly, it just made her even angrier. Bringing an innocent child into this because of their greed? She shook her head. "Fucking *animals!*"

"Was there any information in there about Lucky's whereabouts?" Dante asked.

Grace shook her head. "Dante, if there was, I would be meeting you here to place her into your arms."

Her statement hit Dante in a way he hadn't expected. He hated Grace

Moore. She was an FBI cunt, and he wanted to put a bullet in her skull. She had tried to bust them, to break up his family, to get him the death penalty. And now? Now, she was doing everything in her power, even breaking the law, and risking going to prison, in order to help him get his daughter back. He knew who she was, and what she had done since all those years ago when she was posing as Jonel McNeal, trying to bust them. She was strong. She was the mother to his nephew, Little Damian. She, like so many other women close to his family, had brought about many conflicting feelings inside of him. And that just made her even more of a Reigns woman. They were strong, head strong, and they all made you want to kill them. She was truly a Reigns on the inside, even if Damian hadn't actually married her.

"What about the kidnappers?" Dante asked, swallowing hard. "What do you have on them?"

Grace shook her head. "These are communications intercepts from the National Security Agency. Remember, Galindo and Nuni weren't the original targets, and they only got caught up because of their affiliation with a third party. The NSA wasn't listening for information about Lucky."

"And the FBI doesn't have anything?" Dante asked. "I mean, kidnapping is within the FBI's jurisdiction. They've been on the case from day one, what do they have?"

"They have a bunch of dead bodies all over Texas," Grace told him. "No one's stupid, Dante. They know what's going on, they know where the bodies are coming from, but because it was a little girl who was kidnapped, everyone is looking the other way. But the investigators can't find anything, if your people are getting there first, and then killing everyone before the FBI has a chance to question them."

Dante nodded. She had a point. "They have absolutely nothing?"

Grace shrugged. "We're looking. Just like you are. What do *you* have?"

"I know they're trying to get across the border," Dante told her.

"How do you know that?" Grace asked. "Where did you get that from?"

"Where else are they going?" Dante asked. "They can't stay in Texas. The longer they're here, the greater the chance they'll be discovered. No, they're making an all out run for the border."

"How?" Grace asked, turning up her palms. "Every road is blocked. Every truck stop, every gas station, every restaurant. The Amber Alerts have the entire state on the lookout."

"Underground," Dante told her. "Human smuggling routes, trails, safe houses, tunnels. That's how. That's how they are going to get her out, and that's what I need from you."

Grace raked her hand through her hair, and tucked it behind her ear. She pursed her lips for a few second, before walking back to the driver's side of her car and climbing inside. She opened her glove compartment, and pulled out a map, and then walked back to the hood of her car, where she spread the map out.

"Here is San Antonio," she said pointing. "Where do you think they are going?"

Dante pointed. "Matamoros. Straight down through Brownsville. That's the quickest, safest way."

"I can get the state police to set up check points, along this entire route," Grace said, pointing at the map.

"I wish this map showed all of the damn truck stops and gas stations," Dante told her. "I can get my people to set up at all of the truck stops and gas stations."

Grace stared at him. He could see the uneasiness in her eyes.

"If this is the smuggler's route, then you're going to have to find the tunnels and the safe houses," she told him. "You're going to have to watch a pretty broad swath of territory along this route, and you're going to have to kick in some doors to find out where the safe houses are."

Dante nodded. He was going to have to get heavy handed along that route. Plenty of innocent people were about to get put through hell, just to find the needles in this big ass haystack. But he was prepared to do whatever it took to get his daughter back.

"I will do whatever I need to do," Dante told her. "It would make things a lot easier if you could get me on the right path. I need the location of the safe houses, the tunnels, at least a crooked border patrol officer or two."

Grace exhaled. Giving a crooked cop to Dante was something she couldn't bring herself to do, even if they were crooked. "I'll see what I can do."

"I also need to find Nuni Nunez," Dante told her.

"He's not hard to find," Grace told him.

Dante shook his head. "Not his fortress in Mexico, I know where that is. I need another way to find him. A mistress, a girlfriend, you know..."

Grace nodded. "I'll see what we have. Anything else?"

"The footage from Dominguez State Jail, where they found the car with the housekeeper's body in it. I also need the forensics, and the identities on the men in the car."

"The chances that they'll be in the database are slim to none," Grace told him. "Without a doubt, they were Mexican nationals."

"Most of them," Dante nodded in agreement. "But they had a guide. At least one them is familiar with the United States. Someone has to drive, and someone knew where the state jail was located. No, at least *one* of them is from here. I'll bet you a dollar to a dime that he's in the system."

Grace nodded. He was probably right. At least one of them had to be familiar with this country. "I'll see what I can come up."

Grace folded her map, and gathered her materials. She handed Dante a copy of the top secret communications intercepts from the NSA. Dante took them and peered down at them.

"Galindo's strategy," Grace told him.

Dante smiled, as he read through the document.

"Burn it, once you read it," Grace told him. "You get caught with that, and we're both going to by tried for treason, *and* executed as spies. That's a top secret, eyes only, National Security Agency transcript involving excerpts from intercepts targeting Al Qaeda operatives. Don't fuck around with it, Dante. Burn it. I'm serious. *Burn it!*

Dante nodded. He would burn it before he climbed inside of his vehicle. He didn't want to be caught with it, no more than she wanted to be caught giving it to him. It was poison.

Grace turned and walked to the driver's side of her car, where she opened the door to climbed inside.

Grace," Dante said, calling out to her.

Grace stopped and stared at him.

"Thank you."

Grace nodded, climbed into her small Benz, cranked up her car and pulled off. Dante watched her drive away, thinking about who she was, and what she was now doing. She had gone from a woman he wanted dead, to a woman he was counting on to provide him with the critical information he would need to help him find his daughter. She had gone from an enemy trying to give him a federal death penalty, to an ally given him enough information to destroy the people who kidnapped his daughter. He didn't know what to think about Grace. But if she delivered what he needed, and Lucky was returned to his arms again, then all bets were off. Killing her would be out of the window. And if he couldn't kill her, then he would do the next best thing, he would get Damian to marry her. She had just made another life changing mistake, she had just gotten on Dante's good side.

# Chapter Eighteen

Today's meeting of The Commission was to take place at the JW Marriott resort on the north central side of San Antonio, Texas. The fact that The Commission had chosen to meet not only in Texas, but in San Antonio, the actual city of the Reigns family, was unprecedented. Normally, the members insisted on a neutral site, a site where Dante's men could be seen coming from miles away, and where they could have a reasonable chance of escaping if something went wrong. But these weren't normal times, and The Commission was here to send a message. The kidnapping of Dante's daughter, was not only an attack on the Reigns family, but an attack on the entire Commission.

The JW Marriott Resort was a 1002 suite luxury hotel and spa, nestled on the verge of the hill country. The massive resort hotel overlooked a thirty-six hole TPC golf course designed by golf legends Greg Norman and Pete Dye, and contained a 26,000 square foot spa facility with more than 30 treatment rooms, boasted more than seven restaurants, each with its own distinctive dining experience, and also featured a 262,000 gallon swimming pool with its own 1200 foot lazy river, and massive water park complete with numerous rides and water slides. It was a resort to be envied throughout the country, and one that had in fact become a well known and much coveted convention destination. It was the resort hotel's 262,000 square feet of living space that accommodated those guest. And it was a portion of that very same space, that was hosting today's highly secured, yet secretive meeting of America's infamous drug commission.

Chacho Hernandez called the meeting to order. "Gentlemen, gentlemen, may we all take our seats, please?"

The Commission members arrayed around the conference room all began to take their seats around the massive wooden conference table. The raucous roar from the various individual conversations began to subside, as the members took their seats and shifted their gaze toward Chacho, who was seated at the head of the table. All of the commission members were present. Chacho cleared his throat to get their full attention.

Ladies and gentlemen, were are here today to take care of several items of business," Chacho told them. "I would like to handle the shop stuff before we get down to the big issue. As you know, at the last meeting we officially brought in a few new members, and we would like to ascertain the status of their operations within their individual states. With that said, I will turn it over to each of them so that they can report on the status of their operations, and we can gauge where we are at, and where things need to be. And then we'll move on to the matter of distribution. As we all know, our commodities are once again flowing, although not as freely as we would like, they are nonetheless flowing. We need to address that issue as well, prior to moving on to the primary reason for being here. First, we would like to hear from Bobby Blake of West Virginia."

"There's not much to report," Bobby told them. "My state was relatively easy to secure. My associates and I were pretty much already in charge, so it was relatively easy to gain control over the last few pockets of resistance. Furthermore, my state is in a different position than most of yours, as half of my state's commodities are manufactured within the state. Only half of the desired commodities come from outside of the state, the rest of my state is more interested in Meth and Marijuana."

"That's a great position to be in," Andre Michaels declared, brushing his waves. "White boys love that meth shit, don't they?"

"Fuck you," Bobby told him, pointing his middle finger.

"And so, you don't require any assistance in consolidating your state?" Raphael Guzman of Oklahoma asked.

"My state is fully under my control," Bobby said, confidently. He smirked as he peered around the table at the other new commission members.

"Good," Chacho told him. He turned to the new member sitting next to Bobby. "Vern?"

Vern McMillan of South Carolina thought for a few seconds before speaking. His deeply Southern, Hill Billy accent was thick. "I'm pretty much in the same boat with Bobby. The crackers in my state lean more toward meth than anything else. So, we're pretty good on that part. And I pretty much have most of the state under control. Only problem are the niggers in some areas like Columbus, and parts of Columbia. We're fully in charge in Charleston and all the rural areas."

"You keep using the word nigga, and you ain't gonna be fully in charge of your teeth, White boy!" Andre Michaels told him.

"You and what army?" Vern asked with a smile. "The Union Army ain't around anymore, boy!"

"Union Army?" Andre stopped brushing his hair, stood up, and grabbed his dick. "I got your Union Army right here, you inbred muthafucka!"

"Okay, that's enough!" Adolphus Brandt of Colorado shouted.

"We're not here for that!" Ceasario Chavez told them. "You two muthafuckers can get a room and make out later."

Andre took his seat again, and resumed brushing his waves.

Chacho turned to the next person in line. "Bo?"

"I'm in the same position as this fucking red neck sitting next to me," Bo Henry of Kentucky told them. Vern nudged Bo playfully in his side. "White boys love meth, so my cocaine supplies are adequate, and I'm fully in control of Kentucky. Nothing happens in my state without my permission. If a raccoon shits on the highway, it's because I told him he could."

Smiles went around the table. The three new rednecks around the table had definitely livened up the meetings. Another unspoken consensus amongst the original members, was that the new members seemed to have an inherent advantage over the rest of them. Whereas they all were heavily dependent on cocaine supplies from Mexico, or Colombia, or Bolivia, the new members in the heavily White southern states, were getting half or more of their revenues from meth sales. *And, they were manufacturing it themselves.* They didn't have to worry about border closings, or cartel wars in Mexico like everyone else did, *and* their supplies were steady and endless. In fact, the message was loud and clear. Whenever the cocaine shipments were interrupted from overseas, it would be the new members who would continue to make money and get stronger, while everyone else would have to dip into their savings and get weaker. There was a new balance of power emerging around the table and everyone would have to take that into account. In fact, all of the original members were thinking along the same lines, they all wanted *in* on the meth trade.

Chacho turned to Rick Shorts of North Carolina. "Rick?"

"Well, unlike my esteemed colleagues over here, cocaine still matters in my state," Rick told them. "And I need more of it. Lots more of it. This Commission guaranteed us all reliable supplies, and I've yet to be able to purchase enough to fulfill the needs of my organization. I'm leaving money on the table, which kills me more than I can put into words. *I need more dope!*"

"We're working on that," Damian said, lifting his hand. "We've just re-established the flow of our commodities into this country. It's going to take some time to get everything back up to speed, and to get everyone the amount that they need. Everyone is just going to have to be patient."

"Patient?" Rick shouted. "*Fuck patience!* I'm missing my money! And if we would have taken the deal with El Jeffe, we wouldn't be in this situation! You promised us that you could deliver!"

"And I *am* fucking delivering!" Damian shouted, while banging on the table.

Members around the table quickly shifted their gaze toward Damian. They had never seen him lose his temper or show any kind of anger or emotion. It was surprising to say the least.

"You think you can find some fucking cocaine?" Damian continued, while pointing his finger at Rick Shorts. "Then be my guest, you go right ahead! There is no cocaine to be found in this country, except what I'm bringing in! You think El Jeffe has a magic fucking wand that's going to get his supplies around a closed border? Is that what you're thinking? If so, then you're dumber than you fucking look! No one can get cocaine through, not with a sealed border. And you're lucky that you're getting what you're getting right now!"

"Look, we should all consider ourselves fortunate that we are getting *anything*," Emil said, stepping in. "We are in a better position than most others around the country."

"Also, the limited supply is keeping the prices high," Steve Hawk of Kansas declared.

"Yeah, it means I can charge more, work less, worry about having to store less, and still get the same amount of bread," Baby Doc Mueller of Alabama said laughing.

"How is the control of your state?" Rene Tibbideaux Reigns of Louisiana asked.

Rick sat back in his seat. He felt as though he was now getting it from all directions. "I will have my state under complete control sooner rather than later."

"Sooner rather than later?" Barry Groomes of Arkansas asked. "What the fucks that supposed to mean?"

"It means what I said," Rick answered defensively. "*Sooner* rather than *later.*"

"So you don't have your state under complete control?" Princess asked. She was still the head of Florida, and still had to attend the meeting. And she hadn't taken too kindly Rick's questioning of her brother.

"That's what I said," Rick told them. "I will soon."

"How soon is soon?" Julian Jones of Mississippi asked. He smiled at Princess, who rolled her eyes and looked away.

"Soon," Rick told them.

"Soon, as in thirty minutes, or soon as in next week, next month, next year, what are we talking?" Emil asked.

Chacho lifted his hands, patting the air as if to tell everyone to bring it down a notch. "Calm down, let's give the man a chance to answer." Chacho turned to Rick and asked in a very calm manner, "So, what is going on in your state?"

Rick exhaled. "I've met some resistance in Charlotte. The city is more difficult to get a hold of than I originally anticipated."

"I could send him some help," Vern said with a smile.

"A bunch of rednecks running around Charlotte with no shoes on?" Andre huffed. "That'll do it."

"Hey, fuck you!" Vern shouted.

"Okay, okay, enough!" Chacho said, again holding up his hands to silence them.

"I am bringing in more men from Raleigh, Fayetteville, and Winston-Salem," Rick told him. "I'll have it under control relatively shortly."

"You do understand, that this commission hates publicity," Adolphus Brandt, said, leaning in. "You make a lot of noise, and it brings unwanted media attention, and negative media attention scares politicians. You cause a ruckus, and our political protection will run for cover, and if that happens, this commission will cut its loses. Understand?"

Rick pouted for a few seconds before answering. Like most other people, he hated to be threatened. But the message was very clear. He fucks up, can't take the state, or makes too much noise trying to do so, then The Commission was going to chop his balls off, and find someone else to run the state. And that meant, he would be in a war with the *entire* commission, plus whatever asshole they chose to replace him. It would pretty much mean he was a dead man.

Chacho turned to Andre Michaels of Michigan. "Andre?"

"All of you know that I need cocaine," Andre started off. "And like everybody else around the table, I need to be able to get my hands on more of it."

"And the control of your state?" Adolphus asked.

"Yeah, how's that going for you?" Vern asked with a smile.

"Look, everyone around this table knew my situation," Andre said defensively. "It was never going to be a cakewalk taking over Michigan. Detroit is a mess, Flint, Saginaw, Grand Rapids, all of that shit is nearly impossible to take, and even more impossible to hold. I got muthafuckas constantly coming in from Chicago, Milwaukee, and from all over Ohio, constantly fucking shit up. And the simple fact of the matter is, niggaz in Detroit is unorganized, and ain't trying to get organized on a wide scale. They got they hoods, they got they dope boy clicks, and they fight fiercely to protect they turf."

"Hard headed niggers, imagine that?" Bo Henry said, laughing.

"Fuck you, bitch!" Andre told him.

"But you control the drugs in your state?" Adolphus asked.

Andre began to brush frantically at his waves. "Yeah, sort a. They'll score from a nigga, but they won't organize. Everybody wants to be the chief, and nobody wants to be the Indians."

"So basically, Detroit is a mess?" Barry Groomes said, leaning back.

Looks were exchanged around the table.

"Did we perhaps move too quickly to try to incorporate Michigan into our organization?" Adolphus Brandt asked.

"Are you thinking we should abandon our efforts to bring Detroit into the fold?" Barry asked.

Princess knew exactly what they were asking, and what it meant. They were asking the others around the table if they should kill Andre and forget about Michigan. She peered at Emil, and then Julian, and then at Damian. Would they let him die? Sure, he was young, and brash, and inexperienced, but could he be taught?

"I think that thoughts of abandoning Michigan might be a little premature," Damian told them. He wasn't going to allow them to just kill the brother. At least give him a fighting chance, he thought.

"Besides, Detroit can be very lucrative, *if* it can be tamed," Julian said, jumping in to help. "The amount of money and soldiers that it could provide in case of a major conflict against another organization can't be overlooked. It shores up our power in the Mid West, which is what we wanted, right?"

"But at what cost?" Adolphus asked. "How much money, how many men, and what of our political protection?"

This was normally the part where Damian would volunteer to send in men to help, but he had none to send. No money, no manpower, nothing. He remained silent, and it made him feel weak for having to do so.

"We can get it done," Julian told them. "It may take a little longer than we're all used to, but it'll be worth it in the end. We can postpone sending men in to help secure the state, until our issues are resolved here in Texas, and with the cartel in Juarez."

"If, Andre can hold on," Bobby Blake said.

"I can hold on," Andre said, sneering at Bobby.

"All the Black states are having problems, while the White boys have their shit together," Vern said with a smile. "Just like always."

"Fuck you!" Andre told him.

Damian stared at Vern. He couldn't wait until the time came, when he would be able to put a bullet in him. Usually, it was all about business, and he cared nothing about what another person said, if it had nothing to do with business. But killing that racist redneck would be a pleasurable indulgence that he would allow himself just once.

"We can send a small force to help Andre hold the line until we're able to fully focus on Michigan," Emil suggested.

"Why?" Baby Doc asked. "When we can just dump his ass, and go with someone more powerful within the state, someone who already controls Detroit. That's what he's not telling you. He can't take Detroit, because Detroit has already been taken."

All eyes shifted to Andre.

"Man, you're crazy!" Andre told him. "Michigan is *my* shit, and ain't nobody took nothing, especially Detroit. That shit ain't happened, ain't gonna happen, unless it's done by *me!*"

"You want this commission to fight your battles for you," Baby Doc told him. "You can't do it, so you pretend like it's all good in the rest of the state, you just need a little help with the big cities. Take Detroit, take Detroit, once I have Detroit, that's all I'm hearing from you. But the truth is, you can't do it without this commission. Why? Because you're weak."

"Fuck you!" Andre stood. "I'll show you what weak is!"

Damian rose, walked to where Andre was standing, and whispered in his ear. "The weakest one, is the one who is always shouting, and lifting his fist trying to fight. Don't try to fight the world, Andre. At least not with physical force. There are other ways to win, other ways to get what you want. Your mind is your greatest weapon, not your fist, not your gun, not your soldiers, not your money, but your mind. Always remember that."

Andre nodded at Damian, and then sat back down. Damian walked back to his seat, smoothed out his tie, and sat back down as well.

"I'm glad you got your son to sit down, before he got his ass whipped, " Baby Doc told Damian. He stared at the members arrayed around the conference table. "This nigga has been sitting in here, lying through his teeth. I say we bring to the table, the person who *truly* controls Michigan, and who has already taken Detroit, and did it on his own without any help from us."

"And who is this person?" Adolphus asked.

"A young man by the name of Hassan Ali ibn Gabril," Baby Doc told them.

Peaches spit out the water she had just drank.

"Are you all right?" Princess asked.

Peaches pressed her hand against her chest and nodded. Hassan had been her boy since back in the day. And had tried to kill her ex-boyfriend only a week ago, and had recently tried to set her up as well. Hassan may have even been involved in her shooting. The thought that he would be sitting on The Commission was too much, even for her. Having Hassan as a full blown commission member, with a massive army of niggaz from Detroit, was something she couldn't take. It would only be a matter of time before he tried her, and tried to take over all of Ohio. And then there was the matter of her ex, who was in Detroit trying to make moves on his own, and perhaps even take over the city himself. Things had certainly gotten a lot more complicated. Hassan on The Commission? Hassan, had taken over the city of Detroit? Hassan was buying dope from *her!* And if he had taken over the entire city, then that would explain why he had tried to order so much from her. That brought in the possibility that perhaps he wasn't trying to score big and jack her, but that he actually could move the amount he had asked for. It was all too confusing at this point. Her head was spinning, reeling, she felt herself getting light headed, and coming down with a heavy migraine all at the same time. She needed to be through with this meeting, and she needed to get back to her hotel. She needed her pain medicine, and she needed to lay down for a little while. It was emotional information overload.

"Hassan ain't running shit!" Andre shouted.

Chacho waved for everyone to calm down.

"Look, Andre was voted on to this commission, and he deserves an opportunity to get control of his state," Princess told them.

"How much time?" Adolphus asked. "How much time can we spare?"

"Are we in a hurry?" Princess asked. "We're not going anywhere. At least I know I'm not."

It was a message that she shot to those arrayed around the table. They knew of the troubles in Florida, and she had just made it clear, she was going to hold on to Florida. Bodies were about to roll.

Adolphus shifted his gaze to Andre. "You don't have an infinite amount of time."

The message was clear. Andre not only got the message, but Peaches did as well.  She didn't have much time.  She was going to have to lie her way through this meeting, and hope that she didn't get caught up, or ambushed by another member like Baby Doc had done Andre.  Chacho turned to MiAsia Harris of Missouri.

"MiAsia?"  Chacho asked.

"My state is secure, and one hundred percent under my control," MiAsia told them.  "As far as the shipments go, my supply has been adequate.  I had some of my own supply in reserves to carry me, and like a few of the others around the table, Mizzo has a large population that would rather do meth than coke, and our meth operations are self sustaining.  Missouri is fine."

"What about St. Louis?"  Baby Doc asked.  "I hear there is a problem."

"I'm glad that you've taken such as interest in my state, Malcom," MiAsia told him.  "But, sorry to disappoint you.  There is no St, Louis problem."

"That's not what I heard," Baby Doc told her.  "I hear those boys in St. Louis ain't laying down for you, despite how pretty you are."

MiAsia smiled.  "St. Louis boys?  Which ones are you referring to?"

"I believe they were from the north side of town," Baby Doc smiled.

MiAsia reached into her Nancy Gonzales handbag, and pulled out a folded piece of paper.  She unfolded the paper, and held it up in the air for those arrayed around the table to see.  The headlines read; MURDER IN MURPHY PARK

"I believe these are the young men that you were speaking of?" MiAsia asked with a smile.  "No resistance in my city.  Oh, and another thing.  A few of the bodies that they found in those dumpsters, had Mississippi drivers licenses on them."

Baby Doc's eyes opened wide.  "So!  What does that mean?"

"It means, the next time you send men into my territory to sew confusion, or to get some idiots to rebel and refuse to lay down, I'm going to return the favor.  And I won't just be sending a handful of men down to Mississippi either.  The Delta is going to get real crowded, you know what I'm saying?"

"Bring it, Baby Girl!"  Baby Doc said, rolling his eyes at her.

"I will, *Malcom*," MiAsia told him.  "And when I do..."

"What she has just alleged is very serious," Adolphus said, leaning in and staring at Malcom.

"I don't know what the fuck she's talking about!" Malcom shouted. "The bitch is crazy. They say mixed breed bitches are crazy, and this just proves it!"

Princess smiled. She decided right then and there that she liked MiAsia. The bitch was hard core, ruthless, and deadly, and she did it all with a sexy ass smile.

"Malcom, you sent men into her state?" Damian asked with a frown.

"Like I said, the bitch is crazy!" Baby Doc shouted. "Besides, who are you to ask me about sending men into someone else's state!"

"I can ask you," Cesario told him. "You sent men into her fucking state, *Vato*?"

"For the last time, no I didn't!" Malcom told them. "The bitch is lying!"

"These are serious allegations," Emil said, shaking his head.

"If what she says proves to be true, you're in violation," Julian told Malcom.

"Big time," Chacho said, rolling his eyes at Malcom.

"Fuck you, you, and you!" Malcom said, pointing to Julian, Chacho, and Emil. "I said, that I didn't. Why the fuck I wanna send people into her shit anyway? What fucking sense does that make? I can't stop mutha fuckas from Mississippi from leaving the state and going on vacation and doing stupid shit!"

"Vacation?" Bobby Blake said, staring at Malcom.

"Yeah, White Boy!" Malcom said, nodding. "Vacation! Niggaz take vacations too!"

"Look, this meeting is getting out of hand," Princess said. "There's been some serious allegations thrown around, and some serious matters that need further consideration. We need to take a break, collect our senses, check some things out, and then regroup."

Chacho nodded. "I agree. Especially the part about checking some things out."

All eyes around the table turned toward Malcom 'Baby Doc' Mueller.

"Let's get down to the reason we are here," Chacho told them.

"Yes, let's get on with it," Adolphus told them.

173

"As you all know, a very serious incident has occurred," Chacho told them. "Now, before we get down to the nuts and bolts of this, I have to say something. As you all know, I hate the Reigns family more than just about anyone else at this table."

"I doubt that," Barry Groomes said, interrupting him.

Laughter went around the table.

"I hate those mutha fuckers pretty bad myself," Cesario proclaimed.

More laughter shot through the room.

Chacho lifted his hands, calming them. "Seriously, we have all had our differences, and over the years, we've spilled much blood against one another. But through it all, this commission has endured. This commission was formed as an organization to combat the power of the old mafia. To provide a unifying structure, to help one another fight off those on the outside, and to pool our resources, and leverage our political connections for the good of everyone within the organization. We've done that. And the founding principle of this organization is to protect one another from outside forces, and to come to each others aid, despite our differences. A child was kidnapped from a church, on the day of her aunt's wedding. It doesn't matter what the last name of that child is, the simple fact of the matter is, she was a child. And despite everything that I've done in my life, and I've killed many, I've never involved children in it. Children are off limits. I would hope that everyone around this table, feels the same. You touch a child, you are way over the line. You touch a child, and you die."

Nods went around the table in agreement.

"We are hard men," Chacho continued. "We kill, and we do horrible things to protect our families, and to make money. But I would like to think that we keep our word to each other. If there is no honor among thieves, then there is no reason for us to be here, and if there is no honor amongst men, then there is no reason for any of us to be alive. When they took that child, I thought about my own child. It hit close to home. I will still be Dante's enemy tomorrow, but today... today, I am Dante's brother, and the little girl who was taken from him, was taken from me also. She is my daughter. She is *all* of our daughter. And so, I'm asking you to stand with me today, to live up to your word, the word you gave when you joined this commission, and even beyond that, I'm asking you to stand up and be men. They attacked one of us, and they took our child from us, and now let us join together and show them *and* the rest of the world, what happens when you mess with our family. I am asking you all to vote to invoke this commission's defensive charter, and to declare that the attack on the Reign's family, was an attack on us all."

Chacho rose from his seat. "Who will stand with me?"

Princess rose, and so did Damian. Emil and Julian rose, and so did James Speech of Virginia, who was a distant cousin to the Reigns family. Brandon Reigns who ran Maryland stood, and so did Rene Tibbideaux Reigns, the wife of Damian's brother. And then, after a pause, Cesario Chavez rose, and grabbed Princess's hand. MiAsia stood, and so did Peaches. Adolphus Brandt stood, and he was joined by Raphael Guzman of Oklahoma, Jamie Forrest of Tennessee, and Barry Groomes of Arkansas. Steve Hawk from Kansas rose, as did Andre, Rick, and Bobby Blake. Bo Henry stood, and so did his partner Vern McMillan, and finally, Baby Doc rose.

Princess was not one to get emotional, but she could feel tears welling up in her eyes. The entire commission had risen to stand with them.

Chacho peered around the table. "It appears that the vote is unanimous. For the first time in the history of this organization, we have all voted to go to war together. I feel good about this."

Damian cleared his throat. "I don't want to give some big speech. I just want to tell each and every one of you, thank you. My brother thanks you. I am going to tell him about this moment."

Princess couldn't help herself. She lifted her hand to the corner of her eyes and dabbed away a small amount of moisture. Twenty two states, with thousands of soldiers, had just agreed to go to war with them against the powerful cartels in Northern Mexico. Dante was going to get the soldiers that he needed to do what he needed to do, and the Reigns family was about to given a ton of cash from its fellow commission members. The joining of so many powerful families all with one single purpose, was about to shift the drug world in a massive way. The cartels were about to feel the might of The Commission.

# Chapter Nineteen

Damian walked out of the conference room eager to get back to his office and call Dante. Not only did he want to tell Dante about the meeting, but he needed to know what The Commission was sending him in the form of resources, and check his balance sheets to see what exactly was needed. He had also came up with another idea as well. The Commission would be sending him more men, which meant that he could pull more of his own away from the search and divert them to California. He also remembered that Brandon now had Philadelphia in addition to Maryland, because they pulled out of Pennsylvania. This freed up his cousin Joshua, who used to have Pennsylvania. Josh would be perfect to send to California, Damian thought. He was used to managing a large state, and with the right men on his team to advise him and help him out, and with a significant army behind him, he could reverse the tide in California and began winning back the state. This would allow him to remain in Texas for a little while longer, and manage the war with the Mexican cartels. It was brilliant, he thought. He would have to send for Joshua immediately, get him back to Texas, brief him and then get him into California. Princess had pulled a significant number of soldiers from Dallas to take with her to Florida. Joshua would have to pull soldiers from Houston.

"Why are you smiling?" Princess asked.

Damian stopped and faced his sister. "I just had a brilliant idea."

Princess folded her arms and shifted her weight to one side. "When that happens, it means that I don't get any sleep."

Damian laughed. "No, actually, this idea will give us all a little time to get in a little more shut eye."

"Really?" Princess asked, lifting an eyebrow. "Well, let's hear it then."

"Recall Josh, and get his ass down here, and then send him to California," Damian told her.

Princess nodded, and began mulling over the idea. Josh may be able to pull it off, she thought, but she wasn't sure. Managing Pennsylvania was easy, because of the shear number of soldiers he had in Philly, and Philly was uncontested. Jumping into a state where everyone is rebelling and trying to kill you at every turn was going to be many times more difficult. Not to mention the fact that the underbosses were more powerful than some of the people who sat on The Commission. California was a state where the underbosses and capo regimes had thousands of men, and tens of millions of dollars.

"You think he can handle such a massive state?" Princess asked.

Damian thought about her question for a few seconds, before slowly nodding. "I think he can. With help of course."

"That's the problem, how much help could we actually provide?" Princess told him. "I'll be busy in Florida, You and Dante will be busy finding Lucky, and fighting the cartels, so that pretty much puts him on his own."

Again, Damian nodded. "I see what you're saying."

"I have another idea," Princess told him.

"What's that?"

"Why don't we see if Brandon is willing to give up his state?" Princess asked.

"*Give up his state?*" Damian frowned. "Why would he do that? He's in charge of his own state, with his own family. Why would he go backwards?"

Princess pursed her lips. "C'mon, Damian, let's be real. *His own state?* His *own* family? He's about as independent and separate as my two arms are. Yeah, they're separate arms, but they're both part of the same body. We *gave* Brandon the state, and The Commission approved. He was put there by us as a caretaker, with our money, and our men."

"Well, it's his now," Damian told her.

"Hear me out," Princess told him. "He turns over his state to Josh, and he goes to California and takes care of that for us. Forget the title, forget the seat on The Commission, California is a fucking *promotion!* A *huge* one! More men, more money, more responsibility, more everything."

"Yeah, but he's running it *for* us, instead of it being his own," Damian told her.

"Damian, it's a huge promotion for him, and a huge opportunity," Princess told him. "Brandon will love the weather, he'll love the celebrity parties, the beautiful women, the whole California lifestyle. Trust me. It's a promotion in everything but the name."

"It'll look like a demotion," Damian told her.

"Until he sees his bank account," Princess retorted. "Cut him in, and make sure that he's making more money that he could ever make in Maryland. Money will ease whatever hurt feelings, or sense of shame you'll think he's feeling."

Damian smiled. "He doesn't think like that."

"He's a Reigns, isn't he?" Princess asked lifting any eyebrow. "That means, he's about his money, and he's about business. He'll have more soldiers, more power, more money, than most of the motherfuckers on The Commission. And I know that Brandon can handle California."

Damian bit down on his bottom lip. "I wouldn't even know how to approach him about something like this."

"You want me to do it?" Princess asked.

Damian stared at her. "This requires finesse."

Princess smiled. "What? You don't think I have finesse?"

Damian tilted his head and allowed his silence and stare to answer her question.

"Okay, okay, I'll finesse the situation," Princess exhaled. "You guys act like you're the women with all of this walking on eggs shit."

"*Princess.*"

"Okay, I'll approach it delicately."

"Thank you," Damian told her.

"Damian."

Damian and Princess both turned. MiAsia walked up.

Princess smiled at the two of them. They made a cute couple, she thought. And if not, she would love it if MiAsia played on her team. She would lick that pussy until MiAsia screamed and begged for mercy. Damn, she was fine, Princess said, walking her eyes up and down

MiAsia's body.

"Damian, I just wanted to speak to you away from the others," MiAsia told him.

"Sure," Damian said. He was all smiles.

Princess rolled her eyes. Men, and their dicks, she thought. She knew that all of the blood had rushed from her brother's brain into his pants, by the googly eyed looked he had on his face.

"You know what?" Princess said, rolling her eyes at her brother. "I'll get with you later."

MiAsia smiled at Princess politely, and Princess smiled back, and then departed. MiAsia turned toward Damian.

"I just wanted to tell you, that I am with you a hundred percent, and if there is anything that I can do to help you, don't hesitate to ask."

"Thank you so much," Damian told her. "That brings me great comfort to know that I have friends who will stand beside us in our time of need."

MiAsia caressed the side of Damian's face. "Forget the politically correct stuff, how are you *really* doing? I know that this stuff is tough, and I can't even pretend to know how you guys are feeling. Are you sleeping?"

Damian smiled. He liked her already. Not just because she was drop dead, super model gorgeous, but because she also kept it real. "I'm sleeping. Or, trying to sleep."

"It's hard, isn't it?" she asked, nodding.

"Impossible."

"Are you eating?"

Damian shrugged. "When I can."

"Let's talk," MiAsia told him.

"Sure, anytime."

"How about now?" she asked, allowing a smile to creep across her face.

Damian had to force himself to blink. She was stunning. MiAsia had a natural beauty about her, now that he was seeing her up close. Her face was flawless, and her eyes had flecks of gray and green in them. She had her mother's high cheek bones, along with her father's eyes. Her skin was a light almond with a tinge of olive, while her teeth looked as though they were made of freshly found pearls pulled from the Black Sea. She was the perfect blend of Africa and The Orient. But without a doubt, her body was a gift from the daughters of Ethiopia, as only one of Nubian stock could be blessed with such voluptuousness.

"Now?" Damian swallowed hard. "Yeah, sure. Now would be perfect."

"Good," she said, again caressing his face. "Dinner on me. I want you to eat, and relax, and talk to me. I want you to know, that you have a friend in me."

"Is this friendship only in time of need, or can I count on it always?" Damian asked with a smile.

"Well, that depends," MiAsia told him.

"On what?"

"On how tonight goes," she said with a smile. "We'll see if you know how to treat a lady."

"You ain't said nothing," Damian told her. He pulled out his cell phone and dialed up a number. "Roger this is Damian. Get the helicopter ready."

MiAsia smiled and lifted an eyebrow.

"Ever saw this city from a helicopter?" Damian asked. "The view is absolutely magnificent."

"Really?"

"Oh, yeah," Damian said, placing his arm around MiAsia's waist and leading her down the hall. "We can take the helicopter around the city, and then land at the airport in Austin. I know a wonderful French restaurant in downtown Austin that is absolutely awesome."

"Go on now!" MiAsia told him. "I see you getting your swag back."

Damian and MiAsia broke into laughter as the two of them headed down the hall to the waiting elevator.

Inside of the conference room, Peaches was talking to Andre when Baby Doc approached. Andre and Baby Doc stared at one another for a few awkward moments, before Peaches clasped Andre's arm.

"Peaches, we'll continue our conversation on that issue later," Andre told her. "Suddenly, I have the urge to get some fresh air. It stinks around here."

"Walk away, boy," Baby Doc told him.

Andre turned, and Peaches stepped in between the two of them.

"Ignore him," Peaches told Andre. "Just walk away. I'll talk to you about that issue later."

Andre backed away, mad dogging Baby Doc, before finally turning and heading out of the conference room.

Baby Doc seated himself on the edge of the conference table. "You got lucky."

Peaches turned back toward him. "What?"

"I said, you got lucky," Baby Doc said with a smile. "We didn't get around to asking about Ohio."

Peaches shrugged. "Oh well, maybe next time."

"Will there be a next time?" Baby Doc asked.

"I don't know, will there?"

"You tell me?" Baby Doc told her. "So, how are things going in Ohio?"

"Wonderful," Peaches told him.

"That's not what I'm hearing."

"Maybe you need to check your sources then," Peaches said, gathering her belongings from the table.

"My sources are pretty damn reliable."

"Apparently not."

"What happened to your face?" Baby Doc asked, pointing to the scars on Peaches' face.

"Abusive husband."

Baby Doc smiled. "I noticed you're getting around with a little difficultly. Like you've been shot or something."

Peaches froze. The tiny micro hairs on the back of her neck stood at attention.

Baby Doc leaned in. "You look pale. Did I say something?"

He touched Peaches' side where she had been shot, and she cried out in pain, and then slapped his hand away. She then slapped his face.

"Don't you ever fucking touch me again!" Peaches shouted.

The remaining commission members in the room all turned in their direction. Peaches stuck her finger in Baby Doc's face.

"If you ever put your hands on me again, I swear you'll be drawing back a nub!" Peaches said, through clenched teeth.

Baby Doc laughed.

"Yeah, that's a bullet wound," he said, nodding. "Why would you have a gunshot wound, or two, if you're fully in control of your state?"

"Don't fucking worry about my state!" Peaches told him.

"Gun battles raging in the streets, mansions getting over run, hospitals getting shot up, cars getting shot up, it's like a war zone up there," Baby Doc said, shaking his head. "Looks like you're in some deep shit. You can't deliver Ohio, then it's lights out for you, Baby Girl."

Peaches could feel herself beginning to hyperventilate. Her skin was becoming flush, and her breathing labored. She felt like the walls were closing in, and the room was getting warmer. She had to get out of the room. He knew too much. How did he know so much, she wondered? He knew about her wounds, he knew about the hospital, and about her mansion getting overrun. He could expose her. Hell, he had planned on exposing her. If the rest of The Commission found out, she was a dead woman. Trap was a dead woman, V was a dead woman, Joaquin was dead as well. They would wipe her off the map to silence her, and kill anyone around her whom she might have told about their existence.

Peaches grabbed her belongings, and hurried for the door. She was about to jump through the roof, and she didn't know what she would do if Baby Doc told the rest of them and they stopped her. Her nerves were frayed, and she could feel her legs shaking with each of her steps. Inside, she was praying that she would stay on her feet, and hoping that her legs remained steady enough to hold her up. She felt as if she were going to collapse.

"*Ohio, Ohio!*" Baby Doc sang out loud. "*I love Ohio! Peaceful, wonderful, tranquil Ohio!*" Baby Doc turned to the others in the room. "Maybe we should hold our next meeting in Ohio, seeing as how it's safe and secure!" He turned back toward Peaches just as she was exiting the room. "Tell Kharee that I said hello!"

Peaches made it out of the door to the conference room, and once out of sight, she had to lean against the wall for a few moments to gather herself. Her knees were about to buckle. She could hear Baby Doc's booming staccato voice on the other side of the wall, laughing heartily.

*How did he know*, she wondered? *How?* He knew too much. And how did he know Kharee? *What the fuck was going on*, she wondered?

What kind of games were being played, and by who?

It was too much for her. *Way too much for her.* Peaches slowly began to began to descend to the ground. Her leg was in pain, her side was in pain, and she desperately needed her pain medication.

"Hey, are you all right?" Andre asked, walking up to her. He caught Peaches, and pulled her back up to her feet. She winced and whimpered slightly because of the pain. "Damn, Ma, you don't look so good."

"Just get me to my car," Peaches told him.

"You can't drive," Andre told her. "Let me take you back to your hotel."

"I have a limo outside," Peaches told him. "I'll be all right. Just help me to my limo."

Andre nodded, placed Peaches' arm around his neck, and helped her to the elevator. Peaches didn't know what was going on, but she knew one thing for sure, she was going to find out. She needed to get back to Ohio, she needed to find her brother, find her girls, and get back on her feet. She needed to rebuild, to put things back together, and to finish what she had started. She was going to take Ohio, and she was going to come back stronger than ever. And once she did, she would see about Kharee, and she would see about that Black son-of-a-bitch Baby Doc. She could still hear him laughing down the hall. They would see who would get the last laugh.

# Chapter Twenty

McAllen, Texas was known for little outside of being a bridge for trade between the United States and Mexico. It was a city nestled along the banks of the Rio Grande river that catered to Mexican shoppers, and maintained what was known as a maquiladora economy, which basically meant it manufactured trade goods to send into Mexico. McAllen's proximity to Mexico was the reason for its giant footprint within the framework of the North American Free Trade Agreement; some 30 billion dollars worth of trade goods passed over the McAllen-Reynosa-Hildago International Bridge. McAllen's proximity also meant it had a massive footprint in another kind of trade; human and drug trafficking.

It wasn't difficult to find smugglers in the city, in fact, an entire cottage industry revolved around the illicit trade. The smugglers had their own haunts and hangouts, their own associations, rivalries, language, culture, and even maintained a secret website where they bid against each other for smuggling jobs. They even had their own rivalries, and it was because of such rivalries, that it was easy to find smugglers who were willing to betray others. It was a cut throat business, and it was filled with cut throat players.

Richardo Byza was a veteran in the game. In fact, it was said that he was one of the best ever, in the history of the trade. He had never lost a cargo, or a single person he had been charged with smuggling. He was jokingly referred to as the Harriet Tubman of human trafficking. His skills were so highly praised, that he had plied his trade in other countries. Some say he had worked for the CIA getting people in and out of North Korea, Iran, Iraq, and even Cuba. Others say he had worked for the Russian mob, and even a few terrorist organizations in his time. One thing was for certain though, he loved what he did, and vowed that he would still be smuggling people through the brush while using a cane or a walker. It was this love of the game that had him hiding in the brush to meet his contact and cargo that evening.

"Hoo-hoo," came the sound of an owl hooting in the dark.

Richardo cupped his hands over his mouth and made a distinctive bird call in return. It was his all clear signal.

His cargo this evening were three old women, women who wanted to live in America with their families who had came over a long time ago. The various families had saved up enough money to pay for their grandmothers and mother to be smuggled into the country to live with them. He hated charging them so much, but what the hell, he thought; if he didn't get the money for bringing the old bitches over, then someone else would. He had charged twenty five thousand dollars a piece, because of the women's age. Had they been younger and in better shape, the price would have been roughly ten grand less, but crippled, slow, old ass women were always a burden. You had to stop, they had to use the bathroom, they needed water, food, rest. And the slower you moved, the greater the risk of getting caught, and the greater the risk of getting caught, the more you had to charge. Forget the fact that he already charged an absorbent amount, for this run, he felt as though he deserved every penny he was getting.

Richardo's charges trampled through the dense brush, making their way toward him.

"Old bitches make more noise than a fucking circus," Richardo grumbled.

Soon, his clients came into view. Sure enough, three women dressed in traditional Mexican garb ambled their way up to him.

"Where's the guide?" Richardo asked.

The women all wore scarves over their head, and had their faces partially concealed. The first one peered up at him, and even in the darkness he could tell that something wasn't right. She wasn't old at all. From beneath her large bundle of layered clothing she pulled out a small assault rifle.

"What the fuck is this?" Richardo asked.

All three of the women pulled the scarves from their heads, removing the gray wigs that they were wearing as well.

"Put your fucking hands up, or you're going to die here," the one holding the assault rifle told him.

Richardo slowly put his hands up. He had a nine millimeter tucked into his waist, a forty five strapped to his hip, and a thirty eight revolver in an ankle holster that he carried as back up. But they were all useless right now, as she had gotten the drop on him.

"What is this?" Richardo asked.

Another one of the women walked up behind Richardo and stuck a syringe in the side of his neck. That was the last thing he remembered before passing out.

*****

Richardo woke to find his hands and legs chained. He was lying flat on a hard surface, and the bounds he had on him were around his wrists and ankles, and he was spread eagle. He also realized that he was naked.

The room was dark, and whatever he had been drugged with still had a slight effect on him. He was conscious, but still a little disoriented. This disorientation manifested itself in many ways, one of which was spatial. He knew that the room he was in was vast, but the darkness prevented him from knowing just how vast it was. What he could tell, however, was that a miasmic stench permeated the air.

"Hello?" Richardo shouted. He voice carried, echoing throughout the vast building. "Hello?"

And then someone hit the lights.

One by one, massive ceiling mounted lighting fixtures flickered on, and soon, it was clear that he was inside of a vast warehouse or storage facility of some kind. And it was soon clear that he was not alone.

Men were gathered in the room, and they were watching him. Some spoke amongst themselves in whispers. It wasn't their presence that concerned him, but the look in their eyes. They held a look of utter fear.

Richardo checked the strength of his bonds by tugging on them. They were unbreakable. He turned his head to see what he was chained to, and it mystified him at first, because it appeared as though his chains led to a hook attached to a steel cable, and this cable led to a winch. He turned his head in the other direction, and his other hand seemed to be bound in the same manner. It was completely mystifying. He heard the creaking of a door opening, and then the sound of approaching footsteps. Soon, he could see the face of the man who had entered into the room.

"Dante!" Richardo cried out. "What the hell is going on?"

"Hi, Ricky," Dante said, smiling in the man's face. "How are you doing today?"

"I would be better if I knew what was going on," Richardo told him. "And even better if these chains were removed, and I was allowed to go home."

"Of course," Dante said, as if granting Richardo's request was a foregone conclusion. "But first, before we do that, I have few questions for you."

"Dante, I know what you want, and I know what you're after, but believe me, I had nothing to do with that!"

"Of course you didn't!" Dante told him. "Richardo, at the time of my daughter's disappearance, you were on a plane coming from Europe. Where you had been for three weeks. I know for a fact, that you had absolutely *nothing* to due with Lucky's kidnapping."

"Then why am I here?" Richardo screamed. "What is this for?"

"Like I said, I have questions," Dante told him. "You've worked for me before, right?"

"*Yes!*" Richardo told him. "And I was loyal to you. I never told anything!"

"Of course, Ricky," Dante said, patting his arm. "Very loyal. You are the best, Ricky. The best at what you do. And that's why we are here today. When I need to know something, I go to the best. When I need to know something about an airplane, I go to the best pilot and ask what I need to know."

Dante laughed, and snapped his fingers. "This reminds me of a funny story. You know, I'm a single parent. And as a single parent, and a new Dad, I used to freak out when Lucky would get sick when she was a baby. One time, I actually had the chief of Cedar Siani's Children's Hospital flown in one of my jets because Lucky wouldn't stop crying. Turned out, she was constipated."

Dante shook his head. "I don't know, I guess I've always been that way. Whatever it is, I've always went to the best, bought the best, sought out the best. Damian says it's a severe personality disorder. But me, I don't see anything wrong with it. Do you? Do you think that it's wrong for me to go to the best when I have a question, or when I need a little advice?"

"Dante, what's this about?" Richardo asked. He tugged at his constraints again.

"This is about you being the best, Ricky," Dante told him. "That's it, plain and simple. You're the best, and I need answers."

"Why did you bring me here?"

"Because, you're loyal," Dante told him. "And men like you, don't talk unless you are *encouraged* to do so."

"And you think that torturing me is going to get you what you want?" Richardo asked. "If that's the case, then you know that men like me don't break."

Dante smiled. "Everyone breaks, Ricky. Some are more tolerant of pain than others, but in the end, everyone breaks."

"Then let's get this over with," Richardo said, closing his eyes.

"I need to know all of the smuggling routes, the tunnels, the safe houses, everything," Dante told him.

Richardo burst into laughter. "You might as well fucking kill me! Because that's what you're doing to me! That's what's going to happen anyway!"

"I need all of the smuggling routes, the safe houses, the tunnels, everything," Dante repeated softly.

"You might as well ask for naked pictures of Michelle Obama, or a space ship, or a unicorn!" Richardo said, laughing. "*Ask me for something that I can give you!*"

"I have," Dante told him. "And it is within your power to give me these things."

"I do, and I'll be dead within a week!" Richardo shouted

"You don't, and you'll be dead within the hour," Dante shot back. "Give me what I want, and at least you'll have a week's head start."

"*They will kill me!*" Dante shouted.

"You're that afraid of the cartels?" Dante asked.

"The cartels?" Richardo shouted. "*Fuck the cartels!* Are you fucking stupid, Dante? Are you that fucking blind? Those are not cartel safe houses, you dumb mutherfucker!"

Dante reeled. "What the fuck are you talking about?"

"You want the routes, the safe houses, the connections, the tunnels?" Richardo asked.

"Yeah."

"*They don't belong to me!*" Richardo told him. "*They don't belong to any of us!*"

"Who do they belong to?"

"*To your competition, mother fucker!*" Richardo shouted. "To the biggest fucking drug dealers in the world! *To the United States fucking government!* They're the CIA's fucking safe houses!"

"*What?*"

"Are you deaf, dumb, or just stupid?" Richardo asked.

"How do you think they pay for their little secret wars, while keeping Congress out of their ass?" Richardo shouted. "Huh? They've been in the drug business way before that Iran-Contra bullshit, and they will *always* be in the drug business! Do you really think that a country with that many satellites, satellites that can read the letters on a license plate, can't stop dope from coming in to this country? Are you really that stupid?"

"Give me the safe houses, and the routes!" Dante said forcefully.

"*Go fuck yourself!*" Richardo shouted.

Dante turned to his men and nodded. Richardo soon discovered the reason for the hooks and cables and wenches. Dante's men started up the generators, and the wenches came alive. They each hit a lever on their wenches, and simultaneously, the chains that bound his wrists and ankles began to pull. Richardo found himself being stretched in a way that his body was not designed to to stretched. The pain became excruciating.

"Ahhh!" Richard cried out in a continuous howl of sheer agony.

Dante nodded, and his men threw the levers on their wenches to the STOP position.

Dante leaned in so that his face was only inches away from Richardo's face. "Give me what I want."

"*I can't!*" Richardo shouted. "Don't you fucking understand me? *I can't!*"

Dante nodded, and again his men started their respective wenches.

The 10,000 pound wenches pulled the cables that were attached to the chains bound around Richardo's wrist and ankles. They pulled his limbs in four different directions, stretching his body in such a way as to start rupturing some internal organs. The sockets in his shoulders gave way, as did the joints in his knees. He was literally being pulled apart.

Dante nodded, and again, his men stopped the wenches.

"Give me the routes!" Dante shouted.

"*I can't!*" Richardo shouted. He began crying. "*I can't.* Don't you understand, I can't! *They'll fucking kill me!* And if you fuck with those safe houses, they'll fucking kill you too!"

The blood rose up in Dante's face, and he could feel heat starting to course through his body. He nodded at his men.

The wenches came on once again, and they pulled a man who was already at his breaking point. The distinctive, haunting, unforgettable sound of bones snapping, ligaments tearing, and joints popping could be heard throughout the room, despite the inhuman cries of Richardo.

The joints, and muscle tissue in his arms were the first to give. His arms popped off with a loud snap, sending blood flying throughout the room, onto the clothing and faces of those gathered inside. Many lost their lunch. Richardo's arms flew into the walls, hitting with a distinctive splat, sending even more blood all over the place. Blood spurted from his torso, through the veins that once gave life to his limbs. Dante was covered in it. His smile told those gathered inside, that he *relished* being covered in it.

The result of Richardo's arms being pulled off, was that the wenches connected to his legs pulled his body off of the table the then nearly split him in half before finally ripping off his legs. His screams stopped after a short period of time, as he quickly bled out.

Dante turned to his men. "Take this stump, put it on a pole, and stick it in the ground next to the others."

Dante turned, and walked through massive puddles of blood to exit the room. He was no closer to finding his daughter, or the trails that they would use to spirit her into Mexico, but he felt relieved nonetheless. It felt as if he had just had a gigantic orgasm. He stepped outside, and despite the fact the he despised smoking, felt as if he needed a cigarette to relish the moment. He turned to one of his men guarding the door.

"You got a square?"

The bodyguard nodded, and searched his pockets frantically for his pack of cigarettes. He found them, thumped the packet, and ejected one far out enough so that Dante could take it. Dante pulled the cigarette from the box, and the bodyguard quickly produced a lighter and lit it. Dante inhaled the crisp menthol, and blew smoke into the air. A smile spread across his face.

"So that's what it feels like?" He laughed, as he strolled off into the darkness.

# Chapter Twenty One

DeMarion hung up his cell phone and marched into the supermarket to find Vendetta. He found her standing in the middle of a grocery aisles, with a can of white tuna in one hand, and a can of white chicken in the other. Upon seeing him approach, she held both cans up.

"Which one?" she asked. "Chicken salad, or tuna salad?"

DeMarion placed his hand beneath his chin, as if he were contemplating a life changing decision. "Hmmm, let's see. I kinda dig both. I love chicken salad, but only if you hook it up with Miracle Whip, and lots of sweet relish and shit. And I dig tuna fish, but you gotta dice up some apples and salary and hook that shit up."

Vendetta recoiled. "Boy, ain't nobody making no White folks tuna fish! That shit ain't jumping off around here!"

DeMarion laughed. "Why you gotta go there?"

"What?"

"Why it gotta be White folks tuna fish?"

"Because it is! Black folks don't put no apples and celery and nuts and shit in they tuna fish! Where you been?"

"That's how my Momma made it," DeMarion told her.

"Oh, so yo Momma is a White woman or something?"

"Yeah," DeMarion said with a smile.

"Boy, get the fuck outta here!" Vendetta said, waving her hand dismissively.

"She is!" DeMarion said with a smiled.

"Get out of here!"

"She is!" DeMarion insisted.

"Are you serious?"

DeMarion nodded. He turned up his palms. "Duh? You can't tell?"

Vendetta recoiled and examine him. A closer examination revealed that he wasn't lying. He *was* mixed.

"Get the fuck outta here!" Vendetta told him. "How the fuck are you a Reigns then?"

"Duh?" DeMarion told her. "*My Daddy!*"

"Your Daddy married a White woman?" Vendetta asked with a smile.

DeMarion smacked his lips. "My Daddy married that woman he loved."

"Well, I'll be damned!" Vendetta told him. "No offense, White Boy."

"Ha, ha, ha," DeMarion said, nodding his head sarcastically. "You got jokes today I see."

"So, I guess it's the White folks tuna salad then," Vendetta said, placing the cans in the shopping cart. "C'mon, let's go over here so I can get some damn apples."

"Thank you!" DeMarion shouted. "Now, was that so hard to do? I mean, without insulting my Momma and Daddy?"

Vendetta laughed.

DeMarion followed her to the fruits and vegetable section of the grocery store. Vendetta started checking out apples. DeMarion lifted one, wiped it on his shirt and bit into it.

"Oh my God!" Vendetta exclaimed. "You are so *nasty*! That thing wasn't even washed. If I had any doubts about your genetics, I don't anymore. That was some straight White folks shit right there!"

DeMarion laughed.

"Ask me," he said smiling.

"Ask you what?" Vendetta said, pausing.

"Ask me about the one thing that's been on your mind lately."

"You got a woman?"

DeMarion lifted an eyebrow. "Oh, that's been on your mind?"

Vendetta shook her head. "No. That's not what I meant. Not like that. What is it?"

"I heard from my cousin," DeMarion told her.

Vendetta saw the smile on his face, and realized that it was good news. She threw her arms around him and leaped into his arms. "She's alive!"

DeMarion laughed. "She's alive."

Vendetta showered DeMarion with kisses all over his face. "Thank you, thank you, thank you! I need to talk to her! Can you call her? Can he get in touch with her and put her on three way or something?"

DeMarion held up his hands. "Calm down, calm down. We'll get there. Right now, she's a little tied up with meetings and stuff. She's in Texas."

"*Texas?*" Vendetta said a little too loud. "Texas? How did she get to Texas? What's she doing in Texas?"

"Apparently, my cousin pulled her out of the house," DeMarion explained. "She was taken the the hospital, and then transferred to a hospital in Maryland."

"*Maryland?*"

DeMarion nodded. "It makes sense. Maryland is controlled by our other cousin, Brandon. She's in Texas, because she had to go to a really important meeting. My cousin Darius is with her."

"Thank you!" Vendetta said, clasping her hands. "I just don't know what to say. Thank you! *My sister is all right*!"

"I'm still trying to find out what happened to your other sister, the one that was already in the hospital," DeMarion told her. "Things are hectic right now. People leaving the state, getting moved around, nobody really knows her, and the guys have orders to not make any noise and to be invisible. So they can't really hit the down and do much digging."

Vendetta nodded. She understood. She would find Trap once things cleared up, and once she was fully healed. It would just take time, she thought. Everything would come together in due time.

"Now, about that question you've been wanting to ask me?" DeMarion said, with a smile.

"Forget it," Vendetta told him. She turned, and started checking out stalks of celery.

*****

Damian's motorcade arrived at the entrance to the massive ranch and was stopped by the guards. Damian sat waiting patiently inside the back seat of his stretched Jaguar XJ Portfolio Sedan. He fiddled with the built in iPad on the back of the seat.

"What's going on?" Damian asked his driver.

The driver climbed out of the Jag and lifted his hands in the air. "What's up?"

One of Damian's men from the lead car, who had been talking to the security guards at the entrance walked to the Jag. Damian rolled down his window.

"Danny, what's going on?" Damian asked, after powering down the window of his Jag.

"They won't let us in, Boss," Danny told him.

"*What?*" Damian opened the door, climbed out, and walked to the gate. "What's going on here?"

The two security guards at the gate held up there hands. "We're under strict orders to not let anyone inside."

"By who?" Damian asked.

"Mr. Reigns," one of the men told him.

"I *am* Mr. Reigns!" Damian shouted.

The two guards exchanged glances.

"By, Dante, sir," one of the guards told him.

"Do you know who the fuck I am?" Damian asked.

The two men again exchanged glances. They had a general idea, but the fact of the matter was, they were Dante's men. Hired by Dante, and they worked directly for Dante, and knew little of the family structure.

"Sir..."

"Open the gate," Damian said, through clenched teeth.

The guards were soon surrounded by Damian's men. Again, they peered at one another, and the decision was a no brainer. One of them stepped inside of the guard house, and hit the button, opening up the massive iron gate that allowed entrance onto the property. The second guard lifted his walkie-talkie.

"We got guests," he said, speaking into the communicator.

"*Guests?*" a voice on the other side replied.

"Mr. Reigns," the guard said into the walkie-talkie.

"Dante is back?" the voice asked.

"Negative," the guard replied. "The *other* Mr. Reigns."

Damian walked back to his Jag, climbed inside, and he and his men continued their journey up to the main property.

The trip up to the main property was relatively short. The ranch was massive in scope and size, encompassing some thirty thousand acres along the border, with the Rio Grande running along the southern border of the property. It allowed Dante and his men to pretty much cross over into Mexico at will. It also allowed them to bring people back from Mexico undetected. The ranch's size also ensured privacy.

The first strange thing that Damian noticed, was that most of the activity was not centered around the main house, but far away from it. Dante had set up numerous metal buildings of massive size, deep within the parameters of the property. It was there where the bee hive of activity was taking place. His caravan pulled up and stopped just short of this compound within the ranch.

Damian climbed out of his Jag and peered around. The first thing that hit him, was the smell. It reeked of death. The smell of deteriorating flesh and rotting corpses hung thick and heavy in the air. Damian pulled a handkerchief from his pocket, and placed it over his mouth and nose. His men did the same. One of Dante's main men walked up to him.

"Hey, Damian," Marquis said greeting him. "You should have told me you were coming. I could have prepared for you."

"It was last minute," Damian told him. "Where's Dante?"

"He's in Mexico," Marquis told him.

Damian peered around the area. "What's going on here? What's that smell?"

The strange look on Marquis' face and the fact that he didn't answer raised Damian's suspicions. He knew what death smelled like. The location, the security, and the smell all told him that he was not going to like what he found. He stared at Marquis, as he headed toward the buildings in the compound.

The first thing Damian came across, were men in small, wire, dog cages. The cages were three feet wide, three feet high, and four feet in length. They were big enough for a man on his hands and knees to fit inside. They would not allow a person to lay down, turn around, or do anything else once locked inside. They would not even allow a person to fall asleep, unless he could sleep sitting up on his hands and knees.

The men inside of the wire cages were naked, and the smell of piss and feces surrounded the cages, and he could clearly see why. The nude men had defecated inside of the cages, and were basically kneeling in their own shit and piss. In front of each dog cage was a large pit bull terrier chained to a poll. The pit bulls were barking ferociously at the men inside of the cages.

Damian paused in front of the dog cages, just behind the barking dogs. "What's this?"

"Sleep deprivation," Marquis explained. "It's psychological. The terror of the dogs, the barking all night, the inability to sleep."

"I know what sleep deprivation is and what it does," Damian told him. "What's it for? Who are they?"

"Smugglers," Marquis told him. "From all along the border. Dante wants to find out how the kidnappers are going to get into Mexico so that he can intercept them."

"They can't use the restroom?" Damian asked, pointing at the men.

Marquis' look answered his question.

"Are they being fed?" Damian asked.

"Barely," Marquis told him.

Damian swallowed hard, and continued through the compound. Soon, he came upon a putrid pond, with a gate and a warning sign around it. He turned toward Marquis for an explanation.

"Piranha," Marquis said, giving a one word answer.

Damian continued past the pond. He made his way to one of the buildings, where he peered inside of a dusty window on the door. He could barely make out what was inside, so he was unsure of what he was seeing. He stepped back from the door, and turned to Marquis.

"Open the door," Damian told him.

"You don't want to go inside," Marquis told him.

"*Open it*," Damian told him.

Marquis reached down to his left and pulled some gas masks from a large box that was sitting on a folding table next to the door. He handed one of the masks to Damian, and put one on himself. Damian put the mask on, and stepped aside, while Marquis opened the door to the large corrugated steel building. The smell that had been contained inside of the building rushed out, hitting Damian's men smack dab in their faces. They immediately turned and began to vomit. Damian stared at his men, and he knew that it was bad. He stepped inside of the building, and was he saw was sheer horror.

There were rows of decomposing bodies of men who had been nailed to giant crosses, and the crosses had been stuck in the ground inside of the dirt floor warehouse. It was a literal warehouse of death. Damian had seen enough. He stepped back out of the building, and closed the door. He pulled off his mask and stared at Marquis with a look of sheer fury.

"Talk to your brother," Marquis told him.

"I will," Damian said, storming off. "You're a bunch of fucking animals!"

Damian made his way to another building, where he threw open the doors and peered inside. The smell of rotting flesh was just as bad as in the previous building, but his anger allowed him to control his stomach. Inside, the scene was just as hellish as the first building. Dante had impaled many with large poles, and stuck them into the ground. In this instance, not all of the corpses were intact, some poles had only heads stuck on the tips. Damian turned to Marquis.

"Take them down," he said quietly.

"Sir..."

"*I said take them down!*" Damian shouted. "Bury them. These, and the ones next door, and any others that you have in your fucking sadistic trophy rooms!"

"*Your brother's* trophy rooms," Marquis said, correcting.

Damian glared at Marquis with a fierce stare, before moving along on his gruesome tour. He came to another building, this one considerably smaller. It was not tall enough to do what had been done in the last two buildings. Damian reached for the door.

"Don't!" Marquis told him, clasping his hand.

"Why not?" Damian asked, glaring at him.

"Because, your brother had it filled with ants, and wasps, and bees," Marquis told him.

"Let me guess, he throws people inside?" Damian asked with a frown.

"Only after handcuffing them and covering them with honey," Marquis told him.

Damian slammed the handle back down, re-locking the door. He made his way to the next building, where he reached for the handle and then paused.

"Is this one safe?" he asked, glaring at Marquis.

Marquis returned Damian's stare with one of his own. Damian opened the door and walked into the room. Blood was covering the floor and walls, and there were people inside. Live people. They were naked, and chained to tables that were slightly inverted. Buckets of water were over their heads, and slow drops from the pails were striking them on their foreheads. In this room, their were not only men, but women as well. Including old women.

"What the fuck?" Damian asked, upon coming upon the oldest of the women.

"Your brother," Marquis told him.

"*Your brother, your brother, your brother,* everything is *your brother*?" Damian shouted. "*What about you? What about the rest of you? You didn't have to do this! You didn't have to be involved in this!* You are responsible for *you! You are responsible for what you do!*"

Marquis stood in silence, glaring at Damian.

"What the fuck did she do?" Damian asked, staring at the old woman.

"We found her at a safe house," Marquis told her.

"Found her at a safe house?"

Marquis nodded. "Not just found her there, but she lived there. She maintained it. She's a part of the underground chain."

"And so you brought her here?" Damian ask, throwing his hands up. "To this place!"

"She wouldn't talk," Marquis told him. "She knows the chain. She knows. She had hidden rooms, a hidden basement, maps, boxes of cheap flashlights, stores of dry food, cases and cases of bottled water hidden in her basement. She's a major part of the human smuggling chain. She knows, and she could lead us up and down the chain."

"And so, you've taken a seventy year old woman, and you're subjecting her to Chinese water torture?" Damian asked, shaking his head. He turned and headed for the exit. "Release her."

"What?"

"I said, let her go."

"She knows about this place!" Marquis told him. "*We can't let her go!* Besides, she could be the key to breaking this open and finding your niece!"

"I don't give a fuck, I said let her go!" Damian shouted.

"*Call Dante!*" Marquis shouted.

Damian stopped. "I don't have to fucking call Dante! Dante works for me, and you work for Dante, and I'm telling you, *to let her go!* I'm also telling you, to clean this shit up. Bury the bodies, shut this place down, and then burn it!"

"Burn it?" Marquis shouted.

"*Burn it!*" Damian told him. "Burn it all. I want nothing left. And the people you have, let them go. Don't execute them, let them go. Do you understand me?"

Marquis remained silent.

Damian turned the corner, and ran smack dab into something he could never have imagined. It was a scene out of Dante's Inferno. There were men tied to spits, hanging above a massive pit of flaming red hot coals. Some of the men were still alive, burnt, but alive. Their skin was charcoal in some spots, red in others, missing in some places, and brown and blistered in many areas. They were all being slow roasted, as if they were pigs at a barbecue. Damian lost it. He had seen enough. In fact, he had seen too much. He turned, and grabbed Marquis by his collar and shoved him up against a nearby steel building.

"*What the fuck is wrong with you people!*" Damian shouted. "*What the fuck is wrong with you!*"

Marquis tried to shove Damian's hands away. Damian's men pulled the two of them apart. Marquis straightened his shirt and stared at Damian.

"*You think you've seen something today?*" Marquis shouted. "*Do you?* Well let me tell you, *you ain't seen shit!* You come down here, and you see twenty minutes worth of torture, and you think you've had enough! Well, *we have to live here!* We have to put up with this shit! We live it day in, and day out! You want to get pissed off at us, when all of this..." Marquis threw his hands up and spun around slowly. "All of this, comes from the twisted mind of your brother."

Damian stared at Marquis, breathing heavily. He didn't want to hear what Marquis was telling him, because it was a hard truth to face. His brother was truly a monster.

"And you know what I think bothers you the most, Damian?" Marquis continued. "I think what bothers you more than anything, is that the two of you are cut from the same cloth! His mind is your mind, and your mind is his mind, and this scares you more than anything! Dante didn't do this, *both* of you did. You empowered this terror, you bankrolled it, you gave him Carte Blanche, and then you conveniently looked the other way. This was your doing just as much as it was his. And this is why you are so pissed off, you hypocritical son-of-a-bitch!"

Damian walked past Marquis heading back to his waiting car. There were many more buildings, and much more to see, but he was done. He wanted to get away from this sadomasochistic carnival of horrors.

"Burn it!" Damian shouted to Marquis. "And send every man here, or that's ever worked here, on a one month paid vacation! And when they come back from vacation, each and every single man, is to be reassigned to San Antonio, and they are to report to Bio One's Asa Yancey Medical Center for psychological treatment. *That's an order!*"

Damian climbed into the back of his Jag, and peered out the window. He was in trouble. More than at any other time in his life, because his brother was in trouble. And Dante and he were one in the same. Marquis had been right about that. They were one. They were the Yin to each other's Yang. Dante needed more than just rest. The situation had been worse than he could ever have imagined. His brother's *mind* was gone. Even if he managed to get Lucky back alive, what kind of father would he be? How could such a monster be allowed to hold such and innocent soul? How could hands so bloody be allowed to push her in a swing in the park? He had paid too heavy of a price in this search to get her back, and that price, was his sanity. His brother needed him. Could he be redeemed was the question though? Could he come back into the world of humans? Could he be made to understand morality, humanity, life, love? Never in a million years would he be able to put his brother down, *never.* But that's what was done to rabid dogs that were out of control. In this case, that was not an option. He would have to find another way to save his brother.

# Chapter Twenty Two

Dante pulled into the supermarket parking lot in his La Ferrari sports car and parked in an empty space far from the store. Grace spotted the red exotic, and knew instantly that it was him. To her surprise, Dante was alone. No massive caravan, no dozens upon dozens of security personnel, no armored SUVs, just Dante alone, in his Ferrari. She didn't know which was more dangerous, a Dante surrounded by men who could perhaps stop him from making a stupid and impulsive move, or a Dante who was alone. She pulled her small black Mercedes into the parking spot next to his, and climbed out with her package of goodies. She walked to the passenger side of Dante's Ferrari, opened the scissor doors, and plopped down inside.

"Nice vehicle."

"Thanks," Dante told her.

"Couldn't be a little more inconspicuous?"

"For what?" Dante asked. "We're in San Antonio. No one is going to stop this car."

Grace shrugged. She guess he had a point. He did have the local police under his thumb.

She opened her large handbag, and pulled out a pair of hand held communicators. She handed them to Dante.

"Give one to Damian, and keep one for yourself," she told him.

"What are these for?" Dante asked.

"You can talk to Damian on these," Grace explained. "They are satellite communication devices. Unbreakable. You were worried about the NSA being able to listen in on your communications."

"They'll be able to break these," Dante told her.

"These are from the DIA," Grace told him. DARPA is testing these for the DOD, and they've proven to be unbreakable. Even for the NSA."

Dante eyed her suspiciously. "How'd you get them?"

"A friend," Grace told him.

"A friend?" Dante asked, lifting an eyebrow.

"A *trustworthy* friend," Grace said, hoping to reassure him. "They're safe."

This time is was Dante who shrugged. Ha sat the communicators down on his dash. Grace pulled out a manila envelope, and pulled some papers from it.

"You wanted the video from the parking lot of the state jail?" Grace asked. "There's a zip drive in this envelope that contains the feed from the parking lot cameras. These are the actual stills that the FBI developed from the camera feed. It's dark, the images have been enhanced as much as possible, but the pictures are still horrible. Also, I have a friend over at the agency who is going to see what he can do for me, as far as cleaning up the images."

Dante nodded. "Thanks."

"I've also enclosed the forensic information from the scene, including the car," Grace continued. "There was a bonanza of fingerprints, and other DNA evidence. Unfortunately, none of the DNA was a match with anyone in the system. Apparently, none of the perps have been to jail before. At least not an American jail. We are checking with the Mexican authorities to see if they can provide us with a match or any kind of identification. Of course, it's a long shot. The Mexican Federal Police's criminal database is antiquated, forget about DNA matching. They don't extract DNA from the people who go through their system. But, it's worth a try anyway."

Dante nodded. "Any information on Nuni's location?"

Grace shook her head.

"Damn!" Dante said, shaking his head.

"Hold up," Grace said, holding up her hand. A smile crept across her face. We both knew that getting a fix on Nuni was going to be next to impossible. Other than finding his main residence, which everyone knows the location of. You wanted to find another way to catch him right? Through a girlfriend, a mistress, some quirky secret habit of his. Well, we could find nothing. His shit is wound tight."

Dante eyed her suspiciously. "Then why are you smiling?"

"Because, I got his family's medical records, and his school records," Grace told him.

Dante smiled and closed his eyes. He knew that Grace had found something.

"He has a sister," Grace told him.

With his eyes still closed, and the smile still plastered across his face, Dante leaned back in the seat of his Ferrari.

"She's here," Grace told him. "In the states."

Dante's eyes flew open wide. "*Get the fuck outta here!*"

Grace shook her head. "Not shitting you. Apparently, she left home at a young age, however, she and her brother were, and still are, extremely close. She's his baby sister, and he's concealed her identity to protect her. I have a copy of her passport, her student visa, and her permanent residency card. She's also applied for U.S. citizenship. She originally come over on a student visa. She received a scholarship to a Catholic boarding school on the East Coast as a young girl. It was set up by her local priest, and the archbishop of her diocese. After primary and secondary, she went on to attend college her. Get this, at Princeton."

Dante banged his fist on the steering wheel of his car. "*Yes!*"

He had him. He knew that he had him. If Nuni wanted to play the kidnapping game, then they could both play that game. He would get this bitch, and he would trade her for his daughter. She was going to be his insurance card, in case he couldn't intercept those motherfuckers heading for the border. The game had just changed.

"You want to know something else?" Grace asked.

"Give it to me?" Dante told her.

"She's in Houston. She works in The Woodlands as an accountant for a big oil company." Grace handed Dante the thick manila envelope. "You want me to swoop her?"

Dante shook his head. "No. I got this one."

"Go get 'em, tiger!" Grace said, opening the door to Dante's Ferrari.

"Grace!"

Grace started to climb out of the car, but stopped. "Yeah?"

Dante leaned over and kissed Grace on her cheek. "Thanks."

She was taken totally by surprise.

Dante knew what Grace had risked to help him  She was way beyond losing her job, what she was giving him, was more than just a lengthy prison sentence, she was providing top secret documents from the NSA, radios from the Department of Defense, as well as other classified materials.

"I won't forget what you've done," Dante told her.

"You get her back," Grace told him.  "You kill everything from Amarillo to Chiapas if you have to, just bring that baby home."

Dante closed his eyes and nodded.

Grace climbed out of the Ferrari and walked to her Mercedes, climbed inside, and drove away.  Dante sat inside of his car, rifling through the folder than Grace had given him.  There was a bonanza of intelligence on the Mexican Cartels, and more importantly, on finding Nuni's sister.  He had a special place that he was going to take her to.

*****

Charlie Jimenez unlocked the door to his gorgeous Spanish style home in Parkland Florida's prestigious Parkland Golf and Country Club Estates.  He had a long night the previous evening, partying in Cuba like there was no tomorrow.  And then came the long flight to Mexico, and the subsequent flight to Miami.  The U.S. embargo against Cuba meant no direct flights between the two countries, which was a drag, especially after a long night of mojitos and beautiful Cuban senoritas.  The last thing he wanted to do, was to spend his day listening to the sound of jet engines roaring next to him, which only compounded his hangover.  He wanted nothing more than to fall into bed and sleep for the next twelve hours.

The lights were off, and the house was quiet, which meant that bitch ass wife of his was gone.  His immediate thoughts were that she had found a baby sitter, and was at the club eating, drinking, dancing, and shoveling cocaine into her nostrils by the spoonful.  If only she hadn't popped out two babies back to back, and if only she was still a good lay, and if only she didn't know so much about his business.  He was full of what ifs when it came to her.  What if he had just fucked her and left her ass alone, he often wondered?  No, he thought, you had to bring the bitch home from the club, and make a wife out of her. Or at least *try* to make a wife out of her, he corrected himself. She lived at the club, and only stopped to pop out the two addicted babies that she had given him. He would have loved to have had the benefit of hindsight.

Charlie tossed his keys on the counter as he headed into his kitchen. He wanted to pop an Advil Liquid Gel before heading off to sleep. He hoped that the little blue miracles would work wonders on his pounding head. He hit the light switch in the kitchen so that he could see what he was doing. To his surprise, he had a guest sitting in the dark in his family room.

"*Princess!*" Charlie shouted. His hand flew to his chest. "*Jesus!* You scared the shit outta me! What the fuck are you doing here?"

"Is that any way to greet your boss, Charlie?" Princess asked. She was sitting in his easy chair with her legs crossed,  She had a silenced pistol sitting across her lap.

"How did you get in here?" Charlie asked.

"Questions, questions, questions," Princess said smiling. "We all have questions."

Inside of the kitchen, Charlie opened up one of his cabinets, and searched the top shelf, where he kept a spare pistol.

"It's not there, Charlie," Princess said, from the family room.

Charlie closed his eyes. He knew what this meant. Princess couldn't see him from the family room, but she knew what he was doing. And she had removed his pistol before he got home. He knew that this was not a social visit. He bolted for the door leading to his garage and opened it. One of Princess's men was standing there with a smile. Charlie's heart felt as if it had  fallen to his feet. He turned, and spied the back door. He could now see that there were men on his back porch as well.

"Why don't you come in here and sit down for a minute, Charlie," Princess told him. "Let's chat. Do a little catching up. You know I've been away for a while."

Charlie closed his eyes. His only chance, was to try to bluff his way through the situation. He put on a brave face, and walked into the family room.

"Why didn't you tell me that you were coming?" Charlie asked. "I could have prepared something."

Princess smiled. "I'm sure you would have loved to have prepared something for me. I came unannounced, because I didn't want anyone *prepared*. I wanted to see what's been going on in my absence. You know what they say, when the cat's away, the treacherous, conniving, backstabbing rats will play."

Princess waved her hand toward a nearby sofa. "Please, have a seat. Have a seat, and tell me what you've been up to."

Charlie swallowed. "I haven't been up to nothing. Same shit, different day."

"Really?" Princess asked, lifting an eyebrow. "So, you take trips to Cuba daily?"

Charlie blinked. She knew too much. How much she knew, he didn't know. But one thing was for certain, she wasn't completely in the dark.

"I just needed to get away for a while," Charlie said, shrugging his shoulders. "You know, a mini-vacation."

"Oh, a mini-vacation, I see," Princess said with a smile. "Well, that must have been nice. And convenient. A trip to Cuba and you were able to kill two birds with one stone. You were able to have a mini-vacation, and meet with the Cuban's big boss man to secure your alliance."

Charlie held up his hand. "Princess, it's not like that! It's not what you're thinking."

"Oh, so now you know what I'm thinking?" Princess asked, lifting an eyebrow. "Okay, well then, tell me this. Tell me what I'm thinking right now."

"I don't know," Charlied told her. "That's not what I meant. What I'm saying, is that it's nothing bad, if that's what's going through your mind."

"Nothing bad?" Princess said, nodding. "My capo, cutting a deal with some Cubans in Miami, and then flying to Cuba to solidify the deal with their boss. That's not bad?"

"It sounds bad, if you say it like that."

"What other way is there to say it?"

"I went to talk to them, to see if we could avoid a war," Charlie explained. "And I also wanted to see if we could solidify our supply."

"Oh, so you did this for *us*?" Princess asked. "I see. You did it all for the good of the family."

"Yeah," Charlie said softly.

"And who else has been helping you to do things to help out the family?" Princess asked.

"What do you mean?" Charlie asked, turning up his palms.

"Who else in my organization, has been cutting deals to help me out?" Princess asked. "Arturo? Benny? Daniel? Enrique? Fernando? Gustavo? Israel? Jaime? Who?"

Charlie shook his head.

"Surely, you aren't the only one trying to help out the family, Charlie. Who else?"

"Princess, it's not what you *think*!" Charlie said adamantly.

Princess nodded to her men, who were now standing behind Charlie. They grabbed him.

"*Princess!*" Charlie shouted.

"You betrayed me, and cut a deal with the Cubans, you son-of-a-bitch!" Princess told him. she rose from the chair.

"*I didn't!*"

"You were supposed to be taking care of Miami for me, while I was away," Princess told him. "And look at it! Look at the situation you have me in! I was forced to come back and deal with this shit, despite being needed in Texas. My brother needs me, my niece needs me, and instead of being *there*, I have to be *here*, dealing with a bunch of traitorous son-of-a-bitches!"

"Princess, look at the situation you left us in!" Charlie shouted. "*You weren't here!* You left me to deal with Miami! Well, I don't know if you know it or not, but the fucking Cubans control all of South Florida! They had the connections, they have the political protection, they have the mayor's offices, the police departments, the state representatives, everything! And they have the banks, the money, the manpower, and so when they say deal, *you deal!* I did what I fucking had to do!"

"You took the easy way out, and cut a deal for your own ass, instead of being loyal to me!" Princess shouted.

"You were a thousand miles away!" Charlie shouted back. "I'm here! I live here, my family lives here! The Cubanos, they are *here!*"

"It's called loyalty, *Charlie!* You ever heard of it!"

"It called *survival*, Princess! You ever had to worry about it?"

"You had men, you could have *fought!*" Princess told him. "You could have asked for help. I would have sent you men to fight with!"

"From who?" Charlie shouted. "From where? Look around you! Are you blind? You think Tampa is going to send men to help *me*? Ft. Meyers? Orlando? St. Petersburg? Tallahassee? Are you stupid? You don't have a state, or a family, you have a bunch of different bosses under you, who hate each other! There's no family here. There's no loyalty, no organization. You took over a *mess*, and you haven't spent one day, or one dime, trying to organize it or put it together! You wanted Florida so that you could have the manpower to fight your brothers, and once that fight was over with, you abandoned the state just as quickly as you swept through it. And then, you had the nerve to ask us, the people you left here, to work miracles! I'm Charlie Jimenez, *not Jesus Christ!*"

Princess slapped Charlie. It was not about breaking him, or about his insubordination, but because he had slapped her. Not physically, but slapped her with the truth. She had taken Florida, she had swept through the state like a hurricane, building support against a fat, weak, cigar chomping tyrant, who everyone was happy to see go. The various capos and underbosses around the state were happy to join her and the men she brought with her from Texas. Together, they fought and rid the state of Don Alemendez, and then they happily joined her in her war against her brothers. There was so much optimism back then. They all believed that she was going to return the state to its former glory, restore its position among the pantheon of drug states, and shift the majority of the nation's cocaine entrance points to Florida. This of course, would have meant billions for the cappos and underbosses of the state, and along with that tide of money, the prestige that came with it. In their minds, it was going to be the 1980's all over again. And then, she abandoned them. As soon as the war was over with, she raced back to Texas, and starting to help run her brothers empire, instead of tending to her own. The state's current state of affairs were of her own doing, and it was this hard, cold, indisputable fact that was now confronting her. She had made her bed, and now she was being forced to lie in it.

"Who else is in on this?" Princess demanded. "Who else cut a deal?"

"You think we work together?" Charlie asked. "You actually think that we would trust each other enough to work together?"

"I know that you aren't alone in your betrayal," Princess told him. "When they came to you, they would have told you who else was already on board, in order for you to see the futility of trying to go it alone."

Charlie shook his head. "The north and the south, *are at war!*"

"Yeah, because the southern part of the state is rolling with the Cubans, and the northern part of the state has cut a deal with the Pueto Ricans," Princess told him. "Who else has jumped ship, you fucking rat?"

"Everyone," Charlie said, eying her with disgust. "You are alone, and without an army, with thousands of Cubans on the streets of southern Florida, and with hundreds of Puerto Ricans on the streets of northern Florida. Go back home to Texas, while you still have a chance."

Princess smiled. She nodded at her men once again. One of them punched Charlie in his stomach, causing him to fold. Others started ripping off his clothing. Another one of her men, handed her a large pair of bolt cutters.

"I'm not going home, Charlie," Princess told him. "In fact, I *am* home. Unfortunately for you, you're the first to learn of it. However, I'm confident, that once the others learn that I'm back, and they learn the price of betrayal, they'll quickly return to the fold."

Charlied eyed the bolt cutters and slowly began shaking his head. The fact that her men had stripped him naked told him enough. "Princess, no!"

"Charlie, yes," Princess said smiling, and walking closer to where he was being held.

Charlie began to struggle fiercely, and kick at her. His legs were grabbed by two more men, and he was lifted into the air, and his legs were spread apart.

"Not much there to began with," Princess said, eying his private parts. She rammed the bolt cutters beneath the base of his penis, and then snipped. Blood shot everywhere, and Charlie howled.

Princess adjusted her bolt cutter, and snipped off Charlie's testicles.

"The only reason I'm cutting off your balls, Charlie, is because I like you," she told him. "This will help you bleed out faster. If I didn't like you, I would have just cut off your dick, put a bullet in your head, and been done with it. I'll spare you the bullet. Just relax, and go to sleep."

Charlie continued to struggle and scream. The blood loss was rapid, and his struggling and shouting only increased his heart rate, which made his blood pump faster, which in turn allowed him to bleed out quicker. His resistance quickly began to fade, and his words began to slur.

"That's it," Princess told him. "Don't fight it, just close your eyes, and rest."

Soon, Charlie was out. Her men laid his body on the floor, in a giant pool of his own blood. Princess eyes his penis on the floor, and turned to one of her men.

"Pick up his dick, and stick it in his mouth. When they find him, I want the word to get around that Charlie was found dead with his dick in his mouth. The rest of these motherfuckers will get the message. Princess is home."

# Chapter Twenty Three

Stacia watched in amusement as Infiniti after Infiniti pulled into the park, and deposited its bespoke occupants before pulling away in order to make room for the next SUV. The scene reminded her so much of Washington D.C., and the Secret Service's advance teams that deployed before the President's arrival. Damian had this type of security. In some ways it must be nice, she thought. In other ways, he must feel like a bird trapped in a gilded cage. The world watching him, some for good reasons, and many for bad. Never being able to just live his life, or be himself. Always on guard, never able to just say what he thinks. And it wasn't just because of his *other* life, the life of crime syndicate boss, but also because he was the CEO of a couple of major global corporations.

As the CEO and owner of Bio One, a misstatement from him could cause ripples in the health care market, and cause price spikes that would make everyday medications unaffordable for millions of everyday Americans. And being able to afford chronic care medication, or critical care medication, was a matter of life and death for many. As the CEO of Energia Oil, the wrong statement from him, could cause major ripples through the global oil markets. It could affect the price of not only gasoline, but home heating oil, and more importantly, plastics and other oil based products. And plastic was used to manufacture everything. It was in cars, everyday appliances, medical equipment, military equipment, airplanes, and food packaging. It was a vital global resource, and the price it cost to *package* food, affected the price that consumers *paid* for food. The price to get that food to market, and the price of the fuel used in the combines to harvest the crops that become the food, would also be affected. Higher food prices, meant the ability to buy less of it, which meant less food getting to those who were already on the brink of food insecurity. One wrong statement literally meant life and death for millions. She wondered what it meant to shoulder that kind of burden, to have to live with it constantly, day in, and day out, never being out of the bubble, never having a moment to yourself. Compound this with the fact that he also had many people who hated the fact that he was young and Black, and this coupled with the fact that he had many men all across the globe who wanted him dead. He was the brains of the Reigns family. This was understood not only by rival CEOs, but also by drug cartels all across the globe. All of which would love nothing better than to cut the head off of the Reigns empire, or cut the head off of the snake, depending on how one looked at it. It all made her feel for Damian.

Damian's white Rolls Royce Phantom pulled up and stopped in front of the park bench where Stacia was seated. The bodyguard sitting in the front passenger seat hopped out and opened the rear door for Damian, who climbed out, buttoned his suit, and headed to where Stacia was seated.

"The emperor has arrived!" Stacia proclaimed. She opened her arms wide, and she and Damian embraced tightly. "Hey, Love."

Damian kissed her on her cheek. "Hey gorgeous."

Stacia patted her hair. "Thanks for the lie."

"I don't lie" Damian said, shaking his head. "You are growing more and more beautiful with each passing year. One day, I'm going to trick you into telling me where you've hidden the Fountain of Youth."

Stacia waved off his compliment. "You've always been a smooth talker, Damian Reigns. That's how you tricked me outta my panties when we were young and dumb and full of cum."

"I tricked *you*?" Damian said laughing, and pressing his hand against his chest. "I believe it was you who practically ripped my clothes off and took my... you know..."

Stacia laughed. "After all these years, you still can't say it. Say it, Damian! Just once, let me hear you say it. Say something crude and rude, with even the slightest hint of disrespect. Lite my fires, baby!"

Damian laughed, and waved his hand toward the empty spot on the bench next to where she was seated. "May I?"

"Of course," Stacia told him. She scooted over slightly, to give him more room. "Have a seat, and tell me what's happening in your life. Catch me up on all the good, the bad, and the ugly."

"Which do you want first?" Damian asked. "I'm afraid I only have bad news, and worse news."

Stacia laughed. "That bad, huh?"

Damian nodded.

Stacia slapped him across his knee. "Tell me about it. Some days I think if it wasn't for bad news, I wouldn't have any at all. So, your therapy first, and then we'll deal with my issues."

Damian peered into the sky. "We don't have that much time."

Stacia laughed. "I'm not *that* messed up. Well, maybe I am, but the people around me are used to my psychopathic ways."

"Ahhh!" Damian said, peering away. "Why'd you even have to bring that up?"

"What's that? My psychopathic ways?"

"Anything to do with mental instability is not a good subject at this point."

Stacia nodded. "The search has been pretty hard on you, huh?"

"Yes, but the good thing about it is that I'm still sane. The bad news is that Dante is not."

"Damian, that's not news," Stacia said, tilting her head toward him. "Dante has been crazy, ever since we were kids."

Damian shook his head. "Not like this. Not in this way. He's *really* gone."

Stacia could tell that Damian was serious. The smile she had slowly left her face. "Talk to me."

Damian sat back on the park bench and folded his arms. He stared at the ground. "He has a place. A ranch, near the border."

Stacia nodded. "Go on."

"It's not really a ranch," Damian continued. He shifted his gaze and peered into her eyes briefly. "They call it Little Guantanamo."

Instantly, Stacia realized where Damian was going with it. "Oh, no."

"Yeah," Damian said nodding. "I went there. I mean, I heard the whispers, the rumors, the innuendo, but I just dismissed it. I said, they don't really know Dante. They don't know what he's going through. I rationalized, and blew it off, and ignored it as long as I could. And in the meantime..."

Damian shook his head and lowered it. Stacia caressed his back.

"Come on now," she told him. "Don't do that. You didn't know."

"I *did* know," Damian told her. "Not the details, and I really didn't want to know the details. And because I didn't want to know, those people..."

"*Hey*, Dante is responsible for what Dante does," Stacia said, rubbing his back. "Damian is *not* responsible for this. Get that out of your mind."

"He's my brother."

Stacia nodded. "I know."

Damian shook his head again. "Stacia, I went down there, and there were people in dog cages. There were people...bodies, hung on pikes. There were crucified bodies, hanging on crosses. He had dozens and dozens of torture rooms. I saw rooms covered in blood."

Stacia closed her eyes. "Oh my God..."

"Stacia, I saw men being slow roasted over a pit of hot coals like they were a slab of beef!"

Stacia's sniffled, and rested her hand on her forehead. "I'm sorry, Damian."

"I don't know what to do," Damian said, shaking his head. He began to rock back and forth on the park bench. "I ordered them to shut that place down. I ordered it shut down. But that's the least of my worries. My brother... He's gone, Stacia. And I don't know how to bring him back. How do you come back from something like this? How?"

Stacia began to rub Damian's back once again. "I don't know, Damian. I don't know."

"I don't know what to do!" Damian said, showing his frustration. "I can't give up on him, I can't! Never. He's my brother, and I have to do whatever I can to save him."

"And you don't think this is a result of Lucky being taken?" Stacia asked. "You don't think he'll come back from it on his own?"

"It's wholly a result of Lucky's kidnapping, and I don't know how he can. He crossed the line, Stacia. He went *way over* the line. The stuff I saw, was inhuman. Not just inhumane, but inhuman." Damian shook his head. "His mind..."

"His mind is strong," she said, caressing him. "Dante will be Dante, and he'll come out of it. He'll be okay."

"I saw inside the mind of a pyscho, Stacia. It was like one of those serial killer profiles that you see on T.V. Except this one, was my brother. What do you do, if your brother is the serial killer?"

"He's not a serial killer, Damian. He's a father. I think you are getting the two confused. He's a man who will move mountains to see his little girl safe. That's different. That's a different kind of monster. If he was doing this just on GP, then that would be different. He's doing what he's doing, for a reason, I suppose. What was his reason?"

Damian shrugged. "I haven't spoken to him since I found out. I don't know what to say to him. And he hasn't spoken to me. Maybe we're both avoiding each other, maybe it's the shame of it all that's keeping us from talking."

"If he was doing this, it had to be for a reason," Stacia told him.

"It was," Damian conceeded. "He's trying to find out where the kidnappers are heading. He knows they are heading for the border, and he's trying to get on their path. He's trying to find the safe houses, the tunnels, and who's helping them."

Stacia nodded. "And they must have a lot of help. They set this thing up and planned it and executed it well. They are avoiding all of the roadblocks that the highway patrol has thrown up, and the only way they can do that, is with help. They may not even be road bound. They may have gone off road, and are probably moving slowly, and only at night, under the cover of darkness, with no headlights. He's smart for trying to get on their trail that way."

"He's using a sledgehammer to swat a gnat," Damian said. "His tactics are brutal, sadistic even. It's worse than just a scorched Earth policy, it's mass murder. That place, that compound, it's a place of mass atrocities. Bodies impaled, heads on pikes, it's something out of a Bram Stoker movie, or a Vlad Tepish novel."

"Dante is going to be okay," Stacia repeated. "What he's doing makes sense when you think about it."

"Torturing people?"

"Getting them to talk."

"By torturing them to death?"

"And then leaving the bodies for the next person to see," Stacia

217

nodded. "It shows that he means business."

"They already know he means business," Damian shot back. "Once he takes them there, and they see that place, without a doubt, they know he means business."

"Damian, don't worry yourself into a stroke over this, okay?"

"My brother's insane, and you're telling me not to worry about it."

"Not yet," Stacia said. She gave him a reassuring half smile. "Let him get Lucky back, and then see."

"Do we really want him to have custody over her?"

"Could you even stop it?" Stacia asked, exhaling.

Damian turned away. He couldn't stop it. Nothing short of death would keep Dante from his daughter.

Stacia rose from the bench. She nodded down a long winding road that traveled through the park. "Let's walk."

"Walk?" Damian asked, peering up at her.

"Yes, *walk!* You've heard of it, haven't you? A little exercise is good for you. I'm sure you're not getting enough." Stacia grabbed Damian's hands and pulled him up. "C'mon, lazy boy!"

Damian shook his head. "That's what bother's me about you negroes on the East Coast. You have subway systems, overcrowded streets, and so you want to *walk* everywhere."

"And you negroes in the South want to *drive* everywhere. You'll drive to a store right around the corner instead of getting your fat pork eating asses up and walking."

"*Oh! Oh! So you want to go there!* You're in D.C. now, so now we're fat, pork eating, biscuit and gravy slopping negroes! I see you've flipped the script!"

Stacia laughed.

"East coast liberal elite!" Damian told her.

"Hey, we drive," Stacia said, interlacing their arms, and starting off down the street. "It's impossible to get to Tyson's Corner without some wheels."

"Oh, shopping trips, I see."

"So, have you been getting some exercise?" Stacia asked, lifting an eyebrow.

"Lately, not in your life. Before all of this happened? Sometimes."

"Don't get all fat on me," Stacia told him. "I won't take you back once you're all old and cripple if you're fat too."

Damian laughed heartily. "Oh really? You're going to take me back, are you? I didn't know that you got rid of me."

"Damian, I can't get rid of you. But at the same time, I don't want your shady ass."

"How did I become shady?" Damian asked, pressing his hand to his chest. "Explain."

"You are, and you know you are. But I got something for your ass once you're old and senile."

Again, Damian laughed. "Old person abuse. I'll make sure to have everything set up so that you won't be able to come near me."

"As if anyone could stop me."

"So, you're going to be in your wheelchair, and I'm going to be in mine, and what?"

"I'm not going to be in a wheelchair. I exercise and eat healthy."

"So, you're going to bash me upside my head with your cane?"

"It would only break the cane, Damian Reigns," Stacia said, shaking her head. "Your head is harder than a piece of steel."

Again Damian laughed. And then, he exhaled forcibly. "If only..."

"What?"

"If only it could be like this all of the time," he told her. Walking through the park, watching the kids play, listening to the birds chirp. If only."

"Why can't it be?" Stacia asked. "What's stopping you? Money? You have more than enough. The thrill? You've done it all already, Wonder Boy. So, what's stopping you. What's stopping you from taking your family's businesses public, cashing in on the windfall, and then retiring to somewhere exotic. Buy your own island. Hell, buy a couple of them. Build you a mansion in Dubai, and another one in Paris, and one in Geneva, or Gstaad, or Milan, or Madrid. Hell, build you one in all of them. Buy you a luxury apartment in London. Take that massive yacht of yours around the world. Travel, relax, take care of your health, enjoy life. Live life the way it was meant to be lived. You have enough money, Damian. Cash out, Baby. Take the money and run, and leave the madness behind."

"Damn, that sounds so good."

"Then do it!" Stacia told him. "What's there to think about?"

"Lucky, for one. Dante's sanity for seconds. Princess is struggling to maintain Florida. California is slipping away. Bio One is still facing a massive class action suit. Energia Oil is barely afloat, because we over invested in oil fields, and now the bottom is about to fall out of the oil market. We're one recession away in China from global oil prices collapsing. Let's see, what else is turning me prematurely gray and keeping me up at night?"

"Wow!" Stacia said, whistling. "I had no idea it was *that* bad."

"It's worse. Those are just the things that I could think of off the top of my mind."

Stacia stopped and faced him. "Let it go, Damian. I don't want to lose you over no bullshit. Black men, stress, high blood pressure, you're a ticking time bomb. Let it go. It's not worth your life, none of it is. And your kids, our kids, they are going to need a father to turn to for advice. I need you to be around for them, they need you to be around for them. I need you to be around for me."

Stacia caressed the side of Damian's face. Damian took her hand and kissed it.

"Are you going to put your money where your mouth is?" he asked.

"What do you mean?"

"You expect me to travel to all of those places alone?" Damian asked with a smile.

"I'll come and chill with you in Paris, and Dubai, and Bali, and London, and wherever there is out of this world shopping venues."

"Well, thanks," Damian told her.

Stacia smiled. "No problem. It'll be your money I'm spending."

Damian laughed. "I knew it would be."

"Damian, what would you ever do without me?" Stacia asked.

Damian shook his head. "I don't know. Maybe have more money to spend?"

"You can't take it with you," Stacia said, winking her eye.

She had what no other woman on the planet had, she had access to Damian's money. She had an American Express Centurion Card that he paid, as well as a JP Morgan Palladium Card that he gave her. She also had a debit card giving her access to his personal bank account. Stacia had those things, because she also had something that no other woman currently had, which was Damian's heart. He could marry, she could marry, but they would always love each other.

"I need you here," Damian told her.

Stacia nodded. "I know."

He needed her strength, her advice, her companionship. He needed the strength of a Reigns woman by his side, and Stacia was as much a Reigns as he was. They had grown up together, and she knew more about him than any other person on the planet. She had been his first love, his first kiss, his first time. She was his junior and senior prom date, and more than anything, she had been his best friend growing up. And then, he left for Harvard, and while he was away, Princess had took his family in a different direction. It was a direction that would alter all of their lives. The fact that Stacia's father was the Special Agent in Charge of the FBI's San Antonio field office, cemented all of their fates. He was literally torn apart from the woman he was destined to marry.

"One day, Stacia, one day," Damian told her.

Stacia knew what he was saying. They long ago had stopped needing full sentences, or even words to communicate.

"Is that a promise, Damian? Or a threat?"

Damian laughed and nodded. "With us, Stacia, it's probably both."

Stacia clasped Damian's hand, and the two of them strolled leisurely through the park. Thoughts of what had been, what was not to be, and what was yet to come permeated both of their minds. There was so much between them, so much history, and a vast uncertain future, but both took comfort in knowing that whatever came their way, they would face it together. Both took comfort in knowing that they would always have each other.

# Chapter Twenty Four

Darius walked down the hall of his sister's house, and accidentally bumped into a surprise guest.

"What?" Darius fumbled his words. "What are you doing here?"

"Leaving," Peaches said under her breath.

Darius peered down the hall to his left and then to his right, to make sure that no one was around. "That's not what I meant. What are you doing here, at my sister's house?"

"She insisted that I stay here!" Peaches said under her breath. "She had me leave the hotel and come and stay with her."

"You didn't have to accept," Darius told her.

"Oh, so you have a problem with it?"

"Not like that!" Darius said, shaking his head. "Why is everything an argument with you?"

"Everything is not an argument with me!"

"Yes it is! You've been tripping ever since you woke up in Maryland. Just say thank you!"

"*What?*"

"I *said*, just say thank you!" Darius repeated.

"So, now I *owe* you?" Peaches asked. "Is this something you'll be throwing up in my face from now on? I have to lay down and do what you say now?"

"Dude, what's wrong with you?" Darius asked. "Why didn't you bring your crazy medicine with you? I didn't say anything like that! I'm just saying, you're always tripping with me, and I'm not the enemy!"

"I didn't say that you were the enemy."

"Okay," Darius said, holding up his hands. "Tell me why we are arguing right now? What are we even getting into it about?"

"We're not getting into it. You just acted like you had a problem because I was *here*."

"I knew that you were in town, it just surprised me that you were staying at my sister's house, that's all," Darius told her. "Forgive me if it came out the wrong way."

Darius wrapped his arms around Peaches' waist and pulled her close.

"I was hoping you were in the hotel, that way I could come over and spend a little quality time with you," he said smiling.

"Yeah, right. Here, in Texas? Where your sister and your brothers probably have twenty four hour surveillance on everybody and everything in the city?"

"Forget about them," Darius told her. He leaned forward and kissed her cheek. "How are you feeling?"

"Better," Peaches said, placing her hands on top of his, and removing them from around her waist. "Don't be stupid, Darius. Anybody can turn that corner at any minute."

"Okay, well, let's get outta here then," Darius told her.

"I'm not ready for that," Peaches told him.

"I'm not talking about doing *that*," Darius told her. He *was* disappointed, and hoping that she was up to it. "We can go and grab something to eat."

"I can't," Peaches told him. "I have to get ready to get outta here."

"Where are you going?"

Peaches tilted her head to the side and smacked her lips. "You know where I'm going. I'm going home."

Darius smacked his lips. "Not that shit again."

Peaches shook her head. She didn't want to get into an argument about this again. "Man, there you go. *I have to go home, Darius!*"

"Why? So they can kill you? Blow your fucking skull off?"

Peaches shifted her weight to one side. "I have to go back, because it's *home*."

"You don't have a home there!" Darius said, pointing north. "It's blown to pieces, remember? And what was left of it, is burnt to a crisp."

"I have to find out about my brother," Peaches told him. "You have brothers don't you? Wouldn't you be worried about them? Isn't Dante spending millions of dollars to find his daughter? Well, I want to know about mines too."

"I understand that," Darius told her. "Can you just give me a minute?"

"Give you a minute?" Peaches recoiled and folded her arms. "Give you a minute for what?"

"To let me get some dudes together," Darius told her. "Give us a little bit of time to find my niece, and that'll give you time to heal up. And once we get her back, that'll free up all kinds of men and money. I can get you back to Ohio in style. We can protect you."

Peaches shook her head. "I don't need all that. In fact, it might be better if I can just sneak back into town quietly. If nobody knows I'm there, I'll be safe. I can find my brother and my girls before anybody knows what's up."

"I found your girl, V," Darius told her.

"*What? Where?* How is she?"

"She's with my kinfolk," Darius told her. "He got her outta the city. Took her up to a spot my family has in Michigan."

Peaches felt joy, but it was fleeting. "And my brother?"

Darius shook his head.

"Trap?"

Again, Darius shook his head. "Nothing. Still checking."

Peaches rubbed her eyes. "And when did you find out about V? When were you going to tell me about her?"

Darius held up his hands. "Relax, man! I just found out about her. I was going to tell you as soon as I saw you. I'm not trying to hide nothing from you."

Peaches eyed him suspiciously. "I need to go back."

"Give me a chance," Darius pleaded. "Will you just be patient!"

"Be patient!" Peaches shouted. "My brother could be laying a fucking gutter, or in the morgue, waiting on somebody to identify him or claim his body! And you want me to be patient."

"He could be on a beach chilling somewhere," Darius told her. "See? We can both pull shit out of our ass and just throw it out there!"

"That's why I need to go back," Peaches told him. "I can find out for sure, and I won't be guessing or just pulling shit outta my ass!"

"Give me a week," Darius told her. "A couple of days, and let's see what happens. "Give me time to get some of my kinfolks together, and we'll go up there with you."

Peaches shook her head emphatically. "You can't go up there with me!"

"Why not?"

"Because, you just can't!"

"Why?" Darius asked, turning up his palms.

"Because, it's different. You're not from there, you don't know the city."

"Watching somebody's back, is watching somebody's back," Darius told her. "The principal remains the same, no matter what city you're in."

Peaches thought about Chesarae and Darius running into each other. She saw nothing but gun play coming out of it. And if Ches won, the Reigns family would blame her. If Darius won, then Ohio would label her a cross action bitch, and she wouldn't survive long under that situation either. It was a no win situation. She had to make sure that their paths never crossed.

"You can't go up there," she said, shaking her head. "Not like this. Not the way shit is now. It's too dangerous, and you don't know the city. I can't protect you."

"Protect *me!*" Darius burst into laughter. "I'm going up there to protect *you!*"

"Forget about it."

Darius stared at her. "This is about that nigga isn't it? You still fucking with that nigga aren't you?"

Peaches stared at him. He had hurt her. The eyes that once looked at her as perfect, were now looking at her accusingly, and it hurt her.

"You think I'm trifling, huh?" Peaches asked. "Thanks for letting me know what you *really* think."

"I'm just saying!" Darius told her. "Why the fuck you don't want me in Ohio? And the only reason I can think of, is that nigga you so in love with!"

"You know what, if that's how you want to carry it, then it's whatever!" Peaches said, throwing up her hands in frustration.

"Don't go out like that!" Darius told her. "I know plenty of chicks who got caught, and want to play *that* game! Oh, if you want to say it is, then that's what it is! I'm hip to that shit!"

"What the fuck you want me to say?" Peaches asked. "Hell, you gone believe what you want to believe, so why the fuck I'mma sit here and argue with my damn self!"

"You right, I'm just looking at it wrong," Darius said nodding. "I should have known better."

"What?" Peaches asked, lifting an eyebrow.

"You heard me," Darius told her.

"What the fuck is *that* supposed to mean?" Peaches asked. "*You should have known better?*"

Darius turned and started to walk away, Peaches grabbed him. He knocked her hand away.

"Have a nice life!" Darius told her.

Peaches swung, striking Darius in the back of his head. Darius clasped his head.

"What the fuck are you doing?" he shouted.

"You wanna play me like that?" Peaches asked.

"I'm just saying!" Darius said, still holding his head. "I know when to get the fuck out the way! Three's a crowd, Lil Momma!"

"If you say so!" Peaches said, standing with her fist still balled up.

"Until you say otherwise!" Darius shot back. "What else am I supposed to believe? You got the nigga's birthday, and social security number and anniversary dates and all kinds of shit as your passwords. You don't want me to come to Ohio, so what else am I to believe?"

"What about trust?" Peaches shouted. "Believe in *me*! *Trust me!*"

Darius waved his hand, dismissing her last statement. Peaches swung on him again, and he grabbed her. Dajon turned the corner and stood, staring at both of them.

"*Shit!*" Peaches declared.

Darius turned, to find his brother staring at them. Dajon shook his head.

"It's not what you think," Peaches said, clearing her throat.

"What am I thinking?" Dajon asked.

Darius maneuvered himself so that Peaches was behind him, as if he were about to defend her with his body from a stranger's attack. Dajon let out and half smile, and again shook his head.

"This is not cool," Dajon told them. "You two, are on some dangerous fucking ground."

"It's not like that," Peaches said again, shaking her head.

"I was born at night, but not last night," Dajon told them. He stared at his brother. "What are you doing?"

Darius smiled nervously.

"*She's a member of The Commission!*" Dajon told him. "A *full fledged* member of The Commission! Are you stupid?"

"Dajon..."

"Do you know what would happen if Princess found out about this?" Dajon asked. "Or Dante, for that matter? *Do you?* Did you *think*? Did you stop and take one second to think? And I'm talking about with the head you have on your shoulders, not the one in your damn pants!"

"Bro!"

"*How could you be so stupid!*" Dajon shouted.

"It just happened, okay!" Darius shouted back.

"How could something like this *just happen?*" Dajon asked. "How? Explain that to me, please Darius, because I really want to know. Did your dick just accidentally fall into her?"

"You married Anjounette, and she was a member of The Commission," Darius shot back. "What makes this so different?"

"I went to Louisiana to help her with control over her ex-husbands capos," Dajon explained. "And it just happened. We fell for one another."

"Okay, so did we!" Darius told him. "You, more than anyone else should understand. It happens. You can't help it when it does."

"They are going to say that she's using you for information and influence," Dajon told him. "Dante is going to be suspicious. Princess is going to want to kill her. And both of them are going to be wondering what you are telling her about the family."

"*Dante killed Anjounette's husband!*" Darius told him. "They weren't suspicious that she might just be trying to get revenge and kill you? Or that she was tying to find out stuff about the family to pay us back? Why is there a double standard?"

"Dante is not going to hear that," Dajon told him. "You two are very lucky that he's busy right now."

"I'll go to Damian," Darius said flatly. "I'll tell him everything. I love her."

"Are you stupid?" Dajon asked. "Damian will have you *both* killed."

"No he wouldn't," Darius said, shaking his head.

"Okay, maybe not *you*, but she would be dead in a week," Dajon said, nodding toward Peaches. "And The Commission would go ape shit if they found out. They spent *years* trying to reduce our influence around the table, and now? What do you think they would do if they found out that a new member, a member that we pushed for, was dating Damian's brother? Do you honestly think they would stand for that? She would be a bigger target than Dante, or me, or Princess!"

"Okay, so help us," Darius told him. "What do we do?"

"Leave each other alone!" Dajon said firmly. "Forget about each other. Whatever you had, or *thought* you had, leave it in the past. Chalk it up to a good time, or whatever. But leave each other alone, and never, ever, speak about this again."

Darius shook his head. "Can't do that, bro."

Dajon peered over his brother's shoulder toward Peaches. "What's going on in Ohio?"

"Ohio is under control," Darius told his brother.

"That's not what I heard from the other room," Dajon told them.

"Forget about what you heard," Darius told him.

"My first loyalty, is to this family," Dajon told him. "Make sure yours is as well."

"I'm loyal to this family!" Dajon told him. "*This is not about that!* Would you have given up Anjounette, if Damian had told you to? And don't give me that *for the good of the family* bullshit! This has nothing to do with that. She has her *own* family, her *own* state, and I have *nothing*. I don't own shit, run shit, or r*epresent shit*! And I love her."

Dajon exhaled.

"Help us."

"How?" Dajon said, shaking his head.

"She needs to go back to Ohio," Darius told him. "I need to go with her."

"Darius..." Peaches said softly.

Darius shook his head. "She needs *men*. Not a lot, but enough."

"With the way things are now?" Dajon ask, throwing his hands up, and then pointing toward the border. "Dante has every available man we have!"

"Pull some from New Orleans," Darius told him.

Dajon shook his head. "I can't. New Orleans is already thread bare."

"Bro, please!" Darius pleaded. "She can't go back to Ohio alone. I'm not sending her back with nothing but a shampoo bottle in her carry-on luggage. I'll go myself, and it'll be just me and her, if I have to."

Dajon closed his eyes and shook his head. "I'll pull five from New Orleans, five from Baton Rouge, five from Shreveport, and five from Alexandria. I may be able to pull some men outta Opelousas, and Monroe. That'll give you thirty soldiers. You don't have them for long. Do what you need to do. Get your people back online, and send me my men back."

"Thanks, bro!" Darius told him.

Dajon rolled his eyes at Darius, and then at Peaches. "Don't ever make me regret this."

"You won't," Darius told him.

"And *you don't go!*" Dajon told him. "Those are my conditions. You stay away from that place. You got that?"

Darius peered over his shoulder toward Peaches, who nodded. He turned back to his brother. "Deal."

"Good," Dajon told them. "Now, get outta here, before Princess shows up. And next time, be a lot more careful."

Darius nodded. He turned to Peaches. "I gotta go."

Peaches nodded. "Thank you."

"I love you," Darius said. It was the first time he had ever said it to her. The words hit her hard. He had gone to bat for her once again. Defended her once again. Stood up to his brother on her behalf.

"I love you, Darius," Peaches said softly.

Darius kissed her cheek. "Go pack. I'll make the arrangements. Remember, Brandon still has soldiers up there also. I'll get my kinfolk to meet you at the airport. You'll be safe."

Peaches nodded, caressed the side of Darius' face. "I know. I know that you'll always keep me safe."

Darius turned, and walked to his brother. He put his arm around

Dajon's shoulder, and the two of them headed off. Peaches turned, and walked back to her room so that she could pack. She was going back to Ohio. Brandon had men already in place, Dajon was giving her more men, Darius' cousin was going to meet her in Ohio with Vendetta. Yeah, she was going back home, and boy were they all going to be in for a big surprise, because she was bringing with her, an army.

# Chapter Twenty Five

Damian's Rolls rolled across the tarmac to a private jet sitting on a distant runway. The airport was a small municipal airport just on the outskirts of Kerrville, Texas. It was large enough to land a private jet, and yet not busy enough to for a lot of eyes to see it. The jet was a Canadian Bombadier registered out of Mexico, and it belonged to members of the Yucatan Cartel.

Damian's Rolls Royce rolled to a stop next to the jet. The rest of his caravan quickly dismounted their vehicles and surrounded the jet to provide security. Damian's driver open the door for him, just as the stairs on the jet were descending to the tarmac. Damian buttoned his suit, and jogged up the steps and into the waiting jet. He was greeted warmly once inside.

"*Senor Reigns*!" Johnny Talamantez said. He rose from his creme colored leather seat and opened his arms wide, embracing Damian. "Wonderful to finally meet you in person."

"A pleasure to meet you as well, *Senor...*"

"Talamantez, but please, call me Johnny."

"A pleasure to meet you Johnny," Damian told him.

Talamantez waived his hand toward a nearby chair. "Please, make yourself comfortable."

"Thank you," Damian said, unbuttoning his suit jacket and taking a seat.

"May I offer you something to drink?" Talamantez asked.

Damian waved his hand. "No, thank you."

One of Talamantez's men poured a glass of liquor, and handed it to him. Talamantez took a long drink from the glass.

"Mexican premium Tequila!" Talamantez declared. "The best! None of the commercial stuff they sell in the stores. Are you sure you don't want anything?"

Damian shook his head.

"Well," Talamantez said, sitting his glass down onto a small, but expensive birch wood tray sitting next to him. "I guess you're wondering why we asked for this meeting."

Damian nodded and smiled. "That did cross my mind."

"Well, first off, I want to say that Senor Yanez sends his warmest regards to you, as well as his deepest sympathies for the kidnapping of your niece, and he wants you to know that he prays for her safe return."

"Please tell Senor Yanez, that those words were well received, and they brought joy and comfort to my heart," Damian told him. "The Reigns family thanks him for his kindness, and friendship, and wish nothing more than to continue to deepen our bonds of friendship in the years to come."

Talamantez nodded. He exchanged glances with another person on the plane, and then shifted his gaze toward the third man seated with them inside of the cabin. Damian knew who the third man was because of Nicanor's intelligence briefing. He was Chuchi Espinoza, Don Benito Yanez's killer. He had no idea who the second man was, but guessed that he must be someone of great importance within the cartel's organization. Maybe an accountant or numbers guy he thought. He was wrong.

"Mr. Reigns, please forgive my manners," Talamantez told him. "Please allow me to introduce my associates. "This is Chuchi Espinoza, and associate of mine. And this in Senor Luis Soto, a business associate of Senor Yanez. Senor Soto wanted to meet you in person."

It made sense now. Luis Soto was a powerful member of the Yucatan Cartel, second only to Benito Yanez. He had the second most powerful organization within the cartel, and was a wanted man on four continents. No one outside of the Yucatan had ever seen his face, or met him before, and the American law enforcement entities had no pictures of him. Why he had taken such an enormous risk to fly into the United States made Damian uneasy. *Very uneasy.*

"Pleased to meet you," Damian said, extending his hand.

"It is my pleasure, Senor," Chuchi said, shaking Damian's hand.

"Pleased to meet you," Damian said, extending his hand toward Soto.

"The pleasure is all mines," Luis Soto replied.

"I am sure my boss will be pleased to hear those words you spoke about friendship," Talamantez said, continuing the conversation. "And he wants nothing more than to continue the bonds of friendship that we have established."

Damian nodded.

"How is Dante?" Chuchi asked.

Damian leaned back in his seat. He didn't know how much to reveal to the men sitting inside of the airplane with him. He didn't know how much they knew, or what they knew, or if they knew anything at all. They were important connections, nonetheless, and powerful men in their own right. He knew that he couldn't bullshit them, and also knew that he shouldn't. His principle, was to always fall back on the truth when in doubt.

"He's struggling," Damian said flatly.

The three men in the cabin were taken aback by his candor. They hadn't expected him to be so forthcoming and admit something like that. Men in their business never revealed any kind of weakness or vulnerability. They found themselves staring at one another at a loss for words.

"Sorry to hear that," Chuchi said.

Damian knew that he had thrown them off guard. He pressed forward. "His daughter was taken. His wife is dead, and that precious little girl was his life."

All of the men inside of that cabin were fathers, and the three men from Yucatan all had daughters. They understood completely what Dante was going through. Each man thought about how they would react if their daughters had been taken.

"*Animals!*" Chuchi declared. "Lower than animals. To take a little girl like that."

"They need to burn in hell," Talamantez said.

"If Dante has his way, they will," Damian told them.

Again, the three men exchanged looks.

"How is the search going?" Soto asked.

Damian nodded as he explained. "It's going. Not as well as I would like, but moving forward nonetheless. We overreacted, naturally. We flooded the streets, and basically tried to use a sledgehammer to swat this thing. Our tactics have been heavy handed, and we've blanketed the state. We're hoping that our efforts pay off very soon."

"How soon?" Talamantez asked.

Damian shook his head. "Your guess is as good as ours. The noose is tight, and growing tighter every day. At least that's what we're hoping."

Again, the three men were surprised by Damian's candor. They did find it refreshing however. It totally changed the dynamics of the meeting. They had come to threaten, but Damian had disarmed them with his honesty.

"Your tactics *have* been heavy," Soto told him. "But merited I would think. Is there anything that is being missed? Anyway you can perhaps speed things along. We would like for your nieces return to occur sooner rather than later."

"As would we," Damian told him. "In fact, we would have preferred that it had never happened."

Soto nodded. He realized that what he had just said had been stupid.

"Our primary concern, is all of the *noise* that's being made," Talamantez said. "It is our opinion that once your niece is found, this thing can be calmed down."

"You are making too much noise, Mr. Reigns," Soto told him. "And we do not like noise."

"We explained this to your brother in the beginning," Chuchi told him. "We are not like the organizations along the border. They are animals, uncouth, unruly, bandits, *desperado, vaquero*. They make noise, they love attention. They love to read the newspapers about themselves. We on the other hand, are quiet different."

Damian nodded. He got the message. "I completely understand."

"We need the war between you and the border cartels to be over," Soto told him. "We need this search to be over. Both this massive search, and that back and forth war between your organization and theirs, is causing too much attention. Attention that we don't like, and don't want. You must end this. You must end the war, and finish the search."

"We are desperate to end the search," Damian told them. "But the search cannot end, until she is found. And if she is returned to us alive, that would go far in allowing for the cessation of hostilities. Have you spoken to Juarez? If you could facilitate my niece's safe return, we would be forever grateful. And would be extremely amicable to ending the hostilities."

The three men exchanged glances.

"We don't talk to those animals in the north," Talamantez told Damian. "We stay away from them, we have no relationship, no communication, no nothing. As stated before, they are animals."

"We are not going to stop searching for my niece," Damian told them. He shifted his gaze from one to the next, staring them all in the eye. "She's is innocent in all of this. And her kidnapping, crossed the line."

"They are dogs, Damian," Chuchi said. "What did you expect? You dealt with them all of those years. Didn't you know what you were dealing with?"

"Their decision to kidnap my niece, was a direct result of us *not* wanting to deal with them," Damian told them. "They did this, so that we would not deal with anyone else but them. She's an innocent hostage."

"Damian, how much time do you think it will take before she is found?" Talamantez asked.

Again, Damian shrugged. "We're searching as hard and as fast and as thorough as we can. We want her found more than anyone."

Soto nodded. "We understand that."

"You have thousands of men in Mexico," Chuchi told him. "When will they be pulled out? It is causing a big stir in the Mexican media. It's not only American media we are concerned about, it's our own as well. We don't like it when reporters want to do background, or dig up stuff trying do an expose' and win Pulitzer's. The war in Northern Mexico needs to end, the violence needs to end."

"You do realize that my men are there primarily searching and acting as one big ass roadblock to keep my niece's kidnappers from disappearing if they make it in to Mexico?" Damian asked. "Yes, there is violence, but we are responding to violence against *us*. The majority of the violence is coming from the war between the cartels in Northern Mexico. They are the ones who are causing the biggest stir."

Soto nodded. He understood all of this as well. However, the removal of Damian's men would at least tamp down *some* of the violence.

"You do understand that we don't care if the cartels in Northern Mexico kill each other, we just don't want to be exposed because of our affiliation with *you*."

Damian nodded.

Talamantez leaned in. "The Yucatan consortium voted, and the vote was nearly unanimous. They want to pull the plug on our business dealings, until you get your house in order."

"*Our house is in order!*" Damian told them. He couldn't lose his brand new source. He had just gotten the cocaine flowing again, and to lose it now, would be disastrous. His bank account couldn't take the hit, not with the amount of money Dante was blowing through, not with the number of soldiers they had recruited, not with all of his other companies barely surviving. This, not to mention the fact that The Commission would run back to El Jeffe and Colombia at break neck speeds trying to get supplies. And without a doubt, El Jeffe would cut the Reigns family out of the deal. That would be his price to The Commission. Get rid of the Reigns family, and they could have all of the cocaine they wanted. They would take that deal in a heartbeat, and then, he would have to fight off the entire country, and do it without any cocaine to make money to pay for the massive army it would take to defend himself. He would go broke in a year or two from having to do that. It was a losing situation.

Damian leaned in. "Look, we are going to wrap up this search, and as soon as we do, we are *out* of Mexico. I give you my word, we will end the conflict with the cartels in Mexico, and you will *not* be exposed."

"How long?" Soto asked.

"Give us a month to wrap things up," Damian told them.

Soto shook his head no.

"Two weeks," Damian told him. "Give us two weeks to find my niece, and then, we'll end the search and pull out."

"Whether you have found her or not?" Talamantez asked, lifting an eyebrow.

Damian peered down. Slowly, he nodded.

"Dante would never go for that," Chuchi said with a smile. He knew Dante. And he knew that if he were in Dante's shoes, he would not go for it either. Dante would kill Damian and take over, if Damian tried to pull the plug on the search for his daughter. It would be brother against brother. The thought made him smile. Who would that bitch ass sister of theirs side with, he wondered? It may be fun just to sit back and watch the whole thing go down. But he knew that Don Yanez would not go for that, neither would the rest of the Yucatan Cartel. They were about business. Peace and quiet, was how they liked to do that business. And all of them were loving the profits coming from The Commission. They just wanted The Commission to do things quieter.

"Dante will do what is right for the family," Damian told him. He knew that Chuchi was right, Dante would not go for it. And he knew that if he didn't pull the plug, then they would be cut off, and that would mean Colombia would be back in the game, and the rest of The Commission would have their ass. He always knew that it would come to this. Deep down, he had always known. The price for Lucky would be far higher than anyone could ever imagine. But she was a Reigns, and her blood was more precious than silver and gold to them. Accepting her loss was too heavy of a burden to carry, and continuing the search for her would come at too heavy of a cost to bear. It would mean the end of his family. Was he prepared to sacrifice the one, for the many? Was he prepared to roll the dice and go to war with the world in order to bring his niece back home? The decision weighed heavily on his shoulders.

Soto shifted his gaze to Talamantez and nodded. It was then when Damian realized who was truly in charge, and why Soto had risked coming into the country. He was there on behalf of the Yucatan Cartels, while Talamantez was there on behalf of his master, Don Yanez. Soto had just giving him the blessing of the entire Yucatan Cartel to continue what he was doing for the next two weeks. But the warning was clear, he had two weeks, and not a day longer. The search for his niece had just taken a dramatic turn. They no longer had the luxury of time on their side. The clock was ticking, and the weight of the world was now upon his shoulders should that deadline come and go without the search ending. Could he stop the search? Would Dante allow the search to end? Would this mean he would have to go to war with his own flesh and blood in order to save the rest of his family? War with Dante, or war with the rest of the country? It was a hell of a choice to make. Could he... He shook his head, putting the thought out of his mind.

Chuchi extended his hand. "I will convey your words to Senor

Yanez."

Damian rose, buttoned his suit jacket, and shook Chuchi's hand. He then shook hands with Talamantez, and finally Soto.

"Good luck," Talamantez said, patting Damian on his back.

"I will talk with you again, in two weeks, Senor Reigns," Soto told him, without rising from his chair.

Damian nodded. "Two weeks."

"Have Dante call me," Chuchi said under his breath. He gave Damian a look, and Damian nodded slightly.

Damian turned and headed for the exit. At the door, he paused and peered down the steps. They were now wet and slippery. Rain had come in while they were meeting inside. He peered up toward the horizon, and could see nothing but blackness rolling in. It was clear that a storm was coming.

# Chapter Twenty Six

Dante and his men were seated outside of the massive The Woodlands Mall, just on the northern outskirts of Houston, Texas. For this occasion, Dante had rented several Cadillac XTS sedans in a variety of colors, so as not to be detected. He sat low in the seat, watching the mall's exit for the person he was looking for. His men knew more about the subject than he did, because he had tasked them to investigate and spy on his target. They found her coming out of work one afternoon, and had kept her under constant surveillance ever since. And now, they had called their boss into the picture. He wanted to be there for the grab.

"That's her!" Ahmad told Dante.

"Where?" Dante asked, peering over the dash and searching the entrance.

"Her!" Ahmad said pointing. "The chick with the shopping bags."

Dante saw the one that Ahmad was referring to, and it felt like he had been slapped in the face. He squinted his eyes to make sure that he was seeing what he was actually seeing. He had little doubt.

"That's not her," Dante told him.

"Boss, I've been trailing her for the last two days!" Ahmad said, growing frustrated. "That *is* her! That is Yessenia Nunez, sister of Nuni Nunez!"

"*Bullshit!*" Dante said, shaking his head. "*I know her! I dated her!* I *fucked* her! She's a model. Her name is Paola Catalina, and she's from Madrid! You've spent two days, following the wrong chick!"

"No, I haven't!" Ahmad insisted.

Dante opened his car door and climbed out of the Caddy. Ahmad and several of his men followed. Dante walked up behind Yessenia who was opening up the door on her Porsche.

"Yessenia!" Dante shouted.

She turned. Her eyes locked onto Dante's, and surprise spread across her face. Shock spread across Dante's. Yessenia offered a smile once she saw him, until it registered what name he had called her. And the number of men he had with him also raised her suspicions.

"Dante?" Yessenia asked. "Hi, how have you been?"

She walked to Dante and the two of them embraced.

"What are you doing here?" Yessenia asked, raking her hair out of her face.

"I could ask you the same thing, Paola," Dante told her. "Or is it Yessenia?"

She closed her eyes. "I can explain."

"Please do," Dante told her.

The two of them had shared many nights together, and to this day, still got together whenever she was in San Antonio, or he was in Houston. He had met her at his club, and saw her again at various fashion shows. Finally, he made his move on her while at an art show that Damian was sponsoring, and the two of them hit it off instantly. She had been cool, funny, and real. She was gorgeous, but not pretentious or full of herself like so many other model chicks that he had run into over the years. She made him laugh, and she enjoyed laughing. She was brains *and* beauty, and she just enjoyed hanging out without any strings attached. He liked her. In fact, he liked her a lot. And now, she was standing before him as a completely different person. She wasn't Paola Catalina from Madrid, Spain, but Yessenia Nunez from Monterrey, Mexico. He was at a loss for words. He had never been caught slipping like this. He had been sleeping with the sister of his biggest rival in the world. It had him completely thrown for a loop.

"I didn't lie to you, Dante," Yessenia told him. "I really am Paola Catalina. That's who I was when I met you, and that's who I am today."

"You were born, Yessenia Nunez," Dante said flatly. "You don't think I would want to know that?"

"Why? What difference would it have made? I am not that person, and haven't been for nearly a decade."

"Your brother is a member of the Juarez Cartel!" Dante said through clenched teeth.

Yessenia nodded. "And that's why I ran away from who I was. That's why I changed my whole life around. I am not my brother."

"That's comforting," Dante told her.

"What is this?" she asked, turning up her palms, She stared at the men he had with him. "What is all of this about?"

"Do you know who I am?" Dante asked.

"Dante Reigns?" she asked, uncertain of her answer.

"Yes," Dante said nodding. "Do you know what I do for a living?"

Yessenia shook her head. "You never told me."

"You're not stupid," Dante told her. "Don't underestimate my intelligence, I've never underestimated yours."

Again, Yessenia raked her hand through her hair, sending it back over her head. "I had an idea. And of course, I've heard things."

"I am all of the bad things you heard about me," Dante told her. "And none of the good."

"How can you say that?" Yessenia asked, staring into his eyes. "I know you."

"You don't know me," Dante told her.

"I stared into those beautiful brown eyes of yours, and I saw what was behind them." Yessenia reached out to caress Dante's face. Dante clasped her hand and move it away.

"I am at war with your brother," Dante said flatly.

"What?"

"Your brother, kidnapped my daughter," Dante told her.

"*My brother?*"

"Yes," Dante said nodding. "Nuni."

Yessenia shook her head. "No, that's impossible. You're mistaken. My brother is many things, but a kidnapper is not one of them. He would *never* hurt a child."

"He has my daughter, and I'm going to get her back."

Yessenia peered at the men around her. Everything became clear. "And now what?"

"You are going to help me get her back," Dante told her.

Yessenia nodded. "If he has done what you say, then I will help you get her back. Let me talk to him."

"In due time," Dante said nodding.

243

"Let me call him," Yessenia said.  "I can talk to my brother.  I can reason with him.  He's not a monster."

"Your brother is a monster," Dante told her.  "You know that.  That's why you ran."

Yessenia peered down at the ground, and again, tucked her hair behind her ear.  "I did run.  I ran away from Mexico.  I ran away from my past, my life, my poverty.  I ran away from what Mexico was becoming.  But I did not run away from my brother.  I did not like what he was doing, and I did not like the things I was hearing.  And so yeah, in a sense, I did run away from him.  Not the old Nuni, but the new one.  The one corrupted by Galindo, and his other friends.  I saw the boy I grew up with, slowly turning into something else.  Something that I did not want to see.  But I know my brother.  And I know that despite all that he has done, and all that he has become, that he would never hurt a child.  Let me talk to him.  Let me help you get her back.  He will listen to me, I promise you that."

"I'm counting on that," Dante told her.  "I know that he loves you, and that love for you is how I can get him to listen to reason.  That love that he has for you, will help him to understand.  When something you love is taken from you, it's no easy thing to deal with."

Yessenia nodded.  "I will do whatever I can to help you."

Dante waved his hand toward his waiting Cadillac.  "Come with me."

Yessenia stared at her car.

"It'll be safe," Dante told her.  "Give me your keys.  I'll have one of my men follow us in it."

"No," Yessenia said, shaking her head.  "Leave it here.  Let the police find it.  It will lend credence to the idea that I was forcibly taken."

Dante let out a half smile and nodded.

Yessenia pulled a necklace with a charm from beneath her blouse, and unclasped it.  She handed the necklace to Dante.  "Send this to my brother.  He gave it to me a long time ago.  They are two sea shells from the Sea of Cortez.  We found them when we were children.  I have never taken mine off.  He has one just like it around his neck.  He will know for sure that you have me."

Dante closed his hand with the necklace inside of it.  "Thank you."

He had thought of sending Nuni something else to verify that he had his sister, but this would work even better.

Yessenia headed for Dante's Caddy. "Where are you taking me?"

Again, Dante smiled. "I have a place reserved just for you. A place where you'll be comfortable. It's a nice little ranch along the border."

*****

Palacios de Los Dios, was truly a palace of the gods. It was a stunning, fifty thousand square foot Spanish style mansion nestled on some twenty thousand acres. The home was of the traditional Spanish courtyard style, where the main house surrounded a massive swimming pool and centralized garden. The open courtyard swimming pool was one of only three, but it was the one that was decked out the most. It had Italian marble tiles, gold statues surrounding the pool, hand painted mosaics, and imported marble vases from Brazil. The home itself was finished off in hand cut dry stacked stone, La Habra Plasterized stucco, gorgeous hand troweled walls with pearlized paint, Talavera floors, and custom hand forge wrought iron doors. It was truly a work of art. In addition to being a hundred million dollar showplace, the property was also a working cattle ranch, as its owner was a cowboy at heart. The place was Nuni Nunez's home in Northern Mexico.

Nuni was lounging by one of his swimming pools, relaxing, and sipping on a nice cold mojito. He relished moments like these, times when he could just shut the world off and relax. These moments were rare these days, as the war between the cartels for the control of Northern Mexico's drug trade had consumed all of his time of late. He had wars to plan, strategy to implement, and people to kill. Lot's of people to kill. It kept him busy to say the least.

The war with the Reigns family was just getting started. Dante had sent men into Northern Mexico, and they were clashing almost constantly with his men, and with the men of the other Mexican cartels. He wouldn't admit it to Galindo, but he had vastly underestimated Dante's response, and the number of men the Reigns family could muster. He had no idea that they could blanket Texas with that many men, and still have the resources and manpower to blanket Northern Mexico. They had as many men in Mexico as he had, and this was not counting the number of men they had spread throughout Texas. And these were only *their* soldiers, not soldiers from the rest of their fucking commission. If The Commission got involved an sent soldiers, then he would be vastly outnumbered, and in his own fucking country. He had *grossly* miscalculated.

He hadn't heard from the men he had sent on the mission to bring back his little insurance policy. But the Reigns family was still searching, which meant that his men were still alive, and still in hiding, and still had the little girl. He was counting on them to make it back to Mexico, and he was counting on them to keep the little girl alive. His orders has been that she remained unharmed, and that they were to protect her with their own lives, if necessary. She was not to be frightened, or scared, or alarmed, and they were to make it seem like a fun, but secret game. They were going on a trip, and at the end of the trip, her Daddy would be waiting for her. But she had to be quiet, and they had to hide from everyone, that was a part of the game. If only they could pull it off. If they could deliver her in one piece, then Dante and the Reigns family, would be at his feet. They would *have* to wait. Perhaps he could even influence them to use the soldiers they had in his country, to help him end his war with the other cartels. That would be optimum. And if he could get them to do that, then Northern Mexico would belong to them, and they could work to get the border re-opened, and the drugs flowing again. And drugs flowing again, meant money flowing again. He needed this war to end, he needed the Reigns family to get The Commission to wait and to buy drugs from his organization, and he needed those soldiers that the Reigns family had in his country. It all hinged on getting that little girl. She was the key to it all, she was the key to getting the Reigns family to cooperate. He needed his men to succeed, he needed them to get past the blanket of men that the Reigns family, the FBI, the Texas Rangers, the Border Patrol, and Homeland Security had covered Texas with.

He thought about ways to send them help, but knew that it would be futile. They only thing that trying to send help would do, would be to expose the path the men were taking, and it would get the men he sent killed. He had to wait, and had to trust the men that he had sent, and it was killing him inside. He was never one to just sit around and allow things to take their course. He had to find a way. He had spent hours upon hours staring at a map of Texas and Mexico, trying to figure out a way. His only choice, had been to stick to the original plan, and hope that his men were able to pull it off.

Nuni lifted his mojito and drank. He was supposed to be relaxing today. Clearing his mind. It was with a clear mind that he was able to find solutions. And so, he had taken this day off for specifically this purpose. To relax, to get himself together, to rejuvenate, to clear his mind so that he could attack the situation from a different perspective. He found that copious amounts of alcohol also helped. He was determined to plaster himself with tequila, rum, and mojitos until the spirit man visited and gave him some new ideas.

Nuni watched as one of his men stepped out of the house and made his way around the pool, to where he was lounging. He was carrying with him a small box.

The guard walked up to Nuni and handed him the box. "This came for you. Special delivery, your eyes only."

Nuni looked at the man like he was stupid. "Why didn't you open it?"

The man started to open the box. Nuni slapped the box out of his hand.

"Ever stop to think that it may be explosive?" Nuni asked. "Or maybe even contain poison? Do you know what Ricin is?"

The bodyguard picked up the box, and carried it away from Nuni. Once he was a safe distance away, he opened the box and peered inside.

"Well, what is it?" Nuni shouted.

"A necklace," the man said. He lifted it and held it up.

Nuni recognized it instantly. He rose from his lounge chair and held out his hand. "Bring it here!"

The guard hurriedly carried the necklace to his boss and handed it over. Nuni took the necklace, examined it, and then snatched the box away from the man. There was a note inside.

"Who brought this?" Nuni asked.

"It came by courier service."

Nuni unfolded the note and read it out loud. "A fair exchange ain't no robbery. Signed, Dante."

Nuni clasped the necklace and thought about what had happened. It was his sister's necklace. Dante had his sister. Nuni shoved the guard into his swimming pool, kicked over his lounge chair, and let out an inhuman scream. *Dante had his sister,* was the only thing racing through his mind. Thoughts of torture, of rape, of inhumane brutality raced through his brain. He would have to trade for her. The little girl's life, for the life of his sister. But his plans would be in ruin. He needed the little girl to force The Commission to buy dope from him again. He needed the little girl to force Dante into the war in Mexico on his side. And the biggest problem of all, he didn't really have the little girl in his hands yet. And if Dante and his men found her before his men were able to get her out of the country, then Dante would be holding all the cards. He would certainly killed Yessenia and send her head to him in a box.

Nuni turned, and screamed once again. He held up the necklace, and dropped down to his knees next to his swimming pool. The one person he loved more than life itself, was now in the hands of his worst enemy. It was too much for him to bear.

# Chapter Twenty Seven

Peaches stood in the airport waiting area. She had a carry-on bag with her, and little else. She owned little else. The clothes that Darius bought for her, was what she had. She had little money in the bank, and none stashed. She had just made an enormous purchase of dope before her home got overrun, so her cash was non-existant. She didn't even know if the cocaine she had bought was still in her warehouses. And even the few dollars she did have in the bank, she couldn't access. Her wallet, with her driver's license, her credit cards, and debit cards, had all been lost in the house. She didn't know if they had been burned in the fire or not, but what she did know, is that she didn't have them. She was fortunate that Darius had hooked her up with her plane tickets to fly back home. He was still sore however, about her decision to go.

Peaches thought about Darius, and their relationship. He had defended her against his brothers, he had saved her life when she knew that she was a goner, he had cared for her, built her back up, and during the whole episode, stayed by her side. Sure, they argued, but it was because he wanted her to stay with him. He was worried about her safety. There were plenty of worse things to argue about with a man, in fact, there were plenty of men who wouldn't even give a shit. She needed to ease up on Darius, and she needed to remember what the fights were really about; he just wanted her to be safe.

Peaches also knew that there existed another reason for their discord, a deeper, darker, more selfish reason. Darius was getting too close. Allowing him to get so far in, had been a mistake, she thought. She wanted him close, but not *too* close. It sounded ridiculous, even to her, but she had her reasons. And that reason started with *Ches*, and ended with *Rae*. He was a factor, no matter how much she wanted to dispute the fact, or argue with herself, it *was* because of him. It was *always* because of him. No matter how many years had passed, no matter who she was with, Chesarae would always factor in. They had so much history together, had done so much together, there had been so many good times, and so much pain, that they would always be a part of each others lives. And now that he was out of prison, she needed to clarify where they stood, and what was going on between the two of them, before she could even think about moving forward with Darius, or anyone else for that matter. She needed to talk to Chesarae. They needed to have the conversation that they should have had before he left for Detroit. What was she to him? What was he to her? She needed to know those things now more than ever.

A bouquet of roses was thrust into her face from behind, startling her. She turned, and to her surprise, Darius was standing there with a giant smile on his face.

"What?"

"You didn't think you were going to sneak out of here without me saying good-bye, did you?" Darius asked.

Peaches wrapped her arms around him and hugged him.

"Last chance, I can grab a ticket and go with you?" Darius told her.

"You know what your brother said," Peaches told him. She held her hand out for the flowers. "Are those for me?"

"Of course," Darius told her. He handed her the flowers. "Either they're for you, or for that fine ass flight attendant standing over there by the door."

Peaches smiled and punched him in the shoulder. "Don't play with me. You'll get her and you fucked up in this airport."

Darius laughed. He wrapped his arms around her waist and pulled her close. "Are you going to be okay?"

Peaches nodded. "I'm fine. Everything is going to be okay. Your brother, he's going to have the men there?"

Darius nodded. "They are already in route. They'll meet you in the airport."

"How are they going to know who I am?" Peaches asked.

"I told them to look out for the finest chick coming through the Columbus airport," Darius said with a smile.

Peaches smiled and pushed his hands away. "You sure are a smooth talker. Too smooth."

"I'm just telling the truth," Darius said, kissing her forehead. "And I already made it clear, that if any of them niggaz try to holler, I'm gonna kill 'em. And if they see any nigga in Ohio trying to holler, they better kill his ass."

Peaches threw her head back in laughter. "Boy, you're crazy."

"My cousin DeMarion is heading back to Columbus as well. And don't forget, Brandon has men there. I also just learned that my cousin DeFranz is still up there with Brandon's men. You'll be fine. I'm also checking to see if a couple of my other kinfolks can go up there and help out."

"What?" Peaches asked. "Why are you smiling?"

"Because, you haven't met my other side of the family," Darius told her.

"What's wrong with them?"

"These niggaz is ghetto, with a capital G!" Darius said, laughing.

"Then they gone fit right in," Peaches told him.

"We'll see," Darius said, hugging her again.

"Darius, I'm going to be okay," Peaches told him. She knew that he was worried, by the way he kept hugging her, and by the way he kept touching her. He had to have his hands on her. He didn't want to let go. "You will see me again. I promise. Do you hear me? I promise, you will see me again."

Darius nodded. He leaned in and kissed Peaches on her cheek. "They're calling you to board. You don't want to miss your flight."

"Thank you," Peaches told him. "I don't know if I ever said it. Thank you for everything, for saving me, for protecting me, for staying by my side, for being my guardian angel."

"I'm no angel," Darius told her. "But you *are* welcome."

Peaches leaned in and kissed Darius on his cheek. "Take care. I'll see you soon."

"Take care," Darius told her.

Peaches turned, and walked into the tunnel to board her flight. Darius waved to her. He had the strangest feeling he had ever had. It felt like he was saying good-bye for the last time. Something deep down inside of him, told him that he was never going to see her again.


*****


Damian was seated at a secluded table inside of his favorite restaurant. The lighting was dim, the atmosphere was just right, and smooth jazz was pouring out of the restaurant's sound system. The fact that he owned the restaurant was a big factor in it being his favorite. He had set it up to offer an upscale, soul food and jazz dining experience, and the manager he hired to run the place, had delivered in spades. And the food was awesome to boot.

Damian sat staring at the flickering candle, waiting for his date to arrive. The sweet and spicy smell of Cajun food wafted through the air, while Lena Horne serenaded the patrons seated throughout. He could see his men everywhere, trying to blend in and make themselves invisible, but in truth, he had an impenetrable security wall around him.

MiAsia strutted into the restaurant and found him seated in the corner. She headed over to the table.

"Anyone sitting here?" she asked, waving toward an empty seat.

"Not yet," Damian told her. "I'm waiting for this beautiful woman to join me. You wouldn't happen to have seen her on your way in would you?"

"Oh, you got jokes!" MiAsia said, laughing. She seated herself at the table, and then leaned over and caressed the lapel of Damian's suit. "Ascot Chang. Not bad."

"Really?" Damian asked, lifting an eyebrow. "I'm glad you approved. But my question is, what else did you expect? Sears?"

MiAsia laughed. "No, but I expected you to be one of those Armani type of brothers."

"Oh, really?" Damian asked laughing. "And why is that?"

MiAsia shrugged. "I don't know. That's just how some men are. Most men as a matter of fact. They pick up GQ, read a couple of articles, see the glitzy advertisements, and suddenly they are fashion mavens."

"A fashion maven? Wow! I've never heard that one before. Can a man be a fashion maven?"

"I don't know," MiAsia said smiling. "I just know that most men aren't into bespoke suits from Saville Row. Especially the brothers."

"Damn, that was kinda racists," Damian told her. "Why the brothers can't be up on Gieves & Hawkes, or Henry Poole?"

"I don't know, they just aren't. Especially mafiosos such as yourself."

"Are we going to actually eat, or are you just going to sit here and continuously insult me?"

MiAsia pressed his forearm. "You know what I mean!"

"Okay, I should be wearing a cheesy Italian suit, is that what you're saying?"

"No! Armani is not a cheesy Italian suit. And remember, I'm Black too, so I can keep it real."

"Half of you can," Damian said with a smile.

"Oh, half breed jokes? We going there?"

The waiter came over and left a tray of buttered, Cajun style biscuits.

"Thank you," Damian told him.

"Your drinks are on the way," he said, before disappearing.

"Drinks? MiAsia asked, lifting an eyebrow. "You took the liberty of ordering for me?"

Damian nodded. "I ordered two Swamp Thangs."

"A Swamp Thang?" MiAsia said nodding. "Sounds like it's strong as hell. Are you trying to get me drunk, Mr. Damian? Are you trying to take advantage of me?"

Damian laughed. "I think that it may be just the opposite."

"Oh, really?" MiAsia said, raising an eyebrow. "Why do you say that?"

Damian leaned back and stared at her. "What are we doing here?"

"You invited me, remember?"

Damian shook his head. "No, really. What is this about? Why the sudden interest?"

MiAsia leaned back in her seat and took him in. "Who said that it was all of a sudden, for one? And two, I have a feeling that the interest is mutual."

"Yeah, it is. But what's *your* interest?"

MiAsia leaned in. "I like you, Damian. I think you're cute."

*"Cute?"*

"Handsome," MiAsia corrected. "Harvard grad, business man, very well put together, well rounded, well traveled, well heeled. And you know about my various business interest, so that's not something that I have to hide from you. There are not many men who are on my level. So, when I see one, I'm interested."

Damian nodded. He didn't believe a word she was saying, but he would play along for now. "So, that's what this is? This is about finding a brother on your level, one who you don't have to hide your secret activities from?"

"And one who I know is well educated, well bred, and isn't after a sister for her money," MiAsia added.

Damian laughed. He had experienced the same problem all throughout his life. Finding a sister in the corporate world who operated at the same level he did. Which given his young age, was virtually impossible. Most sisters didn't become CEO's until they were into their fifties. Hell, most men didn't. And finding a sister who wasn't after him just because of his money was equally challenging, so he definitely understood where she was coming from.

"You're not after me for my money are you, Mr, Reigns?" MiAsia asked with a smile.

"At this point, I probably am," Damian told her.

Both of them shared a laugh.

"Spending a lot of money?" MiAsia asked. lifting an eyebrow.

"More than you can even begin to imagine."

"I don't know, I can imagine a lot."

Damian smiled. "I'll bet you can. You *look* expensive."

"I know my worth."

"This search is costing me in the millions," Damian said, once again leaning back in his seat. "And I'm talking daily."

"You've hired a private army," MiAsia told him.

"Dante hired thousands of inexperienced, unvetted, un-tested, un-checked men. I don't know who we have working for us, or how many of them are FBI, DEA, or work for the damn cartel. It's a good thing he's only using them to search, and to put up road blocks. Our trusted guys are doing the dirty work. But still, when this thing is over, he's going to have to let go of a lot of people. Thousands of people. And then slowly, rehire the ones that he's done full background checks on."

"Rehire?" MiAsia asked.

Damian nodded. "They're needed."

The waiter arrived with their drinks, and placed them on the table. "Is there anything else I can get you?"

Damian waved his hand. "We'll order in a minute, thanks."

"Just let me know when you're ready," the waiter said, before disappearing.

"So, why are they needed?" MiAsia asked, once the waiter was out of earshot.

Damian shrugged. He didn't know how much to tell her. She knew anyway. She was a member of The Commission.

"Florida?" MiAsia asked.

Damian smiled.

"California?" MiAsia continued.

Damian nodded, and clapped his hands. "Very good. I see you've done some homework."

"It's not a secret, you know?"

Again, Damian nodded. "I know."

"So, once all of this is over with, you're going full fledged into California and Florida?"

"I'm not waiting," Damian said, shaking his head. "Princess is already in Florida. And I'm sending my cousin out to California."

"Wow, must be nice to have that kind of manpower," MiAsia said, sipping from her drink. She screwed up her face once the liquor hit her. "This thing is strong! You *are* trying to take advantage of me!"

Damian laughed.

"Why didn't you warn me?" MiAsia asked.

"You didn't need a warning," Damian told her. "From what I hear, you can put away some sake."

"Oh, is that what you've heard?" MiAsia asked. "So, you've been checking up on me?"

"A little. We all have our little ways of snooping."

"So," MiAsia said, leaning back. "What else did you find out?"

"A lot." Damian said, smiling.

"Any of it good?"

Damian shook his head.

"I didn't think so," MiAsia told him. "You know, I can help you."

"How?"

"I have friends in California."

Damian smiled at her. "Tell them to stay out of my business, or they'll wake up dead."

MiAsia nodded, and sipped from her drink. She instantly decided that she had misjudged Damian. She was told that he was nothing like his brother, that he was the brains, while Dante was the brawn. That he was more about peace, and business, and politics, while Dante was more about using a bullet to solve all of their family's problems. And now, she realized that Damian could be just as ruthless. Any man who could smile while telling you to stay out of their business or they would kill you, was a vicious, ruthless, killer. He had made her wet.

"I said that, Damian, because I want you to know that I'm a friend," MiAsia told him. "You can come to me and talk to me, and I'll understand. You don't have to hide anything."

Damian took measure of the woman sitting across from him. She was beautiful. Drop dead gorgeous, to be exact. And yet, he saw something in MiAsia that worried him to no end. Her overtures were friendly, perhaps even genuine, and that's what frightened him the most. He looked across the table, and he saw the female version of himself. She was ambitious, well educated, well traveled, well bred, rich, successful, and ruthless. She was a cutthroat in the corporate world, and in the drug world. She would stop at nothing to come out on top. There were only two things that a person could do when they came across their female counterpart, they could either kill her, or marry her and take over the world.

Damian lifted his hand, waving for the waiter to come over. The waiter rushed over immediately.

"Yes, sir?" the waiter asked, pulling out his pad and pencil. "What can I get for you and the Mrs?"

MiAsia smiled and lowered her head. Damian stared at her and smiled.

"Well, Mrs. Reigns, what will it be?"

256

MiAsia lifted her menu, and Damian clasped her hand.

"What will it be?" he asked, staring into her eyes. "Plata o Plomo?"

MiAsia understood what it meant. He was asking her if she wanted silver or lead. Friend or foe? The bribe or the bullet? The silver platter as a wedding gift, or a bullet to the head? It meant all of those things. She smiled.

"I've always been partial to silver," she told him.

Damian removed his hand, and stared at the waiter. "I will have the chef's special, and my wife will have the same."

MiAsia nodded and closed her menu.

The waiter grabbed the menus and nodded. "Very good, sir."

"We'll see," Damian said, staring at MiAsia. "We will see."

# Chapter Twenty Eight.

Arturo Rodriguez loved sex. He loved *uncommitted* sex. And that was what attracted him to whores. He would rather pay for pussy and get it over with, than to bother with a relationship. Who needed the headache, he thought? It was after his third marriage when he developed a penchant for picking up prostitutes in South Beach, and Ft. Lauderdale. As he rose in the drug world, his taste for more exotic women rose with him. He wanted them cleaner, safer, more professional and discreet. And so he turned to more established and professional services to satisfy his cravings.

Tonight, Arturo found himself at The Mandarin Oriental Hotel on the southern tip of the Brickell Key, overlooking downtown Miami. The Mandarin was one of those five star ventures that catered to the elite. NBA, NFL, Hollywood elite, global business elite, and big time coke dealers all frequented the establishment. Arturo had chosen the hotel for its discretion, and for its oriental theme. Tonight, he had put in a special request to his favorite madame, he wanted to fuck something Asian.

Arturo's fantasy's ranged anywhere from the mild to the wild. Sometimes it was a quick wam-bam, thank you ma'am, to a well choreographed and staged erotic fantasy. He had done the African things, with a handful of Black prostitutes, he had done the Roman orgy thing, with a bunch of dark haired chicks in ancient Roman costumes, catering to his every need. He had done the Wild West thing, with chicks dressed up in cowgirl gear, and the prison guard fantasy, where he dressed himself as a jailer, and fucked a bunch of prostitutes dressed as prisoners. He had the money to fulfill all of his sick sexual fantasies, and he did just that. In between killing men, and moving drugs, his orgies were his sole method of entertainment and relaxation.

A knock came to his door.

Arturo excitedly rushed to the door of his hotel suite and opened it. To his wonderment, there was not one, not two, not three, but four women of Asian descent, all dressed in full Geisha regalia. He clapped his hands and rubbed them together, like a kid in a candy store. Tonight, was going to be one of the greatest nights of his life.

Arturo stepped aside, and waved for the women to come in. They each took tiny steps into the suite, as if they were authentic Geisha whose feet had been broken and bound. The sounds of their silk Kimono swishing as they walked along, instantly gave him an erection. Arturo couldn't control his excitement, the madame had delivered in spades tonight.

Arturo pointed to the bar. "Bring me some sake," he told one of the women, while taking a seat on the sofa. He wanted to sip from some sake wine while examining the women. He would have them stand before him and slowly removed their clothing. He wanted to look into each of their faces and see which one was the prettiest, and then he wanted to compare their bodies, and see which one had the best shape. He wanted to fuck the finest one, while staring into the face of the prettiest one.

One of the Geisha handed him a cup of sake. Arturo rubbed her ass.

"Line up right here, my pretty little Jap bitches," Arturo told them.

The women lined up in front of Arturo, who was seated on the sofa in front of them. He rubbed their legs and thighs, caressed their asses, and allowed his hands to find their hidden breast. And then, a knock came to the door.

"*I told you not to disturb me once the girls arrived!*" Arturo shouted. Another knock.

"Dammit! This better be an emergency! Or someone's going to find themselves inside the belly of a fucking croc in the middle of the fucking Everglades!" Arturo pushed the girls away and rose. He walked to the door and opened it. His bodyguard was standing in the doorway with a hole in his forehead. He fell forward into the suite.

"What the fuck?" Arturo shouted. He jumped back.

"Hello, Arturo," Princess said, stepping into the doorway.

Arturo's eyes bulged out of his head. He turned and ran for his gun. One of the Geisha stuck out her foot and clipped him, sending him flying over the coffee table onto the floor. A second Geisha walked up to him, pulled a silenced pistol from beneath her Kimono, and pointed it at him.

"What the fuck is this?" Arturo shouted, staring up at the women.

"You want a little Jap pussy, eh?" one of the Geisha asked, with a distinctly British accent.

Princess walked into the suite laughing. She seated herself on the sofa. The Geisha lifted Arturo off of the floor, while Princess's other men pulled Arturo's other dead bodyguards into the suite and closed the door.

"Princess, what are you doing here?" Arturo asked.

"Isn't it obvious?" Princess asked. She lifted a grape and tossed it into her mouth. "I'm here to kill you."

"Kill me? *Why?*"

"Because, it's time for you to die."

"Princess, I've been loyal to you!" Arturo pleaded. "I have!"

"You're a traitor, Arturo, just like the rest of those snakes. What I want to know from you, is who are the Cuban's you've jumped into bed with, where I can find them, and who else in my organization is working with them?"

"Princess, please!" Arturo said, clasping his hands. "I've been loyal to you!"

"No, you haven't," Princess told him. She held out her hand, and one of her men placed a large caliber, silenced pistol inside of her hand. "I'm not going to even play with you. I don't have time for all of the gruesome and grisly stuff. So, I'll just keep it simple. I'm going to shoot you in various body parts, until you tell me what I want to know."

"And what if I don't know what you want to know?" Arturo asked, breaking into a sweat.

"Then it's going to be a very painful evening for you," Princess said with a smile. She tossed another grape into her mouth.

"Princess, listen to me!" Arturo told her. "I never betrayed you. I haven't jumped into bed with any Cubans. I've been loyal to you since the beginning!"

"Charlie is dead," Princess told him.

Arturo lowered his head and stared at the floor.

"But before he died, he gave me a list," Princess lied. "A list of everyone who has betrayed me, a list of everyone who has jumped in bed

261

with the Cubans. Your name was the first name on the list."

"He's a lying bastard!" Arturo said, spitting on the floor. "May he burn in hell! That son-of-a-bitch never liked me! And you know that! He lied!"

"Why would he lie?" Princess asked, turning up her palms. "He had nothing to live for. He knew that he was a dead man."

"It was a dead man's last act of vengeance against the people he hated!" Arturo told her.

Princess shook her head. She plucked another grape, and tossed it into her mouth. "Who are the Cubans? Give me some names."

Arturo shook his head. "I don't know..."

Princess pointed her weapon and squeezed the trigger. A soft, muffled pop, and then the whistling screech of the bullet leaving the barrel of the silenced pistol penetrated the air. The bullet struck Arturo in his knee, sending blood spurting into the air. Arturo fell, clasped his knee, and screamed like a wounded banshee.

"*No! No! No!*" Arturo shouted, as he writhed on he ground, clasping his bloody knee. "*Please! I have been loyal to you!*"

"Give me a name," Princess told him. She ate another grape.

"I don't have any names to give you!" Arturo shouted.

Princess squeezed the trigger once again, sending a round into Arturo's other leg. This one tore through his thigh. Again, Arturo howled and writhed in pain.

"Princess! I'm loyal to you! I have been loyal to you!"

"Give me a name, Arty," Princess told him. She tossed another grape into her mouth. "Why are you protecting them? They're dead men anyway. Tell me who they are. Who hooked you up? Give me something, Arty."

"I don't have anything to give you!" Arturo shouted. "Princess, please!"

Princess squeezed the trigger once again, this time sending a bullet through Arturo's left arm. Again, he screamed in pain.

"All right!" Arturo shouted. "All right! *Enough!* I'll tell you what you want to hear!"

"Don't tell me what I want to hear," Princess told him. She tossed another grape into her mouth. "I want to know who else has jumped in bed with the Cubans, who hooked it up, and where can I find them?  Who are these son-of-a-bitches who think they can just roll in and take over my shit?"

"They are hitters out of South Florida!" Arturo told her.

"Where?" Princess asked.

"I hear they are based in Key Biscayne!" Arturo told her.  Sweat continued to pour down his face.

"Who hooked it up?" Princess asked.

"Charlie!" Arturo shouted.  "They went to Charlie first, and he came to us!"

"*Us?*" Princess asked, lifting any eyebrow.  "Us as in who?"

"Us!" Charlie shouted.  "He approached all of us!"

"And who rolled over?" Princess asked.

"I don't know!" Arturo told her.  "I never met with anyone else!"

"Bullshit," Princess told him.  She lifted her weapon put a bullet into Arturo's right arm.  Again he hollered.  Blood was pouring from his body, and running over the floor, turning the tiles a slick, dark, crimson red.

"Princess, please..."

"Who agreed to roll with the Cubans?" Princess asked, eating another grape.

Arturo shook his head.  "Charlie was rolling with them, I guess."

"Who else?"

"Princess, I don't know!  We never met again!  I don't know who agreed to jump ship!"

Princess rose from her seat.

"Princess, please," Arturo pleaded.  "Please.  Help me.  I need help."

Princess turned to her men and nodded.  Several of them reached down and began tearing off Arturo's bloody clothing.  They stripped him naked, and then one of them handed her a pair of bolt cutters.  Her men clasped Arturo's hands and legs, while Princess placed the bolt cutters at the base of his penis and then snipped.  His manhood fell to the ground, as he screamed so hard that he passed out. Her men sat him back down on the floor in his own blood.

"You know the drill," Princess told her men.

One of her men bent over, and using a pair of gloves, lifted Arturo's penis off of the ground, opened his mouth, and stuffed it inside.

Princess headed for the door.

"Princess!" one of her men said, calling out to her.

Princess stopped and turned back toward him.

The man nodded at Arturo who was lying unconscious on the floor. "What about him?"

Princess stared at Arturo, and then back at her man. "Leave him, he's dead anyway. He'll bleed out in minutes."

Her men stared at one another, and then shrugged their shoulders. They all followed her out of the suite, locking the door behind them. Inside, they left Arturo, and five of his bodyguards.

The woman who had been dressed as Geisha walked into another suite, where they would change out of their Geisha clothing, into that of hotel housekeepers. Princess wanted to make sure that she left nothing to chance. She wanted them to hang around the hotel just in case there had been something she missed, like a witness who saw them come in, or saw her come in, or in case the hotel's video surveillance camera's had managed to catch something.

Princess took the hotel's elevator down to the lobby, and strutted out of the front door. It was a beautiful night in South Florida, the sky was clear, the evening air was crisp, and a nice breeze was blowing. It was the perfect night. She was back in Florida, back at the top of her game, and everything felt just right. She had forgotten how much pleasure she derived from the business of running and maintaining an empire. It was a lot more fun to take over, than it was to have to sit down and run the day to day shit. And taking over was what she did best. She was fully in her element.

\*\*\*\*\*

Dante was sitting in his apartment overlooking the city. It was the first time that he had been back in the city since Lucky's kidnapping, and it felt weird to him. Not hearing her voice, not getting up in the middle of the night to check on her, not having to tuck her in, or read her a book, or sing to her. Lucky rarely stayed with him at the apartment when they were in town, they usually stayed at his mansion out in Cordillera Ranch. He felt that it was a much better place to raise a child. The open space, the massive yard, having all of her friends in the neighborhood around her, the country club, the neighborhood lake, the river that ran through the community, it was all so beautiful. Out there, she had trees to climb, and acres of land to romp through and explore. It was a place where she could see deer, wild boar, and antelope, all of which would come into the yard to feed. So it was there where they lived when they were in town, and not inside of his downtown apartment, and that made it a little bit easier. All of her dolls, her toys, her clothing were at the mansion, safely out of sight. He definitely would not have been able to take seeing those things, and then manage to get some sleep. Which is what he desperately needed.

Dante's reason for being back at his apartment was two fold. One, because he knew that he needed to sleep. His body was exhausted, and he was on the brink of collapsing. He needed to sleep in a warm bed, his own warm bed, and he needed a couple of good meals, and a nice hot bath. He needed clothing, he needed to rejuvenate, and he needed to confer with his brother, before heading back out on the hunt. He had men everywhere, his trap was set, and he also had the information that Grace had given him about the cartels, and it was vital that he share that information with Damian so that they could come up with a plan. He also had the secure radio that he needed to give to his brother, and then there was the discussion that they had to have about *The Ranch*. He had been informed of his brother's visit to Little Guantanamo, and despite Damian's orders to shut it down, he quickly countermanded that order and had it kept open. The Ranch was a vital part of his strategy, and an invaluable tool in gathering information. He was close to catching the assholes who had his daughter. And now, he had another ace in the hole, he had Yessenia.

Yessenia was the other reason for his presence at the apartment. It was where he brought her to stay. He thought of having her stay inside of the main house at the ranch, but then remembered the awful smell that permeated the air. And so, he had decided to take her to his apartment in the city. The apartment would make for a much better prison anyway. There was no way that she would be able to escape from the apartment if she tried. There was one entrance, and as long as he kept it guarded, she would remain his guest until he decided otherwise.

Dante's apartment in the city was a massive four bedroom unit, and he had assigned one of the bedrooms to her. She could order whatever she wanted to eat, she could go anywhere inside of the apartment, she could even go down to the gym and workout, accompanied by several guards of course, but she was free to move around the building. He wanted her to be comfortable. She was his guest. His special guest. And soon, he would use her to make a call to her brother. It would all fall into place in due time.

Yessenia walked from the bedroom with a towel wrapped around her body, and one wrapped around her wet hair. "Do you have a blow dryer?"

Dante shook his head. "Sorry. But I will send someone to get one. Anything else?"

Yessenia exhaled, and walked back into the back room. She knew what she really was, and she was under no illusions; she was Dante's prisoner.

Dante yawned, and stretched, and lifted the remote and turned off his television. Soon, it would be time to get down the the business of sleeping. He knew that once he hit the sack, his body was not going to allow him to get up again until at least two or three o'clock the next afternoon. He was just that tired. He rose from the sofa, just as one of his men knocked, and walked in with a large box. The box was open, and a strange look was plastered across his man's face.

"What is it?" Dante asked.

The guard sat the box down on the coffee table. "Came by messenger."

Dante tilted his head back and closed his eyes. He knew that it couldn't be good. He was afraid to lift the lid and peer inside. "What is it?"

The man hesitated.

"*What the fuck is in the box?*" Dante shouted.

His shouting brought Yessenia out of her bedroom. "What's going on?"

Yessenia peered down at the box, and saw the look on Dante's face. She hurried to the coffee table, and lifted the lid. She knew her brother, and she knew that he wasn't a monster. Nuni would never harm a child. She was confident in that, and it was this confidence that allowed her to open the box. Inside of the box, sat a giant pink Teddy Bear. But this Teddy Bear wasn't right. It was soaked. Yessenia lifted it out of the box. It was squishy, and covered in red. And that was when they all realized what it was. The Pink Teddy Bear, was soaked in blood. A large gold charm with a tag on it, was around the neck of the bloody Teddy Bear. Yessenia flipped the tag over and read the name on it. The name on the blood soaked Teddy Bear's collar, read: LUCKY.

Dante threw his head back, and let out a wail. He kicked over the coffee table, and dropped down to his knees. He screamed a scream that only a father could let out when his child was in pain. Dante clasped his head, and lowered it to the carpet. His screams became a cry, and his cries became a sob. He could only think about his little girl, the bloody Teddy Bear, and what it all meant. He wondered if they had tortured his little girl, or cut her, or caused her any kind of pain. His mind was gone...

Please be sure to check out other great books by Caleb Alexander, such as;

Peaches' Story
Belly of the Beast
Eastside
Two Thin Dimes
Boyfriend # 2
Just Another Damn Love Story
Deadly Reigns IV
Baby Baller


Please follow me on Twitter at; Twitter.com/CalebAlexander

Please like my Facebook Page.  Caleb The Hit Factory Alexander


Please visit my website and join my mailing list at
www.goldeninkmedia.com


Stay tuned for Deadly Reigns VI

DELETED

**Knight Memorial Library - PCL**

CPSIA information can be obtained
at www.ICGtesting.com
Printed in the USA
LVOW11s1445290317
528916LV00002B/399/P

9 780982 649992